T0113316

THE FRUIT
SELLER

THE FRUIT SELLER

Tales by a 12-Year-Old
American Living in India

Sagar Castleman

authorHOUSE®

AuthorHouse™
1663 Liberty Drive
Bloomington, IN 47403
www.authorhouse.com
Phone: 1 (800) 839-8640

Published by AuthorHouse 10/11/2016

ISBN: 978-1-5246-4496-3 (sc)
ISBN: 978-1-5246-4495-6 (e)

Print information available on the last page.

This book is printed on acid-free paper.

Contents

Cliff

H<small>E STOOD THERE AT THE</small> edge and thought. He thought about his 'friends' back in North Carolina and what they had said. Isaac and Jack. What they had said to him when he hadn't gone in the deep end of the pool. "Wimp!" they had called him.

Isaac had sneered at him. "Come on, Max, you're in seventh grade now, you're a big boy. You think you're gonna get any girls by staying at the three-foot part of the pool?" Jack had splashed water at him. It had gone into his eyes.

Even just remembering it, he could feel the sting of chlorine in his eyes. "Very well, then," Isaac had said. "We'll show you what it feels like being in the deep end."

Then he and Jack had jumped in and sat on him, sat on him until he was spluttering and trying to breathe the water. They sat on him for what felt like forever, until he could almost feel his consciousness fading, and then they finally let go of him and clapped him on the back.

"Now, should we go to the deep end?" But instead, he had gotten out of the pool and had run over and sat down right next to the lifeguard. But even safe next to the lifeguard, he could hear them yelling at him, "Wimp! Wimp! Wimp!" He stayed there until it was time to go.

He took a step forward. And another. Until he could feel the tips of his sneakers at the very edge on the crumbling dirt. They never thought he would do something like this. He saw the tan rocks down below in the middle of the Arizona desert. He saw a vulture flying through the sky and he felt cool air whipping past him. He would prove it to them, he had to.

1

And then he thought some more, this time about his grandfather. About when he had gone to stay at his house and his grandfather had caught a tarantula. "Come on, Max, come and touch it, it's a real beauty."

He had only moved away. "I'll hold your hand." He had moved farther away. "They don't bite. Just look." His grandfather had held out his hand, and inside it, there had been a huge black spider, covering up his whole palm. That was when he had screamed, and fallen to the floor.

"It's okay, Max, here, I got rid of the tarantula," and he had, it had gone out the window. "I'm sorry, Max, I didn't mean to scare you. There, there, let's play cards." But he could see the disappointment in his grandfather's eyes.

So they played cards and ate ice cream before lunch, because mom and dad weren't there, but the whole time Grandpa had looked a little disappointed. And while they played, he saw a photo of Grandpa and Grandpa's father. They were holding a deer carcass, and they had big grins as if they had won the lottery. For them, he realized, it had been like winning the lottery, the hunting lottery, the bravery lottery.

He lifted one foot and put it over the edge. He had thought about doing this for so long, and he now realized that it was the only way, the only way for people to know that he indeed was brave enough to do things. He thought some more. He remembered back at Florence Middle School, when Melvin, the school bully, had approached him as he read his book at recess. "Having fun?" he had asked, but it was clear Melvin didn't care at all if he was having fun or not.

"Um, yeah I guess."

"What book is it?"

"Uh, Divergent."

"Ah, love that book; it's a real page turner. Who's your favorite character?"

"I like, um, Will."

"He's great, I especially like what he does in the second chapter," Melvin said.

"Um, he's not in the second chapter," he said nervously.

Melvin screamed in horror. "Not in Chapter Two, oh no! My whole life's philosophy has been ruined!" he said sarcastically. Then Melvin kicked him hard on his shin, making blood start dripping down. "Get up and fight, you wimp!" But he had only limped inside to his next class.

"Wimp," Melvin yelled after him.

He realized that ultimately, this was the best thing to do. He looked over and saw the huge drop all the way down. They called me a wimp, they'll never do it again. He could feel a burden getting heavier and heavier on his back and he realized that if he wanted it to lighten he would have to jump. "Let's see them do this," he said out loud. Now he was hearing a voice getting louder. "Jump," it yelled.

He tried to push the voice out of his head. I'm doing this because I want to, not because anyone is telling me to do it. He could hear the voice and feel the burden. He looked down at the rocks. He thought about his little sister at the hotel, back in Phoenix, and wondered what she would think about what he was about to do. Would she be proud of him?

He saw the beauty below him, and thought this was the perfect place to go over. And with that, he jumped.

A voice behind him shouted, "Left, sharp left, pull the left string, Max!" He went swooping down and left. He had done it, he was paragliding!

His pilot shouted, "Good job, now slight right." He heard his father cheering for him back on the cliff while proudly videotaping his son.

No one would ever call him a wimp again, he thought, as he felt the cool air blowing like fans on all sides of him.

The Fruit Seller

RAM SHINDARI, LIKE MOST OF the Shindaris in our neighborhood, earns his living by selling things. Ram sells fruits. Personally, I think he has a worse job than all his relatives. His relatives all have actual shops with roofs. Unfortunately, Ram sells his fruits in a cart. Why is that unfortunate? In May and June when the temperature reaches 115 degrees with the scorching sun beating down, he doesn't have a roof to be under. I found all this out one hot May afternoon.

My mother and I were buying fruits from him. I had never seen him look so bad. His eyelids were falling over his eyes. His clothes and face were absolutely drenched in sweat. The only thing that seemed to be keeping him going was a huge juicy mango he was sucking on.

"Hard times, isn't it?" My mother asked sympathetically. Ram sighed as he weighed the bananas.

"Too hard for me. People are just so strange. You see that tree over there?" He pointed to a huge oak tree with leafy branches falling over it. It was right next to the gate we went through to get to our house from the main street. My mom nodded.

"I tried to bring my cart there to protect me from the sunlight. But the man who lives in the house right there told me that it bothered him for me to be so close to his house and he made me come back here." He waved his arms weakly around, to show his open hot area.

For me, it was hard to be out in the sun like that for five minutes; how could he be there for the whole day? "*Namaste, Ram Bhaiya,*" I said, but inside I was already thinking about a way to help him.

4

"Papa, as a foreigner do you have power here?" I asked him that night.

"What do you mean?"

"Well if someone was doing something wrong, would they listen to you?"

My dad smiled. "Okay. What's the matter, kiddo?"

I told him about Ram.

"Well, legally it's the man's land, so there isn't much we can do about that, but we could buy him one of those big umbrellas."

"No, Papa, it isn't his land. The tree was outside the gate. We should call the police."

"Well, unfortunately, the Delhi police do not treat poor vendors very well. If we called them, they would be much more likely to listen to the big rich man than the poor fruit seller."

The chances weren't looking good, but maybe we could still get him an umbrella.

Two days later I found out who 'the man' was. Khan Malhotra was his name. On my way home from school, I looked up at the house behind the tree that Ram had pointed to. I saw the man standing on his balcony.

He was a large man, with short black hair and an overgrown beard. He was wearing a t-shirt that said in blood red letters: **An Education is a privilege, not a right.** He was drinking a huge glass of wine, which was strange because it was 4:30 on a Tuesday. He also had a long crusty cigar sticking out the side of his mouth. There were three large fans on his balcony, all going at top speed. He was reading the newspaper, absentmindedly stroking a huge bulldog that sat next to him. But none of those were the strangest things. The strangest thing was that there was *air conditioning* on the balcony.

I couldn't tell if it was on or not, but there attached to the wall was a deluxe air conditioning unit. That was definitely a waste. He poured the last bit of wine from the bottle into the glass, then hurled the bottle off the balcony. It smashed right next to an old man who was walking by and almost hit him. The old man looked up, his mouth open and ready to start yelling, but when he saw who it was, he just groaned and kept walking. Then a tall servant came onto the balcony and gave Khan another bottle. I decided it was time to leave.

Now I could go through every single time I saw Ram Shindari and how I felt, but I don't think that's really necessary. I'm going to fast forward three weeks.

Three weeks later, I was walking to town with my mother when I saw Ram. But now, he had a huge neon green umbrella stuck to his cart and extending over him. He was slumped underneath the huge oak tree, holding a big red insulated water bottle, smiling. A large, new, battery operated fan whirred happily beside him, blowing air onto his face.

We walked over to him and I asked him how he got all this. Ram gave us each a mango slice, and told us to sit down next to him and he would tell us the whole story. So we got comfortable and started listening.

"Yesterday I was setting up my fruit stand here at about 8:00 in the morning, when Khan Sahib came back from one of his short business trips. I watched him as he walked to his house, but five minutes later he came back out. He was cursing under his breath. He walked over to the man in the market across the street who makes keys. He spoke to him for a while, but I couldn't hear what he said. When he finished, I could see the key maker gave him a polite smile. Then he spoke, loudly. I heard him say, 'Well, I'm afraid I'm busy right now. Come back in a few hours and maybe I can help you.' Khan said something else, but the key maker just sneered calmly. 'I'm quite sorry, but several people have already given their keys in advance. I *am* rather busy right now. Come back in four or five hours and I can help you.' I could see how angry Khan was getting, but he was helpless.

"Khan wandered around the market for a few hours, but he clearly got no help from anyone else. At about 2:00, the hottest time of the day, I was eating a mango, when Khan came along. He was no longer Mr. Cool. He begged for a free mango and tried to convince me that he would pay me back."

At this point Ram paused and I took the opportunity to interrupt. "But you didn't give him one, right? You let him starve the whole day?" I ran my teeth along the skin of the mango that Ram had given me, pulling the strands of pulp off. I always love mangoes but this tasted especially sweet and cool standing outside on such a hot day. I thought this must be how Ram survived being out here on all these sizzling days.

Ram smiled and for a moment I could picture him smiling proudly at Khan and turning him away, into the heat. I definitely would have done that to someone who had bullied me like Khan had bullied Ram.

"Well, I could have done that, and I probably would have if I was in a worse mood. Should I be like the key man? I happen to know, for example, that the key man hadn't had any customers that morning. He just wanted to get back at Khan for how he treated him. But I felt bad for Khan. He told me his story, that his driver was out of town and so he had hired a private taxi to get here from the airport. The taxi driver had stolen his wallet, phone, keys and everything else in his bag. To make matters worse, Khan's servants were on leave, so he had absolutely no way to get into his house. So I gave him two free mangoes. Probably saved his life, it did. He was so grateful, the next day he bought me all this." He gestured to all his new accessories. I felt really happy for him.

I wish I could have such a gracious heart. But it was a good thing that Ram did, and that he had helped Khan, because now his life was better.

Nowadays Ram Shindari lives a life of luxury. Well, okay, maybe not luxury but better than it used to be. And every day I go with my mother to buy fruits and I see Ram Shindari smiling, giving customers discounts, even giving Khan Malhotra free mangoes from time to time. I see Ram Shindari the way he should be.

Always with Me

CHARLIE

I'M PROBABLY THE ONLY STREET dog in India who has a name. My name is Charlie.

So far my life has been a mix of a lot of bad things and a lot of good people. I'm gonna try to tell my story, and please, if you start feeling seriously depressed, the way I feel on some really cold nights when I'm alone and my whole body is starting to freeze, then try to picture your best friend scratching you behind the ears and feeding you warm milk and – wait a minute, I forgot, you might be human. In fact, you probably are. Well if you are, then try to picture your best friend, um, I dunno, playing with jeans in a suitcase. Sorry, I'm currently stuffed upside down in a suitcase underneath some jeans. Where was I? Oh yeah, to get my mind off the pain in my bad foot and all the blood flowing to my head, I'm gonna try to tell my story. Well, here goes.

I was born in a tent inside some broken down brick walls with my mother and four brothers. I was my mother's last puppy. My first couple of days on earth were kind of fuzzy and I don't really remember them. All I would do was sleep and then drink my mom's milk and then snuggle with my brothers and then sleep and then drink my mom's milk and then snuggle with my brothers and then sleep and then drink my mom's milk and then, well, you get the idea. Then one day I awoke in the middle of the night to find my mother howling. I got up to see what was wrong but I saw one of my brothers had beat me to it. Suddenly my brother who had got up let out a squeal. I turned to see why and saw to my horror, that my mother had bitten her own son on his side. Just then I heard two humans talking. They had broken into our house.

"We should let it be. It's nature. We cannot interfere with nature," said one human. The other human looked horror struck.

"And let this crazy dog kill all her puppies? Just look at that cute puppy over there." He pointed at me. "He is probably her next victim!" He was yelling now and he sounded very enthusiastic for talking about such a sad thing. I wasn't sure whose side I was on, but after my mom bit another one of my brothers one human persuaded the other human. Both the humans ran over, grabbed my mom and ran off, pulling my struggling mother. My brothers and I looked at each other, scared and suddenly orphans. It was hard to believe that things can change so fast and you can go from being a normal stray puppy to being an orphan. Without a sound, we cuddled up together and went to sleep.

The next day, I was outside when I heard a human say to another human that he had been at his temple when outside he saw a crazy dark brown dog with a white stripe down her nose. She was apparently jumping around howling even though as far as he could see she was not injured. A few minutes later she just dropped down dead next to the temple. For a second I wondered if my mother was in heaven, before the grief washed over me and I ran home and sank low into our tent.

SAGAR

About a week and a half ago I met a stray puppy, and though I only knew him for a short time, in that short time he became a part of me. Whether he will live on the street, die, or get adopted, I don't know. But since I have some time, I'm going to write down the story of my relationship with him, so that even if I never see him again, I will remember him forever. Here goes.

I had hoped for an awesome international vacation during winter break. Instead I was disappointed when I found out we were just going to Lucknow, a small city- in northern India where my mother's family lives. It was a seven-hour train ride from Delhi, where we lived. I hadn't been in Lucknow for a couple of years and I remembered it being boring. But from the first second I got there, I realized it would be anything but boring.

For starters, the train arrived three hours late. Secondly, our taxi hadn't arrived even though the train came three hours late. When we called, the taxi driver said he would be there in fifteen minutes and then didn't pick up his phone again when my father tried to call him back to check. When he hadn't come twenty-five minutes later, my dad got annoyed and found a different taxi. After all, who needs a taxi that comes three and a half hours late? When we were almost at my aunt's house in our taxi, our original taxi driver called and said he was at the station and asked where we were. We told him he was off the hook and then we arrived at my aunt's house.

We had had to get up at 4:00 that morning to catch the train, so I was exhausted. I had a quick lunch, before spending the rest of the afternoon reading. Right before dinner, my brother, my dad, and I went for a walk in town. I had thought Lucknow would be similar to Delhi, but I was wrong. Lucknow had many fewer people and less pollution, and people here led a much simpler life. We saw a little black and white puppy in town and he seemed nice enough. He let us pet him a little bit. Another way Lucknow was different from Delhi were the animals. In Delhi the only animals you see are dogs. Here there were dogs, but there were also lots of cows, goats, and even a few pigs. After our walk, we came back and had a dinner that tasted delicious. Then I went to bed, and by 8:00 I was sleeping soundly.

CHARLIE

My two brothers who had been hurt by my mother disappeared into our tent. My brother who had been born just a few hours before me had always been a sickly puppy, and without his mother he became terribly sick. He went into the tent too, but unfortunately, inside the tent, he contaminated my two brothers who had been bitten. They barely ever came out except to eat a little.

That left me and my oldest brother. My oldest brother was my favorite brother. He was strong, brave, courageous, and yet cautious at the same time. Our lives were fun but rough. Every morning, before going out, we would wait for the young man across the street to bring us warm milk. We would drink our share and then leave the rest for our sick brothers.

For the rest of the day we would lounge around and have fun. If we got hungry we would either scavenge something, or if we were lucky some shop owners would give us food. We knew the exact right time to be at which shops. We knew that when the samosa man let out a yell, he was going to heat up the oil. (Benefit: we can warm up.) We knew that when the grocer let out a groan, he was sitting down and it would be a perfect time to sneak some food. We knew that about twenty minutes after a particular house's cleaning lady would walk in she would dump water off her roof. (Benefit: we might get to drink some.)

But one day the man who brought us milk brought two human kids with him. One was tall and thin. He had short dark brown hair and thin brown glasses. The other was the smallest human I had ever seen! He had light brown hair and brightly colored glasses. Now usually, when people see me they say things like "Don't touch him, he has lots of little bugs on him!" (which is true of course, but it's not my fault!) or "There are hundreds of street dogs that need our help, you can't expect us to help all of them." (Which is also true, but you only need to help the nice ones!)

Anyway, the point is that these people were different. Usually, the man comes, leaves the milk and leaves. But since the tall boy was petting me and my brother, he couldn't abandon them. My brother seemed to have recognized the boy from earlier. The smaller boy also wanted to pet us, but he would get scared and run away and then come back again. I tried to lick the small human to make him feel more comfortable, but it only seemed to make things worse. Oh well! You can't expect everyone to be perfect on the first try! The man told the boys that our brothers were dead. It made me feel sad, the way he could talk about dead puppies without a note of sympathy. Besides, it wasn't true – my brothers were sick, but they were alive.

After a while the tall boy seemed to sense that the man was getting annoyed and so they left. But just four minutes later the tall boy was back, this time alone, and was petting me and cuddling with me. And as he sat there playing with me, I realized that I had never met a human like this, who would pet me just for the sake of petting me.

What was that? A shoe! Gee whiz, how many things do they have in this suitcase?

SAGAR

The next morning was a lazy morning. I hung around, had breakfast and lounged around. Then my older cousin told me that he was going to give some warm milk to the puppies that lived across the street. I loved puppies and so I decided to come too. Then my brother, who always does everything that I do, came too. So the three of us set off.

The abandoned brick house was right across the street. Inside of what was left of the house there were two puppies frolicking about. I recognized one as the puppy I had seen in the market the other day. He ran over to see me and the other followed his lead. The other one was brown, black, and white and liked me too. My brother, wanting to be like me, would try to pet them and then get scared and run off and then come back again.

"Where are the others?" my cousin asked himself, "Dead from the cold, probably." It made me feel sad the way he could talk about dead animals without a note of sympathy. I could tell my cousin was getting annoyed about me staying there, petting them, so I got up and left with my brother. But I wanted to spend more time with the puppies, so a few minutes later I came back by myself and started petting them both. The puppies loved it and leaned in to get more. I liked it, but I was hearing lots of loud squealing noises. I realized that the noise was coming from the tent. I decided I would investigate it later.

When I was done I came home and told my parents about it. I showed them the puppies and they both liked them. But I was getting more and more concerned by the squealing. Finally, I went and looked into the tent, afraid of what I would see. I could tell the puppies didn't want me to check, but I was determined. I looked in and saw to my horror three sick puppies. Two of them were a tan shade of brown and were lying there, probably asleep. The third was an albino with plain white fur and bright red eyes. He was awake but his half closed eyes were fluttering.

I bit my tongue to stop from making any noise, and silently stepped away from the tent. The puppies outside scurried to my heels, but I paid them no mind. I walked into my aunt's house, into my parent's room, and spoke, jerkily, my voice trembling.

"Inside the tent there was, there was, there were puppies, their brothers. And, and they were dying."

My parents could see how disturbed I was. My father talked to me for half an hour, and by the end of it, I understood what he wanted to teach me. This was one of those things that was not in my control.

CHARLIE

The whole next day was like heaven. It was sunny, for one thing, and I always love sunny days. But it wasn't mostly about the sun, it was because of the tall boy with the thin brown glasses and his brother and the man who seemed like his father. My brother and I lounged around on the road in the sun. Every hour or so the tall boy would come out by himself or with his brother and play with my brother and me. We had a lot of fun. And for the first time since my mother had died I thought there might still be hope for me. I could imagine myself every day until I became a full grown dog hanging around with my favorite person – my brother – waiting for the tall boy to come out and playing with him and sometimes his sweet little brother. But that night, just when I was beginning to think things would be okay, everything changed.

SAGAR

The whole next day was like heaven. I had always wanted a puppy as a pet, but this was much better. I didn't have to worry about them like I would if I owned them, but I could still see them whenever I wanted. Plus, they were free, not stuck in my house. Every hour or so I would go out to play with them. I could tell they liked it, because every time I came they would jump up and run over to me and sometimes my brother, if he came. Even though I knew that I would be in Lucknow for nine more days, I was already thinking about how I would miss them when I left. I knew they wouldn't need me, and I would not need them, but I would still miss them, and I hoped that they would miss me. And I had absolutely no idea that something would happen like what happened that night.

CHARLIE

Okay, this next part will take a lot out of me just to think about. I better get comfortable in my suitcase, get some jeans on my fur- THUDD!!!! Whoa! I'm not upside down anymore! (Nice sound effects, right?) Good, now that I've gotten comfortable, it's time to tell the worst part of my story, about ten times worse than even when my mother died. Here goes.

After playing with me most of the day, the tall boy with the thin glasses went somewhere in a car and didn't come back until night time. It was the coldest night that I had ever lived in. I was shivering madly and my teeth were chattering so much they smacked into each other about once a second. I wanted to go into our tent and cuddle up with all my brothers, but I had this bad feeling that cuddling with them would make me ill too. So my brother and I cuddled up outside our tent together. As the night went on, it got colder and colder. My brother tried to comfort me, and cuddled up with me like my mother used to do. Soon I had dozed off.

When I woke up it was the middle of the night and was freezing cold. I saw that I had woken up my brother. I was shivering and my teeth were chattering. My brother went to check on my brothers in the tent and I wondered that if I was this cold, how would my brothers be? When we looked in we saw that two of my brothers were lying there, dead. My brother had seen what I had seen, and he looked down at me and scratched his paw on my back. My third sick brother was breathing heavily and coughing every few minutes.

My brother tried to hold him, but he jumped up and, coughing, fell down the stairs of our broken down house. My brother bolted down after him, but stopped stiffly at the bottom of the stairs. I looked down and didn't see my sick brother, and then something caught my eye. A tall, dark human was biking down the street and in his bike basket I saw the dark coughing silhouette of my sick brother.

I trotted down the stairs to find my brother, but he was gone too. I looked closer at the disappearing dot that was the bicycle and then saw behind it the galloping shape of my brother. Behind that a motorcycle, illuminating everything in front of it, zooming toward the side of the bicycle where my brother was galloping. Then I saw my brother hear the noise of the motorcycle. He turned around, but the motorcycle paid no attention, ran right over my brother and continued on its way.

SAGAR

The next morning, when I got up, I wanted to immediately check on the puppies. I got up, put on my slippers and walked across the street, only to find that it was freezing cold. I went back in, put on my jacket and went out again. This time, though, I found that a tall sullen boy was standing by the crumbling house. He was very skinny and had bony cheekbones jutting out of the side of his face. His dark hair fell down over his forehead and he seemed to be blocking my way.

"Ya don't want to go in there," he mumbled, almost like he was talking to himself. "Dead. All of them."

"No, wait a second-"

But the boy cut me off again. His eyes had a wild look in them, and his hand wrapped around my shoulder. "They're dead," he was half mumbling and half sounding very determined, and the combination was not good.

I started to talk, but then realized he had to be right. There was simply no reason that he would lie to me. I turned around quickly, and started running home. When I told my dad about it, he immediately came to see. We found a crowd of street kids about my age and they started telling us what happened.

"Four of them died from the col-"

"No, no, three of them died from the cold-"

"Yes and the fourth got hit by a car-"

"The fourth was the one who he played with, he-"

"I heard one is in the market-"

"No, only two died from the cold, one got kidnappe-"

"You idiot, he wasn't kidnapped, he was adopted-"

"Adopted! That's you. Always making everything seem perfect. They all got murd-"

"That's a flat out lie, you jerk!-"

Suddenly a fight broke out between the two kids. They started shoving and pushing each other. When my dad broke up the fight, we got out the real story of what happened. Of the three sick brothers, two died of the cold and one had been adopted. The fourth brother (the one I had seen in the market) had been hit by a motorcycle. However, the last one, whom I had been closest to, had survived and had run into the market.

CHARLIE

I didn't know where I was going. I was running into the dark street, farther and farther away from home, the only home I had ever known. Was this all that life was? Pain, then brief happiness, then pain again. Well why should I be happy? I've tried to keep myself together, I shook it off when my mother died, and tried to still be happy. I tried to still be happy when two of my brothers died, but this was the last straw. My brother who meant more to me than anybody was gone…... Fine, the boy with the thin brown glasses would be there, but how was I supposed to know he wouldn't die too? How was I supposed to know he wouldn't get hit by a car? Or die from the cold?

And then a terrible image came into my mind. There is an old, thin, bony brown dog that always lurks around. His skin is nearly gone in some parts, and if you get in his space, he eyes you warily. His eyes are hungry, and his gaze is so intense that when he looks at you, his message is clear: Don't bother me, and I won't bother you.

He has no friends, he steals from everyone, and he bites humans. He is old, but has fast reflexes. He's fought with countless dogs and humans. Whenever a shopkeeper sees him he shoos him away.

I imagined myself like that dog, lurking around, caring for no one, without any friends and with no one to love, stealing from everyone. No, I told myself firmly, I was not going to be like that. I had the boy with the brown glasses, I had his brother, and I had his father. With that, I turned around and slowly started trotting back.

By the time I had walked back about a kilometer, I was very tired and even colder. I hadn't realized how far I had run. I decided, however, that I was not going to go back to my home. I couldn't sleep there by myself. It would constantly be a painful reminder of my mother and brothers. When I could walk no further and was practically frozen from the cold, I stopped. I didn't dare go any farther, because otherwise I would be drawn to my old house. I stepped up to the rows of shops and saw an old cloth bag lying there. I got comfortable on the bag but I was still freezing. However, I just couldn't fall asleep. Whenever I started to fall asleep, the image of the motorcycle running over my brother would flash in my mind. Finally, just when the first rays of light were coming into view, I fell into a sound sleep.

As I slept, I had a terrible nightmare. In it I was driving a motorcycle, something I had always wanted to do. I was dressed up like a lot of humans I had seen on motorcycles, wearing a leather jacket, black jeans, slippers, and sunglasses. Suddenly, I saw my brother in the distance. He jumped up to embrace me, but while he was in midair, I ran right over him and continued on my way.

I woke up with shooting pain in my foot, the smell of motorcycle gas in my nose, and the drone of a motorcycle in my ears. I opened my eyes and saw a motorcycle zooming away from me. As I was half awake and half in my nightmare, I thought it was the motorcycle that had just run over my brother. I got up to chase after him but I collapsed in pain over my leg that the motorcycle had run over. I felt like an idiot for thinking that the old bony brown dog was my enemy when here was a silver and white metal motorcycle that stops for nothing, definitely not puppies.

SAGAR

A few minutes later, my dad and I went out to find the puppy. When we found him, he was curled up on a cotton bag shivering madly. When he saw me, he trotted over to me but he seemed to be limping. I picked him up and took him to our house. As I walked I could feel his body shivering crazily. When we got home, I tied an old scarf around him.

I decided to name him Charlie. I named him after a great dog I had known: my grandfather's big Bernese mountain dog. He had been big, but soft and gentle.

My dad and I bought some buns to dunk in warm milk and feed him. Charlie ate them happily, but he was still shivering terribly. Then finally we let him go back to his cotton bag to warm up.

Only yesterday, I had asked my father, "Papa, what is the percentage chance that the two puppies will live?" His answer had made me feel relieved.

"Definitely at least eighty percent. They seem to be happy and healthy. I can't say about their brothers, though."

Now I asked him the same question, but his answer was much darker. He looked at me, and I could see that he was thinking about how to tell me what he thought. "Maybe thirty percent, but I'm not sure. We can try to help him, but I don't think it will do much. Even if he doesn't die from the cold, his leg is going to make it much harder for him to hunt for food."

We went back and had some *parathas* for breakfast. They are like *roti*, which is an Indian dish made out of dough, but *parathas* are filled with warm potatoes and bits of cut up vegetables. When I had eaten maybe two thirds of my *paratha,* I resisted the urge to eat the rest and patiently waited until everyone was done, before running out the door to give the rest to Charlie.

When I found him, he was curled into a ball about the size of a soccer ball. He was inside of a small house made out of bricks outside a shop. Two large bricks were stacked on top of each other on either side of him and one more was balanced on top of them serving as a roof. The house had been built by the owner of the shop where Charlie was sleeping, and I was glad to see that I was not the only one in the neighborhood who was trying to take care of him. I quietly left the *paratha* next to where he was sleeping and walked back home.

CHARLIE

Before I continue with this dramatic part of the story, I must say that if my leg had been run over by the motorcycle a few minutes ago, I might be able to describe how it felt very well. But it happened about eight days ago, which makes it a bit fuzzier in my head. So, instead of detailed description, I will just simply say how I felt.

Back to the story.

My foot hurt a lot. I fell back down onto my cloth bag and lay down, licking my foot that had been run over. Sometime later the boy with the brown glasses came over with the man who I thought was his father. The boy picked me up and took me to his house. He then tied some sort of itchy scratchy fabric onto me. I trusted him but this felt really annoying. Then they bought me some warm milk and some sort of bread in it. It tasted amazing. After I finished slurping the warm milk they took me back to my cloth bag. A little while later, a man came over and built a small house around me of bricks and I started dozing off.

SAGAR

Well, surprisingly enough, Charlie did live. The next few days went by fast as my family and I were travelling around Lucknow, visiting relatives and old friends. Even so, I still found time to play with him, but not too much time. We would buy him milk and bread and occasionally we cooked eggs for him and he seemed healthy enough because of all we were feeding him, but that made me more worried. He was only living because of all we were feeding him. And as the time of our departure grew nearer - only six days now - I was afraid of what would happen to him after I left, with no one to take care of him, feed him or play with him.

Eventually he even figured out where our house was so if he was hungry or wanted to play, he would come and whine with his head under our metal gate. My aunt can't stand stray dogs and she would shoo him away with the back of a broom unless I came out to play with him.

He was a great dog, always happy and ready to play, and soon I didn't think about him as a cute stray puppy. I thought of him as my own pet puppy. Whenever I came up to see him, he would run up to me and try to jump into my lap. If I brought food, then he would smell it and try to take it from me. What more could you want from your own dog? We would play games like hide and seek and even tag. I would run down the street and he would run after me. For hide and go seek I would hide and he would look for me. Of course it wasn't as much fun as it would have been if he hadn't hurt his leg because now he was limping hard. As time went on, I started realizing that I wasn't feeding him and playing with him and checking on him because I wanted to save him and help him. I had helped him and his brothers at the beginning because I hadn't wanted them to die. But now it was more than that. I already knew he wasn't going to die while I was here. It was because I enjoyed spending time with my dog.

CHARLIE

The days went on and the boy and his father continued to feed me at least twice daily. We played games, though my leg often made it hard for me to do well in these games but I tried hard anyway. My leg was not getting much better but with all the food they were feeding me I was getting stronger overall. The boy with the glasses somehow reminded me of my brother. He would hold some food in his hand and run and I would run after him or play other games like that.

The boy's whole family started calling me Charlie. I thought it was a nice name and was glad to be given the same respect humans got. I decided to learn the boy's name as well, since he had learned (made) mine. When I listened closely I could hear people calling him Sagar. From that moment onward, I thought of the boy as Sagar, not just "the boy". Personally I thought Charlie was a better name.

I played with Sagar less often because he was often gone but when we did play together it was more fun than it used to be because we would actually be playing. I realized that as long as he kept feeding me I didn't have to worry about my bad leg because I wouldn't need to hunt. Sagar and his father would feed me as much food as I needed.

But I decided that I needed to know something. If I was going to depend on Sagar, his father, and brother, then I needed to know where they lived. And once again I pictured myself as the old thin bony brown dog, though this time not with hate and bitterness but with admiration. Even though no one likes him, everyone knows that he is easily the best smeller in the neighborhood. He can smell a piece of rotten chicken or egg from so far away that when a dog gets very, very hungry he will just hang around the old bony dog and follow him so that eventually he gets some food. I have an okay sense of smell for a dog. I try to use listening more than smelling. Sure, sometimes with my brother we would smell the warm sweet fresh scent of samosas or jalebis, and I can always smell the boy and his father and the food they are bringing me. But I never really exercised my nose. Usually if Sagar came without food I would try to follow him back but eventually he would make me stay, either by coaxing me to sleep or getting me food or just running off. Even if I did follow him, I would be focusing so much on trying to follow him that I wouldn't pay attention to the directions to get there.

This was all going to change now.

The next time when Sagar came, he came by himself. That was good because his father seemed to be very clever. When he left, I pretended to stay back but when he wasn't paying attention to me anymore I slowly started following him, sticking to the sides of the road. It was hard to see him through all the people but I could remember his scent and I tried very hard to maintain it as I walked through the side streets. When he walked into his gated house I realized it was quite an easy walk to get to. So from then on, if I was hungry or cold or bored I could just whine and put my nose under the gate.

SAGAR

The time soon came for my father to go home to Delhi to go back to work. He was leaving four days before me, my mom and my brother. That night before he got into his taxi, he went to say goodbye to Charlie with me and my brother. He bought him a goodbye treat of an egg and leaned down to pet him and say goodbye. "Hang in there buddy, okay?" he said to Charlie. "I'll miss you." He left that night, and as I said goodbye to him I realized again how in exactly four days from now, it would be me leaving train station, probably never to see Charlie again.

The very next morning I got up to check on Charlie, to find him curled up next to a bonfire that some men had made. He was lying so close that when I petted him, his fur was hot. He seemed so happy sitting there curled up next to the fire that I began to think that he might be fine after I had left after all. When he got up to see me, his tail was curled in a loop and he was not shivering at all. He jumped up to meet me, and I slowly stroked his fur. Usually when my father left early on a trip, the whole rest of the trip I would miss him and want to go home, but this time I wanted to stay longer in Lucknow and the reason was sitting in my lap.

Later in the day my mother, brother, and I went to The Royal Cafe for lunch. I think it was the fanciest, best tasting food I had ever eaten, yet my mind was constantly wandering to Charlie. I kept thinking about how much I would miss him when we went home.

When we got back I played with Charlie some more. Charlie was running as well as he had ever run, and it occurred to me that Charlie didn't know that I was leaving. In fact, I thought to myself, as I halfheartedly ran down the street, Charlie at my heels, he might even think I will live here forever.

CHARLIE

When Sagar was not in the house, I spent time with the other kids in the street and shop owners. They were nice, but not like Sagar was. Sagar really wanted to play with me. He would leave his house to come play with me. The other kids usually did their own thing and I would watch. The shop owners would give me food. I liked Sagar's food more than the shop owners' though. The shop owners' food was very salty and heavy, and I tried to mostly eat Sagar's food. Plus, it gave me an excuse to go to Sagar's house. I liked my new life, with Sagar and his father and his very cute brother.

But one day something happened that horrified me and made me think about something I had never thought of before. One night Sagar's father came with Sagar, but the father did most of the talking. He said some stuff I didn't quite get, about hanging somewhere, but then he said something that shocked me. "I'll miss you."

When he said that it made me think of something. There were some humans that I had known since I was born. Some of the shop owners, the man who brought milk, some street kids, people like that. But as I stood there watching Sagar and his father become smaller and smaller specks in the distance, it occurred to me that he and his father had never been one of those people.

They had just appeared one day and since then they had been nice to me and I had expected them to stay with me forever. But now that seemed just silly. They had only been here for about ten days. I should have realized at some point they were going to leave. That was why the father had said that he was going to miss me. So they were all leaving. Today. That was it.

All my dreams of staying with them forever had just been crushed. So I decided that I would just forget about the boy and his father. I was used to this sort of thing. I had, after all, tried to forget about my brother and mother. So without thinking another thought about the boy, I went inside my favorite shop owner's shop, and, without him knowing, went to sleep.

SAGAR

When I got up the next morning, the first thing I realized was that I was only going to spend two more full days here in Lucknow. I liked this town a lot, the people, the animals, the stores, everything.

A few minutes later I got out of bed and went to check on Charlie, only to find that he was gone. I looked everywhere for him but couldn't find him anywhere. I was starting to think that he had been run over by a motorcycle or car like his brother, when I finally found a kid who told me where Charlie was. Apparently a dog had gotten locked inside of a shop overnight and was inside whining. I found the shop that he was locked in. It had a big metal grate closed over it so I couldn't even see in. I leaned against it and called in "Chaaarlie!" Inside I heard lots of whines and I started feeling very scared. Today was Saturday. If the shop was closed during the weekend, then he wouldn't get out until Monday. Even if he was still alive after more than two days of not eating or drinking anything, I would be gone by then. I ran back home to tell my mother. She assured me that no shops were closed over the weekend in Lucknow. I was relieved, but I went to check every half hour.

Sure enough, two hours later the shop opened and out came Charlie, who seemed very eager to get out!

CHARLIE

When I woke up, it was pitch dark. I didn't know if it was nighttime or daytime because of how dark it was. My first instinct was to find a way out. So I started walking one way in the dark. I kept walking until I hit a wall. I turned around and walked the other way. I hit another wall. I walked the third direction and I hit something that was like a wall, but harder, like metal. I walked the fourth way. Guess what? It was a wall. There didn't seem to be any apparent way out, so I tried to remember what I had last been doing. When a little bit came back to me, it all came back to me. I realized that if I was correct, Sagar would be gone forever by now. I knew where I was and why. The shopkeeper didn't know that I was here and so he had closed up the shop, oblivious to the fact that there was a dog in his shop.

Humans are like that. They sometimes fail to notice certain obvious things.

Finally, I started hearing voices outside the metal wall. They were hard to understand but I recognized them as voices of the other kids I sometimes played with when Sagar wasn't here. But in the chaos of voices, one voice stood out to me. Sagar's voice. He hadn't left! When I heard his voice calling my name I let out a howl and then a whine. Again I ran toward the wall from which his voice was coming from. It was the hard, metal one, and I let out a squeal. I realized that since there was no way to get out I might as well sit down. The voices of the other kids continued for a long time, but Sagar's voice wouldn't come for a while and then would come back again.

Finally, after a forever of waiting, the door flung upwards. The light blinded me but even so, I still ran out as fast as my three legs would carry me.

SAGAR

The rest of the day flew by quickly with Charlie. It was lots of fun and it seemed to go by way too fast. Before I knew it, I was going to sleep for my second to last night in Lucknow. I had trouble falling asleep that night, for I thought about Charlie and how I would probably never see him again. My mother had told me that when street dogs get older they wander from town to town for the rest of their lives. Even if Charlie didn't wander away, it would still be hard for him to hunt because of his leg and he wouldn't have the healthy food that I gave him. And what if...... what if I came back in six months, only to find a big gruff brown street dog who didn't care for me or remember me. I could picture myself arriving in Lucknow, yelling, "Yes! He's here. I told you he would be here, Mamma, I told you!" And then I would walk over to the dog and shout, "Chaaarlie!" And then I would start running expecting him to run after me, but I would turn around, only to see him slowly trudging the other way, snooping in some garbage. I would wonder what was going on and I would go over to pet him, but then he would bite me. And I would be completely forgotten. Forgotten. Forgotten.

The word echoed over me, and it made me feel so sad that this dog would forget me. I had saved his life, fed him when he couldn't hunt, I had played with him. Every day he would come to our gate and whine because he wanted to play with me, and yet in a few months I would be forgotten.

CHARLIE

After I got out of the shop, Sagar and I played for the rest of the day, and he fed me as well as he ever had. We would play a game where he would run and I would run after him. We would run everywhere until we ended up back where we started. This game would have been easier if I could use all of my legs. Then I might have even been able to catch up with him. A game that I liked better was when Sagar would hide somewhere and I would try to find him.

Anyway, that night I lay in my brick house trying to go to sleep and I thought about something I hadn't thought about for a while – my family. I tried to remember my brother. I thought for a few minutes, until I had his picture in my mind. When I thought of him, I felt in awe. He had helped me survive before Sagar came. He acted like my mother after she had died. But that was nothing. He had died, trying to save my other brother. Next I thought of my mother. It was much harder to see her in my mind. When I could picture her, I didn't see her with nearly as much admiration. What had she thought she was doing, giving birth to five kids she couldn't take care of? I could see it now, in my head, my mother sinking her teeth into two of my brothers. But I decided that I had to move on from that. I had to stop thinking about them. I had a new family now, with the Sagar, his brother, and his father. (By the way I haven't seen him recently. Wonder where he is?)

SAGAR

The next day was all fun and games. I spent more time with Charlie that day then I had any other day because we weren't going anywhere, we were just staying home and packing since it was the last day we would be spending in Lucknow. I spent as much time as I could with him, but all too soon I was going to sleep for my last night in Lucknow. Our train left at 3:00 the next afternoon.

The next morning, I checked in on Charlie, made sure he was okay, and then came back in to have a big breakfast. After that, I was packing, looking at the presents my aunt had given me, playing with my cousin, and getting ready to leave. After lunch time my cousin started watching a movie and since I had never watched it I sat down to watch it with him. The movie was two hours long and by the time it was done it was time to go to the train station. I dragged my suitcase out the door toward the taxi, when my mom told me I had forgotten my retainer in the house. I ran back to get it, hurled it into my suitcase, threw my suitcase into the trunk of the taxi, and ran out to say goodbye to Charlie.

I ran to his brick house, but he wasn't there. I ran down the street looking in both directions, but saw no sign of him.

The taxi driver was yelling for me to come. I looked one final time down the street, then stepped slowly into the car. Ten minutes later, as we arrived in the busy train station, I said to my mom, "I didn't even get to say goodbye to him." My mother looked at me for a second, as if there was something obvious that I didn't understand.

Finally, she spoke. "Sagar, Charlie will always be with you. You saved his life, you gave him a new life that he had never dreamed of. Wherever you go, wherever you are, Charlie will always be with you." At first I thought that it was just one of those cheesy things adults say to make you feel better. But after I thought about it for a little bit, I realized she was probably right. Someone you do so much for, you can never forget. Yes, Charlie would always be with me.

CHARLIE

The next day I had lots of fun playing and I had started getting used to spending my days like this. So I was completely unprepared for what happened the day after that. I saw very little of Sagar that day and that afternoon something happened that made me stop short. I was sitting on the curb next to Sagar's house, when Sagar came out lugging a suitcase, his face red and sweaty. And at that second I understood everything that had happened. Sagar's father had pulled out a suitcase like this on the day when he had said, "I'll miss you." And then he had left and I had not seen him again. Now Sagar was leaving with his mother and brother. As he came out I heard him mutter, "I have to say goodbye to Charlie." But then something else happened.

Now when I think of myself, I don't really think of myself as Mr. Lucky. My mother and four brothers all died and all. But at this second nothing luckier could have happened to me. Here's what happened. A voice came ringing out of the house. "Sagar, check if you packed your retainer." Sagar opened up his half empty suitcase, let out a groan and ran inside, leaving the open suitcase outside. Without a second thought I jumped into the suitcase, burrowed myself into some jeans and laid down as flat as I could. Sagar came running out, threw something on me, put the suitcase into the car and without a second glance went running out.

So that's where my story ends. Here I am now in that very same suitcase up on a rack above the boy, listening to him talk. I don't know what this new life will bring for me, but it will be an adventure and I like adventures. Besides, I will always be with Sagar and he will always be with me. Here I am signing out. Charlie, a street dog, the only street dog in India who has a name.

SAGAR

So here is where my story ends. Right now I'm sitting in the train, telling my story. The tea cart is just in time because I'm done writing my story and getting thirsty. Amidst the smells of gasoline, tea, and cigarettes, I can make out a faint wet dog smell. The smell reminds me of Charlie and how he will always be with me wherever I go.

Johnson's

A S A RESULT OF MOVING to India, many things happened. Most were expected, some were not. One of the 'not expected' things was our cuckoo clock going cuckoo. At random times the bird would pop out and cuckoo thirteen times. There was no pattern. Some days it only came out once or twice, some days every two minutes. Eventually, we shut it up in a box and locked it in a cupboard in our guest bathroom.

Finally, after we had settled into our new house, we decided to take the clock in to be repaired. We did get it repaired, and it is ticking obediently as I write this. But how we got it repaired is a story, and one that captures the unique experience of living in India.

The first place we went was Priya market, which was close to our house. Stores there usually had most things we needed, and what they didn't have, the store keepers could tell us where we could get it. We went to the hardware store in the market. The man there had a blue tag that said, Hello my name is Rish. When we asked him if he could repair it, he burst into laughter.

"Me, repair this clock from Switzerland? I'm just a simple man and do not know how to. For this first rate craftsmanship, you need someone special to repair it. Maybe-" CUCKOO, CUCKOO CUCKOO CUCKOO CUCKOO CUCKOO CUCKOO CUCKOO CUCKOO CUCKOO CUCKOO CUCKOO CUCKOO CUCKOO said the clock. The man gasped. "Yes, sir you need him to repair it."

"Who do we need to repair it?" My dad asked.

"You need the best clock store in India. The store is right here in Delhi. I have its business card right here." He walked over to a row of five filing cabinets. He opened the middle drawer in the third cabinet. It was full of business cards. It took me a moment to realize they were all the same card. The cards were navy blue, with white text. They all said the following: JOHNSON'S, the Best Clock Store in India. Call 991-8CL-OCKS. Inner Circle Connaught Place.

The next weekend, my dad and I went to Connaught Place. It was very hot, and we were hoping to finish this outing quickly.

As soon as we got there, we saw a small clock shop, and we went inside. It seemed to be a family business. There were two young men who were doing the physical work running around carrying clocks and watches. An old man was the cashier. A man my father's age was actually doing the clock work. A boy and girl my age were listening to the customers' problems. It seemed to be a decent business, but it wasn't Johnson's. We asked the cashier if he knew where Johnson's was.

"Of course I know where the best clock store in India is. Just go straight for a little bit, take the second right, the first left, the fourth right, and you will get to a fake dead end. Find some steps and go down them, take your first left, third left, and you will see a big sign that says Johnson's on it." My dad and I exchanged glances. This guy definitely seemed to know where Johnson's was.

We followed the cashier's directions until we got to the 'fake' dead end. There weren't any apparent steps. We found a much smaller watch repair shop and peered in. Inside, a small man was stooped over a little table. He had his back to us and was holding a small phone and shouting into it. "No! No! I will not have you bunking classes! Do you hear me? Do you think I put all my savings into sending you to college so you can skip classes to eat-" At that moment he turned around, and saw us. "Ahem," he said. He tossed his phone into a desk drawer and turned to us. "What do you want?"

My dad looked at him. "Do you know where the stairs that lead out of this dead end are?"

"Ten rupees, sir."

"Excuse me?"

"It costs ten rupees."

"Look, all I want to know is how to get to Johnson's."

"Johnson's! You should have said so before. Follow me." He took us around his shop and we saw some stairs. My dad sighed and I could hear him mutter under his breath, "Johnson's better be good."

Ten minutes later I was thinking the same thing. The first left was easy to find, but the third left was much longer. The temperature by now felt like it was definitely above 100 degrees, and we had finished all our water. Just when I was about to suggest we go back and let the family business repair our clock, we found the third left. We walked down it and sure enough we saw a huge banner at the end of the street that said Johnson's, the Best Clock Store in India. Below the words was a huge arrow, pointing to what I could only guess was the store. Finally, with our goal in sight we started walking determinedly toward the best clock store in India.

The sign was much farther than it looked. Twenty minutes later we were still walking and the sign seemed only a little closer. Our faces were dripping with sweat; even the bottle of Minute Maid orange juice that we bought didn't help. Twice we had considered giving up, but the sign always hung in front of us, beckoning us forward.

Finally, after a half hour of walking, we got to the end of the street, where we finally reached the gigantic sign. It seemed as if our shirts were plastered to our bodies with sweat.

The arrow on the sign was pointing to a neon orange tarp on some stakes. Underneath the tarp was a dusty stool. Sitting on it, reading a book, was a tiny man with a small mustache and a bowler hat. We were about to ask him where Johnson's was, when he spoke up.

"Hello, may I assist you? I'm Johnson."

The Keeper

I

Louis Parkinson danced across his lawn. It was spring vacation, and the green grass was so bright it almost appeared as if it was reflecting the sun. He jumped over a stump that had been cut down by a gardening team a few months ago. Jumping over it, he felt a little upset, remembering the day when he had watched unhappily as the tree fell down. But it was nothing, and the smile returned to his lips, only slightly dimmer than it had been before.

It was only then that he noticed the tall, handsome stranger approaching. The stranger had combed back blond hair, crystal clear blue eyes, and a long face with freckles. Louis walked across the lawn and brightly asked, "Who are you?"

The stranger smiled. He had a genuinely happy smile, and already Louis trusted him, which wasn't saying much, because Louis trusted anyone with a happy face. At first glance it looked like a genuine smile. But if you were to look closely, you would see the strained expression on his face, beneath the false smile.

"I'm Henry Terk. Pleasure," the man said in a smooth strong voice. "And am I in the presence of young Louis Parkinson himself?"

"That would be me," Louis said. "Want to play checkers?" It was hard to find someone who would play checkers with Louis, so he asked everyone.

35

"Checkers? With Louis Parkinson himself? I'd love to." His voice seemed to have a touch of sarcasm, but either Louis didn't notice or he didn't care.

Louis ran back into his house. He looked over his thirteen different checkers games. Which one should he choose? After taking a good five minutes, he finally chose his ivory board and started running back excitedly.

"Who are you playing checkers with? Your latest imaginary friend?" his sister Lisa asked. She was flopped on the couch, watching TV, her hair loose and tangled. Louis glanced at the screen. There was a man and a woman, lying in bed, madly kissing each other.

Lisa was pretty mean to Louis sometimes. She was always watching something like this on TV, and Louis was never sure why. He never asked her, and he certainly wasn't going to ask her why she was watching what she was watching right now. He was too excited.

It had been seven months since he had played checkers with anyone, and checkers was his favorite game. Louis didn't have any friends at school. No one wanted to play with a kid who was so spoiled. It wasn't Louis' fault that he was spoiled. His parents never spent time with him. His father was a colonel in the US Army and was almost never home. His mother was a full time lawyer. They thought that since they couldn't spend much time with their son, the best way to make him happy was to buy him whatever he wanted. But even when either of his parents did have free time, Louis wouldn't play checkers with them. They always beat him in checkers. When he played with his imaginary friends, Louis always won.

Louis didn't mind that he didn't have friends. He had lots of imaginary friends, and anyway, what he really liked was to sit down and read fantasy books.

He was eleven years old and his mother often told him to go get some exercise. Usually he would just dance across the lawn, as he was doing earlier.

He ran outside where Henry was waiting for him.

Henry looked anxious, but he still greeted Louis with a smile. "Finally! Ready to play, Louis?"

"I guess the better question is, 'Are you ready to lose?'" Louis asked. Henry gave a good-natured laugh as he set up the board.

They played nine games and Louis won seven of them. Louis had never had so much fun, but after their ninth game, Henry stopped.

"Now Louis, let's get right down to business. The real reason I came here, believe it or not, was not to play checkers. I want to invite you to a party, this very Saturday night. And you Louis, you, will be the guest of honor. There will be about fifteen kids there, and all of them will want to meet you and shake hands with you and get your autograph. Aside from that, the party will be a board game party. It will have all your favorite games, since you will be the guest of honor."

Louis was amazed. Was this actually happening? This was what he had always wanted. He sometimes dreamed about everyone playing with him and for him to be the center of attention.

"Will there be books?" Louis asked, wondering if this could get any better.

"Books? How could I forget? There will be books of every type. There will be hundreds of antique bookshelves filled with fantasy books taking place in faraway lands. There will be bookshelves with Kindles, so packed they will be falling out. There will be the latest-"

"Now just wait a minute." Something seemed a little strange. "Who's going to be paying for all this?"

"Haven't you ever heard of The Keeper?"

Louis shook his head sadly. "I'm afraid I don't know too much about people from outside."

"The Keeper is a multimillionaire who supports fun and games and pays for parties like this."

"Will I get to meet The Keeper?" Louis asked.

"Well of course, you are the guest of honor after all. But enough talk about The Keeper. So the party takes place next to the Imagine Mosaic in Central Park at 11:00 pm and-"

"11:00! But my bedtime is 8:30!"

"No. Louis, listen closely. On Saturday night, you are going to sneak out of your house and come to the party. By 3:00 am you'll be back in your bed."

Louis didn't think about it for a moment. "I'll be there." he said confidently.

II

Trent Rugster was sitting outside on a lawn chair playing a video game on his DS. He was immersed in shooting the little zombies popping up all over the small screen. If he could only shoot 350 more zombies, he would get the 550 bonus coins and then he could purchase the grenade blaster which would make it much easier to kill all the zombies.

His thoughts were interrupted, however, by a voice saying, "What are you playing?" Trent put the DS on pause and looked up to see a handsome stranger peering down at him. His blond hair was combed back and was illuminated in the morning sun.

"It's called Zombie World. You probably haven't heard of it, 'cause it's not very well known."

"Zombie World! I love that game. I work at a video game company myself, Trent. I've met the creator of that game."

"Cool! But how do you know my name?"

"Well, your, um," the man's freckled face turned red. "Well if you must know, you're kind of a celebrity here at Nintendo. I mean you're so good at gaming and all."

"Wait a second. If you work at Nintendo, then do you think you could finish this level for me? I just need to defeat 350 more zombies. I'm saving up for the grenade blaster."

"Listen, I have a method that's much easier than having to actually shoot them. Watch this. You can do this trick whenever you're more than halfway done with a level. I call this trick the Turkish method because my name is Henry Terk."

Henry laughed, then pulled off the battery at the bottom, and started fiddling with it. "Now if you pull the pointy end, it will become just a little bit pointier. Now jam the battery into the hole here and… just wait a second."

Trent's face was glowing. If there was one thing he liked more than video games, it was technology tricks.

Henry continued. "Now once the battery has been jammed, it will make this token pop out. This token has all the data of the DS. This might look alarming, but if you pull very hard, the token will break in two and out will come this. This is called a microchip. The microchip is the specific part of the token that holds the data. All you have to do now is put everything back together. Slide the microchip back into the token. Jam the token back into this slit, and put the battery back in. Now watch."

He turned on the Play Station and there was a picture of lots of zombies holding a sign that said "Congratulations! You made it to level 496"

"Awesome!" Trent shouted.

"Now Trent, let's get right down to business. The real reason I came here, believe it or not, was not to show you how to get to level 496 in Zombie World. I want to invite you to a party this very Saturday night. And you Trent, you, will be the guest of honor. There will be about fifteen kids there, and all of them will want to meet you and shake hands with you and get your autograph. Aside from that, the party will be a video game party. It will have all your favorite video games including Zombie World, since you will be the guest of honor. The other kids who are invited will be amazing at video games too, but obviously not as good as you."

"That's so cool; a party just for me? But will it have lots of video games or just my favorites?"

"Trent, this party will have every video game ever invented. Aside from the games themselves, there will be 15 Wiis, 15 DSs, 15 Play Stations, 15 X-boxes, 15 laptops, and

15 tablets. You will get to play for as long as you want and then every single person will get to keep one of each of these devices. The money to buy these things for the party will come from The Keeper, a kind multimillionaire gentleman who supports video games and holds parties like this all over the country, not just in New York."

"This is going to be so fun! It's on this Saturday, you say? What time?"

"You might be surprised that the party will be at 11:00 pm. I know your parents will not allow you to go so late, so you must sneak out in the middle of the night and walk to the Imagine Mosaic in Central Park."

"But why does it have to be so late?" Trent asked. "I mean, why couldn't it be in the afternoon?"

"Trent, have you ever played video games at night in the Park? It has got to be one of the greatest feelings in the world. Please come. Trent, the party will have to be cancelled without the guest of honor."

Trent had already made his decision. "I'll be there," he said confidently.

III

Bernard Peterson sat in his tree house, surrounded by textbooks. Math textbooks, English textbooks, science textbooks, music and art textbooks, technology textbooks, French, Spanish, and Latin textbooks.

Scattered among all the textbooks were two laptops, one with a complicated diagram of a bee, the other with a 96-page research article on the causes and effects of lung cancer. In the mix there was also a tablet, and buried beneath three biographies of Molly Pitcher, a smart phone. Bernard was engrossed in a biography of Hans Christian Anderson when his learning was interrupted by a handsome stranger swinging himself into the tree house. The stranger had combed back blond hair and blue eyes.

"Are you Bernard Peterson?" the handsome stranger asked. Bernard's eyes narrowed into slits.

"What's it to you?" Bernard asked arrogantly.

The man's eyes flashed, and Bernard saw him clenching his right fist, but just as quickly he relaxed it.

"Perhaps this is not the right Bernard. The Bernard I had heard about was a genius. In fact, the New York Department of Education told me that you were "destined to be the next Leonardo de Vinci" according to Tom Wilthrow, Head of the Department."

"What! You know Tom Wilthrow?"

The man laughed. "Do I know him? Well, if you want to know the truth, I'm Tom's boss. My name's John Flintson, I'm the head of the Education Department down in Washington DC."

"I think I've heard of you."

"So what I'm here for is to invite you to a party. The party's rule is basically this – smart kids only. There will be geniuses from all over the country. You, of course will be the smartest, which is why the party is being held where you live. So what do you think, Bernard? Will you come?"

There seemed to be something very strange about this man. Bernard felt so comfortable with him, although usually, well, he wasn't someone who trusted everyone he met.

John had his eyebrows cocked up, as though he was already thinking about what he was going to say next. Bernard frowned.

"Sir, I'm, I'm really glad you came and that you think so highly of me. But to tell you the truth, well, I can't really trust you. I mean you are a stranger after all, to me at least."

The man looked at him with a sad smile on his face. "I did so much to prepare for this party. I had professional chefs make your favorite foods. I designed huge organized competitions about trivia. Nonetheless, I understand completely if you don't want to come. After all, I could be a terrorist." He gave a sly smile.

"Now wait a second. I didn't say I didn't want to come and I definitely don't think you are a terrorist. But first I have a few questions. When is the party? Who is holding the party? Why are you having this party?"

"The party will be on Saturday at 11:00 at night. I know it is past your bedtime, but it's linked to one of the contests. Just sneak out of bed and come to the Imagine Mosaic in Central Park. You will be back in bed by 3:00 am. The party will be sponsored by The Keeper, a multimillionaire who sponsors educational parties like these. So can you come, Bernard? Please?"

Bernard was swayed by the man's confidence. He didn't hesitate. "I'll be there," he said confidently.

IV

At 11:00 that Saturday night, 15 kids snuck into Central Park, each with different expectations. As they snuck in, each coming from different places, a medium height pale man approached them. The man wore a long black cloak and black gloves that nearly reached his elbows. His dark clothes, jet black hair and dark eyes contrasted with his pale face. When he spoke he had a light English accent yet everyone understood him perfectly.

"Welcome, welcome," he said. "I am The Keeper. I am quite glad you all made it here *safely.*" He gave a laugh. There was an outbreak from the children. All of them were yelling for different things.

The Keeper held one hand out as if he were a traffic officer. "Please children, I'm sure you are all wondering where your party is. Do not worry. Everyone wanted to have a bigger party so it was moved to another part of the park. Please just get into this truck here and we will take you to the party."

The back of the truck was empty with just a big open space, and somehow none of the kids were very enthusiastic to get in. Whatever motives they had had for coming here didn't seem so exciting now.

One by one, though, with the right amount of urging, each child stepped into the back of the truck.

A small man in the front was driving, and The Keeper sat shotgun. The kids were nearly piled on top of each other in the back. After they had been in the truck for about fifteen minutes all the children began to think the same thing.

They were in a huge truck piled on top of each other with a stranger driving, without anyone knowing they were there.

When they had been in the car for thirty minutes, a boy who had come to see a Lego sculpture display shouted at The Keeper, "Where do you think you are taking us?"

The Keeper spoke softly, but with menacing clarity. "I will not tolerate yelling, please."

"I DON'T CARE WHAT YOU TOLERATE. I WANT YOU TO TAKE ME HOME," the boy screamed. With a jerk, the car stopped. The Keeper's eyes flashed, and he glared at the driver.

Despite the apparent warning from The Keeper, the driver laughed with malice. He pulled out a metal instrument that looked like a ruler, reached back and touched the boy's face with it. The boy's face contorted with pain, and he started screaming. But no sooner had noise come from his mouth when The Keeper turned and yanked the instrument off the boy's forehead and spoke sharply to the driver, "What are you thinking? You have no right to torture the subjects."

For a moment, it looked as if the driver was going to object, but he closed his mouth, gunned the motor and started driving once again.

Eleven hours later the truck was still driving, and now it was in Aroostook, Maine. The kids hadn't eaten anything, but The Keeper and his driver had each had a plate of pancakes a few hours ago from a restaurant. Now that the kids could see the driver, they saw he was a short man with uneven brown hair and green eyes. He was handsome, but there was something surreal about him, almost as if he wasn't really there. Since the driver had hurt the boy with his instrument, the kids had been too scared to do anything, even talk. But finally, after they had been driving for about fifteen hours, the truck stopped, and The Keeper stepped out. Trent, who was closest to the window, looked out and, to his astonishment, saw the driver coming out of a building, at the same time that he was sitting in the driver's seat!

V

The Keeper stepped out of the car and walked over to the driver's twin. The twin had come out of a large, flat, grey building. They seemed to be in the middle of nowhere. Besides the building and the land around it, it was just yellow fields stretching on forever. When the twin saw The Keeper, he ran over, faster and faster, until he was right in front of him, at which time he started speaking angrily.

"Commander, where have you been? I thought you were going to get some kids who knew stuff about earth and come back. You've been gone for months. We've been getting more and more calls from The Governor asking about your whereabouts. He's not happy. He said that as soon as you get back, to communicate with him. I know you think you are smart and can do everything by yourself, but this is getting to be too much. We should just go back to Neptune and forget about this."

"Who asked your opinion? I don't care about the stupid Governor. I am your commander. If I tell you I have everything under control, then I have everything under control. I teamed up with an earthling and I got the –"

"What! Now you are teaming up with humans? If The Governor finds out –"

"I don't care about The Governor!" The Keeper bellowed. "The human I teamed up with will be taken killed in the end. He is my servant, just like you! I-"

"And you are The Governor's servant. This is getting to be too much. The next time I talk to The Governor, I will tell him what you're doing. Teaming up with humans, coming here in human transportation!"

"I will have no more of this nonsense. These kids are all good in their own ways. They will be used like the human I'm working with. Once they have been used to their full potential, they will be killed too. Now I will bring them in."

The Keeper left the twin there and walked back to the truck. He motioned to the driver and the truck window opened halfway. "Welcome to your new home. As you may have figured out, you are all good at different things and you will all be helping me since I am *new* here. I'm sure you all have questions and many of them will be answered inside. For now..." he whipped out the driver's metal ruler instrument. "Come on out."

The door opened and the kids slowly started filing out of the truck. The twin took them into the building.

The youngest kid in line, a nine-year-old girl who thought she had come to attend a math convention, was crying. She had big brown eyes and looked at The Keeper sadly. "Please, Mr. Keeper, can I go home?"

For a moment, it almost seemed like he was considering her request, but at the last second his face hardened. "What is your name?"

"Katie."

"Katie, why do you want to go home?"

"I miss my house?"

"What do you miss about it?"

"Every Sunday night, our whole family gets a fire going in the fireplace, and we eat mint chocolate chip ice cream, and we talk about our favorite parts of the weekend."

The Keeper suddenly looked sad. "Perhaps you will like it here too. Please walk inside, Katie."

Although the weather was nice outside, strangely it was freezing inside the building. Each child was handed a thick woolen jacket to wear. It was colder than it was on even the coldest, snowiest days in New York.

They were taken into a large dining room. At the door of the dining room stood two men who were dressed strangely, with baggy green pants and shirts. But their clothes were not the strangest thing about them. They looked exactly like the driver also. In their hands they each held a metal ruler like the driver's. The kids gaped at them as they were ushered in by the first twin.

The last kid, who had come to see the biggest robot exhibit in the world, was being followed by The Keeper. After all the kids and The Keeper had sat down at the dining table, The Keeper, who was sitting at the head of the table, cleared his throat before speaking.

"I call this place Mini-Neptune. As I'm sure you've realized, it is quite cold, though not nearly as cold as the real Neptune. This keeps it comfortable for us and reminds us of home. Each of you will be taken to a room where you will be helping us understand our new surroundings. You will be asked questions and you will truthfully answer."

A boy raised his hand, but spoke before anyone said anything. "What if we refuse to answer the questions, Mr. um, Keeper." The Keeper's eyes flew nervously around the room eyeing the six driver twins who all held the ruler instruments.

"The people who ask you questions are not known for their kindness. Trust me when I say that you don't want their instruments on your skin. Is your question answered?"

"Yes, Mr. Keeper."

VI

Each of the children was taken into a small room, where the only furnishings were two uncomfortable looking chairs and a small round table. Each room had one of the people that looked like the driver, except for Bernard's room. With Bernard was The Keeper himself, peppering Bernard with questions about U.S. history. In each of the other rooms, a similar process was happening with one of the driver twins interrogating each of the kids.

Abby Flark, a girl who knew all there was to know about great literature, was hurriedly giving a bored looking driver twin a detailed description of Fyodor Dostoevsky, Victor Hugo, Charles Dickens, Mark Twain, Leo Tolstoy, and L. Frank Baum. The door flung open and in walked The Keeper. He listened for a few moments then interrupted when Abby started talking about how the books of Mark Twain could make you feel like you were really floating down the Mississippi River.

"Perhaps you misunderstood me, my dear. You must answer the questions truthfully." The voice of The Keeper startled Abby.

"But this is the truth, sir, you do feel like you are there." The Keeper raised his eyebrows. He snapped his fingers and another driver twin rushed in. "Get me Huckleberry Finn by Mark Twain!" he ordered.

A few minutes later, when the twin returned with the book, The Keeper tucked it under his arm. "I will read this tonight. Thank you for telling me about this."

Nick Williams, a robotics genius, was explaining to a driver twin the many different types of metal and engines used to make a basic robot as well as how to make a human automaton out of tin. Suddenly, the door opened and The Keeper walked in holding a tablet. He listened for a little while before speaking. "These robots can impersonate certain things that humans do, yes?"

"That is the idea of it," Nick said.

"Almost like a clone," The Keeper mumbled under his breath. He started searching on his tablet. The longer he looked the more shocked he became. His eyes had a certain wild look in them, as though he were discovering exciting things that he had never imagined before. It was two hours before he left.

Trent Rugster was giving a thorough description to a driver twin of how to play Wii tennis, DS, X-Box and many other video games he excelled in when The Keeper walked in. He listened for a little bit about Wii sports before interrupting. "So the idea of Wii sports is that you get exercise as part of an electronic game?" The Keeper sounded skeptical.

"Well, if you don't believe me, why don't you let me show you?" Trent asked with a small smile. Within minutes, The Keeper had ordered a Wii set from a driver twin, and he spent the next 90 minutes engrossed in various Wii games under Trent's instruction. He might have stayed with Trent the rest of the day had he not been called away by an incident in another room.

Jeane Bileson, whose father was a professional astronaut, was telling a very interested driver twin about the Mars Rover and Curiosity when the door burst open and in walked a very angry young man with blue eyes and blond hair.

"Where is The Keeper? I demand to see the liar right this instant!" the man shouted.

"Wait a second," Jeane said. "I know you. You're the man who invited me here in the first place. You told me this was a party for kids who knew a lot about astronomy. Your name is…. Henry. Henry Terk."

At that moment, the door opened again and The Keeper himself came in, looking annoyed to have his Wii lesson interrupted.

"What is all this yelling about? You should be doing a better –" he saw Henry and stopped. "Ah, Henry. Perhaps you better step outside with me for a moment."

"I'm not stepping anywhere with you until you give me the $5,000 you promised me!" He was no longer the calm man Jeane remembered. His eyes were now bloodshot and his light hair was wild and tangled. His handsome face now had a dirty sneer on it and his khaki pants were torn and muddy. It had apparently been a rough trip for Henry to get here.

"Henry, please leave. If this comes to fighting you are greatly outnumbered."

"We'll see about that," he snarled. Suddenly, he threw himself on top of the Keeper. But no sooner had his hands wrapped around The Keeper's throat than the driver twin drove his ruler into Henry's forehead. Henry started screaming and his face looked horrified.

The Keeper looked at Jeane and calmly said, "You may leave now. Go straight out and turn left to get to your um, uh, dormitory."

The 'dormitory' was a medium sized room with seven bunk beds crammed into it. Jeane was sleeping above Katie Slivik, a girl who seemed to know quite a lot about math.

Jeane knew there was something strange about The Keeper and his driver twins. He claimed to be *new* here but he didn't act like a foreigner. He spoke amazingly good English and so did his driver twins. He talked about Neptune, but Jeane knew enough about astronomy to know there could not be life on Neptune.

Jeane tried to think about what was probably going on in Manhattan right now. The police would have looked everywhere only to find no trace of a kidnapper. But somehow The Keeper didn't seem like a kidnapper. Not like she had ever met one, of course.

Despite getting angry, The Keeper acted polite and seemed genuinely interested in what she and the other children were telling him. Jeane tried to convince herself that he was bad, but even in her mind when she saw his calm face and his interest in learning everything she told him, she found it hard to stay angry at him for long.

Meanwhile, Henry was taken downstairs into a small circular room. Two driver twins escorted him into a room with long metal rulers at their sides.

VII

That night, The Keeper slipped into the room where the fifteen kids were sleeping. He walked over to where the smallest one was, and picked her up in his firm grip.

He walked out the door, and into a large room that was made of stone. There was a huge stone fireplace, already blazing with a huge fire. There were three comfortable green armchairs, and The Keeper dropped the girl into one of them. When he did so, she woke up.

"What am I doing here?" Katie's eyes fluttered open.

The Keeper smiled warmly. "It's Sunday night, Katie."

"You're joking," she said.

The Keeper was about to respond, when someone else entered the room. The tall figure of Jeane Bileson came in. "What's this? A midnight party?"

The Keeper stood up, almost defensively. "How did you wake up?"

"Katie was sleeping below me. I heard some noise and followed you out."

"You're pretty brave. Well, there's one seat left; why don't you join us?" As Jeane sat down, The Keeper said, "Do you like mint chocolate chip ice cream?"

"I love all ice cream."

The Keeper picked up a large carton and an ice cream scoop, and served a white scoop glistening with chunks of chocolate into three bowls.

As they were eating, The Keeper said, "So Katie, what do we do now?"

"We share what the highlight of our weekend was."

"Okay. Jeane, what was your highlight?"

"Well, I know a lot about space, so a few months ago, I had applied for a math/science magnet in another school.

Only a few people in my school made it into the school, and yesterday I learned that I had gotten in. So that was definitely my highlight."

A dreamy look appeared on The Keeper's face. "I also once made it into a school because of my knowledge of space. It was called Dex, but......"

"But what?" Katie asked.

"It was a long time ago. It doesn't matter anymore. What was your highlight, Katie?"

"Well my older brother has special needs. He-"

The Keeper broke in. "As in, he needs more than others?"

"No, silly! As in he's, well, not normal. He starts shouting sometimes, and his voice is strange. Anyway, my highlight is that yesterday we took him to a doctor who said that there's a new treatment out nowadays, and tests have proven that the medication brings in good results. And -"

The Keeper interrupted again. "You took him to the doctor?"

Katie looked confused. "Yeah. So?"

"They didn't turn him in?"

Jeane leaned forward in her chair. "Excuse me, sir, but on what charges would the doctor turn in Katie's brother?"

"Well, um, never mind. So is your brother getting better?"

"Well he's starting on the medication on Monday."

Under his breath, The Keeper murmured, "He doesn't realize how lucky he is."

"But what about you, Mr. Keeper? What was your highlight?"

The Keeper smiled. "Last Thursday, I went to Coney Island. I came back yesterday. It was the most beautiful place I've ever been to."

"Yeah, it's great," Jeane said, yawning. "I'm going to bed now. Goodnight Mr. Keeper. Thanks for the ice cream."

"I'm going too," said Katie. "I just want to say, this was almost as fun as when we do it at home. But tell me, when will I get to go home?"

The Keeper looked at her sadly. "Soon, Katie. Soon."

VIII

That night, after the ice cream party, The Keeper was sitting in his office when a clone came into the room.

"Master, you are getting a communication signal from The Governor.

"I don't care about The Gover-"

"He threatens to exile you from Neptune if you don't answer."

The Keeper's jaw clenched. "Take me to the communication room." The clone led The Keeper through the dark hallways of Mini-Neptune, until they arrived in a rather small room with a large white screen on the biggest wall. A tablet was sitting on a very small desk. The clone pressed a few buttons on the tablet and suddenly the screen flew to life. A huge man was on the screen. He had very short brown hair and cruel dark eyes.

"You there!" The man on the screen pointed at the clone. "Get out!" The clone left quickly, tripping over his feet in his haste. "Humbert!" the man yelled.

"I prefer to be called The Keeper, Trink," The Keeper was trying to be calm but it was clear he was furious.

"Just as I prefer to be called The Governor," The Governor sputtered. "Anyway, let me get straight to the point. You need to come back to Neptune immediately. Somehow people from Uranus know that one of our most powerful men is not here. Just yesterday half the Empire was burned to ashes. I hate to say this, Humbert, but we need you here."

"Trinket, the civilization on Earth is fascinating. My plan is going perfectly. The kids know a lot about Earth and once we know everything there is to know from them, we will no longer need them, and I can..."

"No! Humbert, dispose of any traces that you have been there, including the kids, the clones I provided you with, and any other humans that have helped you. Then return immediately. Communicate with me once before you leave."

"Trinket, Earth is amazing. In many ways they are ahead of us on Neptune. If we could get them on our side, we could easily beat the attackers from Uranus."

"You dare suggest an alliance? You know what happened the last time we tried to grow our empire through other planets. Neptune partners with no one, Humbert!"

"But the beauty, Governor. I went to a beach yesterday. It was ten times more beautiful than you described it. Come for yourself, and you will never want to leave."

"You did not come to Earth to go to beaches, Humbert!" The Governor bellowed. "If you are not back on Neptune in two days, then you will be exiled forever. For all I care, live the rest of your shameful life on Earth with human kids. Do I make myself understood, Humbert?"

"But-"

"Good. Farewell until next time."

The next morning, The Keeper walked through the hallways of Mini-Neptune. He walked into the same room he had walked into the day before. He pressed some buttons on the tablet and in a moment Trinket's pudgy face appeared on the screen.

"Humbert, yes. I hope you have made a good decision and are coming immediately."

The Keeper spoke quietly and formally. "Yes, I have made a decision. Everything here will be disposed of. But tell the army not to wait for me. Goodbye Governor."

The Keeper tapped on the tablet, picked it up and exited the house.

EPILOGUE

Two weeks later, at the Empire State Building a crowd of tourists pushed their way to enter the building. Among them was a medium sized man with jet black hair, eyes and cloak. He stopped, however, when he saw a family of three coming through the crowd. The boy ran toward the man.

"Hey, Louis, how are you?"

"I'm good. I have a new best friend – Trent! Thanks for introducing him to me." The boy's parents came over.

"And who is this, Louis?" his father asked. The Keeper stepped forward.

"I've chaperoned at Louis' school a few times."

"Well, nice to meet you," the father said. The men shook hands and then the father said,

"My name's Jack, what's yours?"

The Keeper gave a small smile, as if sharing an inside joke with only himself. "I'm Humbert. Well nice to meet you all, I have to go." Humbert winked at Louis before disappearing into the mob of tourists.

Life in Las Vegas

T HE THREE OF US SAT, cross-legged, on a comfortable blue carpet: my Father, my brother, and I. It was Saturday night, and delicious smells wafted out of the kitchen. But all three of us paid no attention to our surroundings. We were immersed in the board laid out in front of us.

I spun the spinner. It landed on a 9 but after 6 spaces, the space I had landed on said: Stop! Day of Reckoning.

"What does that mean, Jacob?" my Father asked me. I wasn't sure, so I flipped over the box that said LIFE on it to see what the instructions said about Day of Reckoning. I read it aloud:

You must STOP on the Day of Reckoning space.

1. *Receive $48,000 for every child.*
2. *Pay back any promissory notes at the rate of $25,000 for every $20,000 borrowed.*

In this turn you must make a big decision. You must do one of the following:

A) *Go on to become a MILLIONAIRE. If you think you have enough money to win, spin again and move toward the space marked MILLIONAIRE.*
B) *Try to become a MILLIONAIRE TYCOON. If you have little or no money, place all that you have (your car if you're broke) on ONE number on the number strip. Spin again. If your number is spun then you become a MILLIONAIRE TYCOON, the WINNER, and the*

game is over. If you lose, the bank takes your money, and you sit out the rest of the game at BANKRUPT.

As long as there is no TYCOON, the game continues with players becoming either BANKRUPT or MILLIONAIRES.

"I have $463,700, Papa. How much do you have?"

My Father grinned. "Is that all? I've got $1,500,000 right here." He pointed to a neat stack of $100,000 bills at his side. "As for Charles, well, he's got almost twice as much as me."

I grimaced. Even if I did get a 1 and land on the space that said, *Find Buried Treasure! Collect $600,000*, I still wouldn't be able to win.

"I want to become a Millionaire Tycoon," I said bravely.

"Am I going to win?" Charles asked. That was all he cared about, winning.

"You sure are, Charles," Papa said to my four-year-old brother.

"Not necessarily," I said slowly. "I choose the number...." I had never felt so nervous, even though it was just a game. "9, I think..." Soon I had piled all of my money onto the green space marked 9. I got ready to spin, but at the last second I stopped.

"Actually, instead I'll make it 6." I don't know why I changed, but I did. I moved all the money down the strip and onto the red 6. I put my hand on the spinner and got ready for the most effective spin in the history of The Game of Life. I twisted my hand all the way around on top of the spinner, so much that creases showed in my skin, and spun as hard as I could. The spinner kept spinning for about 30 seconds, a blur of colors, until it finally started slowing down, more and more, until I could see the numbers it was landing on. 4, 3, 2, 1, 10, 9, 8, 7, 6, 5.

"NO!" I yelled, for it had passed the number I needed, but when I looked again it was still spinning, just very slowly. 2, 1, 10, 9, 8, 7. Once more it looked like it was going to stop but as if using its final burst of energy, it managed to turn onto the 6. And this time it really stopped.

"YES! YES! I WON! I WON!" I was screaming at the top of my lungs.

That night as we ate dinner, I took everyone through the story of exactly how I had spun it, what numbers it had landed on, how much I had been losing by. All Charles could manage to say was, "Did I win second place?"

* * *

All this comes back to me in a flash as I sit down on the armchair in the casino in Las Vegas. The bright lights shine down on me and all the other men and woman in the 'rest' area of the casino. I try to do some mental calculations. All together I've probably lost $200,000 today. There is no way I can get that much money back in a few hours. I look at my watch. 11:30 pm. My flight back to New York leaves at 7:00 tomorrow morning, less than eight hours from now. I think about what I had promised Rachel, my wife. "Don't worry, I won't bet more than a few hundred dollars." Here I am having completely lost all of our life's savings except for.... $450. I sigh. I decide to look at all the little gambling stations to see if there are any where I can get back some serious big bucks.

I have looked through almost all of them when something in the corner catches my eye. It is a Roulette wheel. A short stocky man dressed in a tuxedo is the croupier who is running it. After reading the sign I realize this might be my chance to win.

The Roulette is a large wheel with thirty-six sections, half red, half black. The numbers 1 to 18 come up twice on the wheel, once on a red section, once on a black. The croupier spins the wheel and also tosses a ball, which falls onto different sections. Eventually, as the ball loses momentum, it falls on a number and color. If you just bet on a color and the ball lands on that color, then you win however much you bet. But if you bet on a number and a color, and the ball lands on that number and color, then you win thirty-six times as much as you bet. It seems almost too similar to the MILLIONAIRE TYCOON in the Game of Life. I feel a shiver run down my spine as I decide to go for it. I bravely step out of the casino and across the street to the bank.

The banks in New York aren't open at midnight, but here, so close to the casinos, they have special branches that stay open all night for gamblers. The banks in New York are clean and nice, but here they feel more like pawn shops that you might find in an alley. The bank is a large, airy room, yet it still seems rather old. It is crowded but there is still one borrowing counter that has no one in line. The man behind the counter has a pipe dangling out the side of his mouth and a glass half full of brandy on the counter. The banks back in New York don't allow their tellers to drink and smoke on duty, but things are clearly different here.

The air smells musty, and when I put my hand down on the counter it upsets a thick layer of dust. When I start speaking, my voice trembles so I cut myself off. Here in Vegas, I have to be confident of whatever decision I make. Finally, when I think I'm ready, I look the banker straight in the eye. "I would like to borrow…. $463,700."

Half an hour later I am standing next to a bunch of other men also betting at the Roulette table. Besides me, there are a total of six other men.

"Let's see," says a tall man with wavy brown hair. "I think $10,000 on black."

"$110,000 on black," says a man who I'm sure I have seen in the Business section of the New York Times.

"$50 on black." This comes from a man who looks like he's at a little league game, not in a place where people can lose their entire savings in a few hours.

"$30,000 on red," says a thin man with an unusually long nose.

"$55,000 on black," says a middle aged man, about my age, dressed in a suit.

"$2,000 on black two," says an old man with a raspy voice. This is the only man who has bet on a specific number and he bet very low.

Everyone looks at me expectantly. I pause for a moment. I have to sound determined. I casually snatch a glass of scotch from a small man carrying a tray, drain it, then place it back on the tray before speaking.

"$463,700 on red six." Some of the other men stare at me, surprised, but the man running the Roulette looks bored. We all place our chips, then the man gets ready to spin.

I don't know much, but somehow I think my chance of winning is more than one in thirty-six. If I don't win, I don't know what I'll do. Run away, maybe? I can't walk into my house in Manhattan and tell Rachel we are $463,700 in debt, and our house is now the property of some Las Vegas bank. I look at the huge wheel and suddenly I feel a bit dizzy, knowing my whole life depends on that wheel and as I spot the red 6, I know that just as I won that Game of Life long ago, I'm going to win this too.

I close my eyes as the man who runs this dangerous game brings his arm back and gives the wheel a mighty spin.

Ten Minutes

THE MOMENT I SAW ALL the foods on the list at the international food fair, the one thing I was most excited about was the lasagna. My favorite food is lasagna. And my second favorite. And third. And fourth. And - well you get the point: I love lasagna.

As soon as we got to the fair, I zipped over to the Italy tent and saw one thing - pizza. Lots and lots of pizza. I walked over to the woman in the tent and asked where the lasagna was. She said that they had made it and put it in the oven a while ago so it would be done in about ten minutes. Okay, I thought, it will be ready soon. Plus, it was homemade, even better!

I wandered through the rest of the tents. Some of the food looked good, but I wanted to wait and have the lasagna. Besides, the best things had meat in them and I am vegetarian. At times like this, I really wish I weren't vegetarian. About ten minutes later I went to check on the lasagna again. This time someone else was there. I asked where the lasagna was and he replied, "Ze lasagna is in ze oven. It will be done in ah, say, ten minutes perhaps."

"Oh great," I thought. "It will still be ten more minutes."

I roamed through the rest of the tents, but most of them had meat. Why couldn't they have more vegetarian options? I bought some desserts and ate them. They were okay, but I really wanted some good lasagna.

I went to the lasagna tent again and found yet another person there. Then I realized that I knew her. Her son was a good friend of mine, Enzo. I asked her about lasagna and she said it was in the oven and would be out in ten minutes. I groaned. We talked a little bit and then I left.

Ten minutes later, I was back at the tent and found a tall, bony man working there. "They must have a lot of people working here," I thought.

When I asked if they had lasagna, he said, very clearly, "Yes." I was about to whip out some money, when he added "Yes, ve have lasagna, it said so in ze menu, it is just cooking in the oven. It vill be done in about ten minutes."

Well after that, I kind of gave up.

About half an hour later my dad and I were eating some falafels somewhere else, when Enzo's mom came by and said," The lasagna is done, do you want some?"

My dad and I were at the tent labeled ITALY, before you could say, "ten minutes."

When we got there, where the pizza had once been there was now lasagna. I was already imagining its tasty, cheesy goodness, when yet another person who worked there said, "One piece of chicken lasagna coming on up!" I froze. All of this waiting and running for *this?*

Then I remembered something. The menu had said there would be chicken lasagna and vegetarian lasagna.

"What about vegetarian lasagna?" I asked.

The reply was probably the worst thing that she could have said.

"Ah yes, of course, ze vegetarian lasagna. I believe zat zey are putting it in ze oven right now. Don't worry, it will be done in about ten minutes."

Just Call Me

THE BRIGHT LIGHT OF THE chandelier reflected off my aunt's glasses as she spoke. Her name was Aunt Alena, and her sister Aunt Cosette. The two of them were visiting my family's house for dinner on a humid summer evening. Outside, the sun was still shining as brightly as usual, and my summer holidays were going perfectly. In a few days we would go to Miami Beach, which was a vacation favorite in our family, and Aunt Cosette might even come with us, which for me was great news.

Aunt Alena was telling us some story about when she was younger. She was pretty, and her grey hair was tightly curled, almost in an afro. "I was a camp counselor in Pennsylvania," she said, and I could tell that she enjoyed having everyone's attention. "A couple of guys from New York were also counselors. They had found a cheap car they wanted to buy. The laws of Pennsylvania said that to buy and register a car, you had to have a Pennsylvania license."

I was only ten, and it was hard for me to understand everything that she was saying. Aunt Alena wiped the sweat from her brow, and continued. "They asked me to let them borrow my license for the car. Of course, on one hand, I wanted to be a pal. I wanted to say sure, Andy, sure Mike, you can borrow my license. So I said fine. I was getting ready to make the deal, when I heard a voice in my head, the voice of my mother."

I stared at her, enthralled, although I noticed that other people at the table were starting to lose interest. My dad finished the last of the meatloaf, and my mom was wiping her mouth with her napkin. Aunt Cosette was looking at her sister, but I wasn't sure if she was actually interested. "I was in a dilemma. On one hand I wanted to be a friend, but on the other hand, I had an instinct that it wasn't the best thing to do."

My older brother Jake shook his blond hair and rolled his eyes. "May I be excused?" I was officially the only one still interested.

Dad glared at him. "Wait till the end of Aunt Alena's story. You on the other hand, Jim," he looked directly at me, "This story may not have a happy ending, so if you're disturbed, you can leave."

When I heard my name, I spun around. "No, no, I want to stay. Continue, Aunt Alena."

"Finally my mother's voice won out and I told them that I wasn't going to do it. They went and got someone else to agree to help them. Once they did, they bought the cheap car for only fifty dollars, and then they took it for a spin. But it was an old car, and the emergency brake was worn out. Two days after they bought it, the car was parked on a hill and rolled down and smashed into another car. It caused a lot of damage, and the insurance company didn't agree to pay. If I had been the legal owner, it would have all come on me. I remember thinking to myself with relief that boy, had I made the right decision."

Jake stood up. "Now can I leave?"

Mom nodded. "Go ahead, Jake." Then Mom went and started clearing plates, and Dad took the leftovers back to the kitchen. Aunt Alena went to change into night clothes.

So it was just Aunt Cosette and me left. Aunt Cosette was one of my favorite people in the world, and I trusted her with everything. She had long grey hair and greyish blueish eyes. She had wrinkles, which made her seem wiser. "Did you like Alena's story, Jimmy?"

"I'm not sure. It was kind of sad."

"Jimmy, soon you're going to be in middle school. And after that, high school. In high school, kids sometimes drink alcohol in parties. You might be with friends who are drinking alcohol. If they invite you to go with them in a car, just call me. You know I live close to you. Even if it's three o'clock in the morning, you can call me."

If anyone else had said that, I would've thought they were just saying it to make me feel better. But not with Aunt Cosette. "Okay, Aunt Cosette," I said confidently.

"I don't want to lose my number one boy," she said, wrapping me in a hug.

"Jimmy, are you in or out?" says Andrew. His cheeks are rosy, and his eyes are flashing.

"I'm not sure. Is there space?" I ask in a voice I try to stop from trembling. It's late at night, and we're leaving Katie's party.

"What do you mean, is there space? I'm the only one with a car here, so you either come," he points his thumb towards his car, "or you don't come." He points in the other direction.

"I mean, you already have five people."

Will laughs. "Don't worry," he says, with a lopsided grin. "Lucy can sit on my lap. We'll have fun."

Lucy grabs Will's hand, and digs her fingernails into them. "You wish," she says, pushing her dark hair behind her head.

Suddenly, I remember back when Aunt Cosette told me that I could call her in a situation like this. I remember Aunt Alena telling me about the boys whose car crashed. And I think to myself, *what're the odds, Jimmy?* Aunt Alena has probably gone in hundreds of car rides with friends who had been drinking a little. So has Aunt Cosette. They only remember the bad times.

So I nod at Andrew. "I'm coming as long as I don't have to sit on anyone's lap."

Some people laugh, but I'm feeling a sense of dread as I step into the car. *It's not too late,* I think. It's only about midnight. Aunt Cosette will be proud of me, I know she will.

But what about my friends? They'll laugh until their sides ache, if they see a van pull up with an old grey haired woman inside, and see me step inside before the car cautiously pulls away into the right lane.

Andrew leans behind his seat, laughing and blowing kisses at his girlfriend, Senna. I'm sitting in the back, between Will and Senna, with Lucy actually sitting on Will's lap. Shotgun is Benjamin, sitting quietly, texting on his smartphone. Lucy is touching Will's cheeks, with Will leaning back in his seat, a content smile on his face. He lets Lucy ruffle his jet black hair.

It's then that I notice with a shiver down my spine that Ben is the only one wearing a seat belt. Glimpses from the party come into my head, and suddenly I don't feel so good. I see Andrew practically inhaling beers, Senna crazily dropping a wine glass, and watching the wood floor soak up the alcohol. I see the calm contained eyes of Aunt Cosette, who doesn't drink at all. I see twelve-year-old Jimmy making his poster with friends about not drinking and driving. And then last of all, I see myself, Jimmy, slurping up drinks at the party, with Katie's arms looped through mine.

I'm shaken out of my thoughts by Senna screaming a curse.

Then I hear Will swear loudly, and feel a huge jerk. We've crashed into a wall. I see Andrew, already unconscious, with blood streaming down his forehead. My head goes forward through the gap between the front seats, hitting the dashboard, which is already bloody from Andrew. I vaguely see Lucy getting out of the car, screaming with a voice of pure fear. Ben is already outside, walking in the steady way he always does, going I hope to get the police. He walks without the unsteadiness that Lucy has, and recall how Ben had not been drinking at the party.

That's when I notice the quantity of blood all over me. Things start getting blurry as I try to open the door, and then I fall out of the half broken car. I fall onto the hard street, the gravel soaking up blood and sticking to me, pain searing through every part of my body, just as everything goes black.

Trust

A FTER HAVING MY PASSPORT FOR a good five years, it eventually came time to renew it. In Delhi, the place to renew American passports is the American Embassy. Now, my parents had not yet bought a car, so my father had been going to his office every day in a three-wheeler. A three-wheeler is a small green and yellow vehicle. It has two wheels in the back, with a bench where the passengers sit, and one wheel in the front with a little seat for the driver. Depending on their size, three or four people can fit inside one three-wheeler, but in India you see three wheelers all the time with more than five people packed into them. A few days before I went to get my passport renewed, my father had arranged with one particular three-wheeler driver to meet him in front of our house every morning to take him to the office.

Based on what I had seen of him, the driver, whose name was Kuldeep, seemed like a fine fellow. He was pretty old, short, with broad shoulders, paper white hair, and deep brown eyes. He always dressed in a heavy brown overcoat instead of the usual three-wheeler driver uniform.

When the day for my passport appointment arrived, before I went to school and my parents went to work, Kuldeep picked us up to take us to the embassy. Kuldeep talked to me the whole way, asking about my school and telling me about his son who he told me was my height but was two years older than me. Because three-wheelers are open and do not have doors and because there is so much traffic and honking in Delhi, Kuldeep had to keep turning around and shouting to talk to me, which seemed to make my parents a bit nervous.

We got to the embassy, told the driver to wait, and got in line to enter. The embassy was very crowded. On one side was a door with a crowded group of Indian citizens applying for Visas. They were talking loudly, and a young American man from the embassy was trying to get them into a line. Meanwhile the other door was for Americans. It had about five people standing neatly in line.

We were almost inside when a young uniformed guard told us that no electronics were allowed inside, from pen drives to iPads. Among the three of us, we had three phones, a laptop, two pen drives, and an iPad. We had a few options in front of us.

The first and safest solution was to cancel the appointment, go home and reschedule. The problem with that was that you have to reschedule at the embassy at least thirty days in advance, and even then it's sometimes full. We had made the appointment for today and had taken time off from work and school to come, so we wanted to get it done.

The second solution was a bit riskier. We could rush home, drop off all the electronics, and hopefully make it back in time for the renewal. The problem with that was with all the traffic, it was unlikely we would get back in time, especially given how strict the embassy seemed to be about appointments. Then we would have spent the morning rushing back and forth to the embassy and would still have to reschedule.

The third solution was the riskiest. We could give the three-wheeler driver all our electronics to hold onto, while we renewed my passport. The risk from this option was obvious: we had only known Kuldeep for a few days and for that matter we didn't really know him – he had just taken my father to work a few times. We didn't know where he lived or anything about him, other than that he had a son who was about my height.

After thinking it over quickly, my parents decided to leave the electronics with Kuldeep. We put all of electronics into my father's laptop bag and walked over to him. After my father spoke to him for a few minutes, Kuldeep wedged the laptop bag between his feet in the little space where three-wheeler drivers sit in the front of the vehicle. I wondered why he didn't put it in the trunk until I realized that three-wheelers don't have trunks.

"I'll take good care of them," he said, smiling. It seemed perfectly fine to me. So I didn't understand why creases of worry came into my father's forehead, and he whispered something in my mother's ear.

Nor did I understand why he was so anxious the whole time we were waiting at the embassy, and even while the man there was asking me questions. By the time we finished renewing my passport 45 minutes later, his face was bone white.

A few years ago when we were on vacation in Washington DC, we had gone to the Washington Monument on a tour bus. There too, we learned that electronic devices weren't allowed. I vividly remember my father, without batting an eye, handing over his laptop to the bus driver, along with the other members of the tour, and calmly telling him to take good care of the stuff. It had been a great day, and I had no memories of my father having even a shred of anxiety. And that was the first day that we had met the bus driver.

After we completed the passport renewal process, we went outside, and my father quickly ushered us to the roundabout where we were supposed to meet the driver. There were lots of three wheelers there, but Kuldeep's white hair and overcoat were not to be seen.

My father told my mother and me to wait there and he sprinted down the street toward the next roundabout. As he ran, I could see him turning his head back and forth searching for Kuldeep's three-wheeler. I saw him in the distance reach the other roundabout and dart around, peering in the four or five three-wheelers that were parked there. Apparently, none of them were Kuldeep because he then started running back toward my mother and me.

As he got closer, I could see his red face and his furrowed brow. The only other time I had seen him this anxious was one day back in the U.S. when we were at a shopping mall and my younger brother had wandered into a shop and for a few minutes we weren't sure where he was.

When my father finally reached us, he looked like some combination of helpless and furious. "You both stay here in case he comes here," he barked abruptly to my mother and then bolted off again in the other direction to keep looking for Kuldeep.

My mother shook her head sadly. I took a few steps away from her, just as a three wheeler zoomed up beside us. The driver stepped out, cheerful as ever, "I've come, Bhaiya," he greeted me.

"Kuldeep!" I don't know how my father had got back here so fast. "Where were you?" he yelled, but I could see the relief in his face and his brow started to gradually relax.

"I am here, sir. I just went to that side for a few minutes. You came early, sir." He saw my father eyeing the space under his feet, and I noticed a hurt expression in his brown eyes.

"Your things are all okay, don't worry, sir. See for yourself." He handed my father the laptop bag bulging full with our electronics. His face had lost its usual cheerful expression.

We piled into the little vehicle, and headed off toward my school. We rode in silence. The whole trip, not once did Kuldeep turn around and say anything to me. He just looked straight ahead and drove. I watched my father's face and saw it gradually relax back to normal, though he looked at Kuldeep a few times with a strange expression on his face. I tried to see Kuldeep's face but from where I was sitting I could only see the side of his jaw, which twitched every now and then.

When we got to the school, I got out and said good-bye to my parents. Kuldeep zoomed off, and I watched the green and yellow vehicle disappear into the Delhi traffic.

A Biography
of Humbert Clarence

I N A SMALL, CRUMBLING ROOM, a couple was sitting on thin folding chairs; both appeared anxious. The room had fabric nailed against the walls, and the only light came from a small candle flickering in the corner. The man had short brown hair that was a mess, and his green eyes seemed to be the only thing alive in the whole room. He was dressed in some of the same brown fabric that was on the walls, but he only had enough to wrap around his waist and over his shoulder. You could see his body was trembling, not just from anxiety, but from the cold.

His wife had dirty brown hair that looked like dirty cloth. Her warm brown eyes were deep and filled with kindness. She too wore rags, but hers covered her entire body. It had cost a small fortune to buy, but her husband had insisted that although they had little, the least they could have was decent clothing. Even if they were poor, he said that he didn't want them to become like the spitters, the men and woman outside who walked around naked, slowly going crazy from the cold. They were called the spitters because their only source of warmth came from when they spit on each other, letting the saliva warm them.

Despite her clothing, the woman's hands were red from the cold, and they clutched her husband's for warmth.

Finally, a woman stepped out from behind a door, and both the man and the woman stood up. The woman had tears in her eyes. "Mr. Clarence, we have cleaned your baby, and it's ready to be seen. It's a boy, sir."

"Excellent," the man said. "And please, call me Ward." It was then that he noticed the tears. "What's wrong?" His voice was icy cold.

"He won't make ……." the woman burst into tears.

It was then that his wife spoke. She walked over and seized the nurse's arm hard enough to make her wince. "He won't make what, Ms. Yark?"

The woman looked up fearfully and spoke. "He won't make it through the night, Mrs. Clarence." At this, Mrs. Clarence started crying as well.

Ward Clarence wrapped his arm around his wife. "There, there, Keileen, it's all right." He leaned over to kiss her, but she pushed him away.

"How can you say that, Ward? Our first child is going to die, and you're saying it's okay?" She was screaming now, and Ward wrapped his arms around her.

"There, there. Can we see him, Ms. Yark?"

"Of course," she answered, regaining some control. "Follow me."

"Come on, Keileen," Ward coaxed, pressing his lips against her cheek. "Don't you want to see our little Blit?"

Keileen managed to stand up, and she followed her husband, who followed the nurse. The candle flickered out, leaving them in complete darkness. They walked out of the room, outside into the bitter cold. Everyone's teeth started chattering, and they rushed down the road into the little nursery. The nursery was a small room, packed with babies lying all over the ground, with nothing between them and the floor other than a thin piece of brown fabric. Each baby was wearing nothing, and the room was quite cold. Most of them looked pretty strong, except one who had red spots all over it. Another was wheezing. Finally, they came to the very last baby.

"Meet your son," Ms. Yark said, smiling. He was naked like the rest of them, and had almost no hair. His big eyes were baby blue. His skin was extremely pale. He looked like most of the other babies except for one thing. His size. He was about half the size of the other babies.

Ward reached down and picked him up. "Hello Blit," he said, tickling him under his chin. The baby had a twinkle in his eye, and he head-butted his father. Ward laughed, and he gently lifted his son high in the air. "Look, Keileen," he said. "Look at our handsome son." His wife was starting to smile. "Do you want to hold him?" He gave the baby to his wife, who held him, giggling. Even the baby seemed to be smiling. "Now why don't you take him outside, and I'll pay Ms. Yark?" He patted a small pocket that was sewn into the fabric and some coins jingled.

Keileen nodded, and smiling, took the baby out. As soon as the door had closed behind her, Ward's face turned deadly serious. He turned to the nurse. "What is this?" He pointed to all the babies lying on the ground naked.

"I'm afraid I don't understand, Mr. Clarence." Her face had genuine confusion on it.

"Why don't you clothe the babies?"

"But sir, this is the cheapest hospital on Neptune. Even the spitters have their babies here."

"I'm aware of that. But how many babies die of cold here?"

"About five every week."

"Five every week. This is probably also the reason that my baby, for instance, my baby that my wife has been waiting years to have will die in her arms. And to you...... To you it'll just be another baby who didn't make it. Maybe you'll come to the funeral. You'll probably forget in another week about my darling Blit! And meanwhile, my wife," he choked back sobs. "My wife will live her life in depression. As head nurse, you are responsible for all these babies." He paused for a moment, and the nurse cut in.

"You must understand sir; the living conditions of the babies is not my decision."

"I don't care about whose decision it is." Ward bellowed. Some of the babies were starting to cry from the noise.

The expression on the nurse's face was strained. "I know how you must be feeling, Mr. Clarence, but -"

"No you don't know how I'm feeling, *Ms. Yark.* If you ever have kids, you'll probably have them at the hospital in the Empire."

"We have had many successful babies here. The plurality of babies born on Neptune are born here."

"I don't need statistics right now, Ms. Yark," Ward's face was white with rage, but his voice was a bit quieter. "What I will tell you is this. If Keileen and I were to have a baby again at, say, the Himbo hospital, he would be a perfectly normal child, possibly even brighter than normal. I would pay maybe two hundred yert, four times as much as I paid here, for the birth of a normal child."

"I'm afraid you're mistaken, sir. The hospital has nothing to do with the overall health of the patient."

"Oh yeah? Do you want to bet?" Ward's voice remained quiet, but there was an aggressive edge to it.

The question took Ms. Yark by surprise. "We're not allowed to bet with patriates' families here, but since I'm trying to make a point, I'll make an exception. How much?"

"How much?" Ward laughed grimly. "I'll bet you two hundred thousand yert that we can have a normal child at Himbo Hospital." Betting was common on Neptune, and Ward knew two things about Ms. Yark that led him to such to make such an aggressive offer. First, he knew that Ms. Yark loved to gamble and had trouble resisting a bet. Second, he knew that she was due to inherit a fortune when her uncle, who owned most of the hospitals on Neptune, died. Her uncle wanted her to learn the business from the ground up, which was why she was working as a nurse – that and because he didn't trust her love of gambling.

Ms. Yark hesitated for just a moment, and then replied excitedly, her cheeks turning slightly pink. "Fine then. There's obviously something wrong with either your genes or your wife's, which is why he's like this. So the bet is close to a sure thing for me."

"Something wrong with me? With me! You're the one who has all your babies lying on the floor shivering and naked, and you're saying something's wrong with me! Shake my hand then, if you think there's something wrong with me. Shake my hand if you think we can't have a normal kid at Himbo." He stuck his face right in front of hers. "Shake my hand, and we shall bet."

Ms. Yark, stuck her hand firmly into Ward's. In his anger, Ward squeezed with a bone crushing grip, so that when he let go, her hand fell limp. He dropped a handful of carefully counted coins on the floor, coins that had taken him months to earn. With that, he walked out the door.

Seven years later, at Naita academy, school was over, and kids came running out, slipping on the ice, and laughing. It was the last day of the first semester, and everyone was huddled together with friends, talking about what grades they probably got. Only one person was alone. Blit Clarence trudged slowly through the snow, thinking about the big orange envelope his teacher had given him.

Even if he had done well in school and hadn't been as small as he was, he wouldn't have had friends anyway. He was the only one dressed in brown rags. Naita was one of the best academies outside of the Empire, and his father had spent weeks arguing with the oil company where he worked. He said he would quit his job if they didn't pay for his son in Naita. And today, today was the day his parents would finally realize how bad he was in school by looking at his grades.

He looked up and saw that the rest of the kids were far ahead of him. He started walking a bit faster, but then slowed down. He wanted to never reach home. When he got home, his parents would realize how bad he was. But it wasn't just that. It was much more than that. He had heard the story of how the nurse had said he was going to die. And he knew he probably would have died if his parents hadn't taken the huge loan of one hundred thousand yert in order to have him sent to the Empire to have him completely remade.

And a single thought had haunted him ever since that day when he had heard the story. The thought that one day, one day when his parents realized how bad he truly was not just at school but at everything -- sports, humor, tricks, intelligence, popularity – one day one of his parents might think in the back of their minds, *was it worth it to pay that much money for this failure?* He would reassure himself that this wouldn't happen, that his parents would always love him for what he was. But, in the back of his mind he knew that there would be a day when that could happen.

He had finally reached his 'house', which was just about three hundred bricks stacked like a square. He was about to open his wooden door, when he was struck with curiosity. He reached into his bag and took out the orange envelope. He sat down beneath the tin sheet that was his roof, and began to read.

> *Dear Mr. and Mrs. Clarence,*
>
> *We are sorry to inform you that your child was not selected to be at Naita Academy next year. Although Blit is a sweet child, he lacks the skills that are needed to be at Naita. His intelligence is well below that of his classmates, and he has made no friends in the three months that he has been here.*
>
> *I hope you understand our decision.*
>
> *Thank you,*
> *Brent Gaslo, Naita Headmaster*

It took Blit fifteen minutes to read it, not just because he was a poor reader, but also because reading in English was extremely hard. If this had been written in Mondelf, the previous primary language of Neptune, he could have read it in five minutes. But English was hard, and only about a quarter of the people on Neptune used it regularly. The Empire had recently made it a law that people had to speak English, but since most of the people in the Empire couldn't read English, some writing was in English and some was in Mondelf, and the Empire didn't actually care much. The only English writing they had learned was from the Men from Mars, who got a lot of English from explorers from Earth. Naita boasted being the only school outside the Empire that taught reading and writing in English.

Despite the time it took him to read it, Blit read the letter twice more, each time hoping he had read it wrong before. But no. It was correct. He had not been selected to continue at the Academy the next year. It didn't surprise him. He was, after all, quite poor in school. But the thing was, he knew this wasn't how it worked in Naita. There was no selection for next year. All students were allowed to continue. He understood what was really happening. He was being kicked out.

He opened up the door to his house, pushing the tears back from his eyes. When he looked inside the single room, he saw his father sitting on the ground.

"Why are you home so early, Dad?" Blit asked, trying to remain calm.

"I got the day off early," he said, smiling. "Sit down. Your mother and I have a surprise for you."

A surprise? What could it be? Taken over by curiosity, he sat down next to his parents on the worn out floor. His mother had a nice little smile on her face, and Blit hadn't seen her this happy for a long time. "Your mother," his father said, "is going to have a baby."

A baby? Blit had not seen that coming. He had thought they might say something like he was going to a new school, or something like that, but not a baby.

"Every month since you were born, no matter what happened, no matter how big a loan I had to take, I would put at least two yert into a box that I have. And now after eight years of doing this, I have two hundred yert in the box, which is sufficient to pay for the hospital bills."

"Two hundred yert! But fifty yert is enough to pay for our town hospital."

"Oh no, Blit. We're paying for admission at Himbo hospital."

"Himbo! Is it a boy or a girl?"

"A boy. He'll be born next week."

"Do you know what his name will be?"

"Oh yes. We chose his name quite a while ago. His name will be Humbert."

Ten days later, in the midst of winter break, Blit gratefully left his house to meet his baby brother for the first time. He trudged through the snow, making one footprint after another, without thinking about anything except that he was going to see his parents again. Last night had been the first night that he had ever spent alone, and it had troubled him, haunted him to be alone in the house where he had slept every night of his life. But he had said to his parents that he could do it, and he had done it, and now he was going to see his parents again.

And of course, there was the baby. Blit was excited to see him too, just not as much as to see his parents. It took him two and a half hours to walk to Himbo, which was more than it should have taken because he had been disturbed by a pack of spitters on the street. Although he was shivering, he felt much warmer when he felt his fabric after seeing the red naked bodies of the spitters. One of them had collapsed and died right in front of his eyes.

The thin, shivering body of the spitter had coughed up some spit and snow, and then lay there, his eyes still open, but in a dead sort of way. It wasn't unusual, of course. He had seen spitters die before, but none when he was alone. None without his parents or schoolmates, even if they weren't his friends.

Nevertheless, he eventually reached Himbo. He stood in front of the hospital in awe of it. It was at least an acre big, and had been constructed completely of dried mud, and now had a thick layer of ice over it. The door was not just the plank of wood that was used everywhere else, but had hinges, and a doorknob.

Standing outside the door was a young man dressed in the same fabric that Blit was wearing. He gave him a little grin despite the cold, and said, "How may I help you, young man?"

"My parents are in the hospital with their newborn baby," Blit said slowly.

"Well then come on in," the man said, opening the door.

Blit stepped inside, and saw he was in a small room, about twice the size of his house. There was a small table with a woman behind it. "Miss, I'm here to see my parents," Blit said in a small voice.

The woman gave him a small smile, and asked what his parent's names were. When he told her, she said, "Yes, they said you were coming today." She pointed to a door. "Just go in there, and up three flights of stairs. They'll be in the room there."

He did as he was told, and finally was in front of the door. He was about to knock, when he heard something odd. His father's voice.

"He was born from a bet!" his father's voice said, laughing.

Born from a bet? Who? Humbert? It was too much to think about, so he just knocked on the door. It opened, and then he was in the middle of hugs and kisses, and questions, but finally when it all stopped, he saw his brother for the first time.

He was small, but not nearly as small as Blit had been when he was born. He had dark eyes that were alert, even at this young age. He already had a large crop of jet black hair, and his cheeks didn't have the pinkness that most babies had. He was dressed in the piece of fabric that they wrapped around babies' middle when they were born, and he had another piece wrapped around his chest to keep him warm.

Blit had never seen his parents so happy. His mother's eyes were alight with joy, and his father kept laughing and tickling the baby. "Here at Himbo," he said to Blit, "they do a little Intelligence Assessment on the newborn babies. And this one," he pointed at Humbert, "this one got the highest score they have ever given in twenty-three years."

Blit knew his father wasn't trying to make him feel bad, and he knew that he too should feel happy, but he couldn't. His parents had tried to be nice about his getting kicked out of Naita, but he had been able to see how upset they were. And never, not once in his eight years of existence, had he ever seen his parents as happy as they were now.

He realized that he was jealous of his newborn baby brother, but he didn't even care. Choking back tears, he turned around and walked toward the wall so his parents couldn't see him. He tried to stand upright and normal, but he lost control of himself.

He collapsed on the floor, his eyes pooling with tears. He saw his mother walking towards him, but he just started screaming. It was too much. Everything that had happened to him since he was born started flooding onto him: the stories of him nearly dying when in the hospital, his parents spending all their savings to allow him to live, getting kicked out of Naita, seeing the spitter die, having some genius baby brother, all of it. He kicked his mother in her shin, and his throat was already hoarse from screaming. Then he finally saw a nurse approaching him. He brought back his fist, ready to hurt her too, when she injected something in his arm. It brought searing pain for a moment, and then all was black.

Eight years later, Naita academy received a letter. Brent Gaslo, the Headmaster, tore it open, already laughing. "Ward Clarence? If I were him, I would've moved to Mars. What does he think he's doing, sending me another letter? He was one of those failures right, Charin?"

His secretary nodded. "Not just any failure, though. His son was Blit."

"Blit!" Brent rolled over in his seat, trying to control his laughter. He weighed about as much as the standard house on Neptune, and his thick, greasy hair was the color of a rotten peach.

His secretary, on the other hand, was as thin as a pencil, and had thin, silky, straight, black hair. "I believe Blit was diagnosed with keylice recently."

Many centuries ago, Neptune had been locked in a deadly war with the people from a small sub-planet far from Neptune. The strongest power the small planet held was a concoction they had created. If even one drop of the concoction was drunk, it caused the drinker to go crazy. The victim would lose his memory, spend most of his waking hours screaming, and his intelligence would drop drastically. Before the war began, people from the other planet had started coming to Neptune and getting jobs as drink sellers. They would mix some of the strange brew into the drinks. When ninety percent of Neptune's population had gone crazy, they attacked.

The new people won the war and they ruled Neptune for a long time. Finally, there was an uprising, and the Neptunites rose to power again. Of course they tried very hard to dispose of all traces of the potion. And they were sure they had, until one day a baby had the symptoms of drinking the potion. When that had happened, the Empire made a new law. They called the disease keylice, declared it to be contagious, and said that anyone with it would be killed instantaneously. From that day on, keylice seemed to infect random people, and those infected would always, always, be killed.

"Keylice? And he's alive?"

"I believe the Empire is practically pushing down their door. It'll only be a matter of time before his death."

"Well, then I take back what I said about Mars. I hope his family moves to Venus."

Even his secretary had to smile at that. Venus, Mars, and Neptune had always had an alliance, until recently, when Venus suddenly attacked Neptune. Luckily, Neptune was well prepared for this kind of attack, and after keeping its defenses up and crushing Venus, they had sent back their own counterattack, in which Neptune had wiped out the entire population of Venus. The last Venusian had died about four months ago. Since then, there had been no contact with Mars. The Empire was spending a huge amount of money on rebuilding their defenses, as they were expecting an attack from Mars.

"Well, read the letter out loud, sir," the secretary said.

"Dear Mr. Gaslo," the headmaster began mockingly. "I am writing to enroll my son, Humbert Clarence, at Naita academy. I know that generally if someone has been dismissed from Naita, the school does not admit their siblings, but I feel that Humbert is different. I ask you to let him in for just two weeks. If you are not satisfied, then we will happily accept your decision. In case it helps you make your decision, then I will pay ten yert a day for the two weeks that the school is testing out Humbert. Yours truly, Ward and Keileen Clarence.' Ten yert a day! Since when did the Clarences have so much money?"

Charin, who knew practically everything that happened on Neptune, shrugged. "The Empire has been after them for years. Since Humbert's birth, they seemed to suddenly have a huge amount of money. Ward claims he had just been playing in an illegal lottery, and happily gave the money for the ticket. But the authorities found no record of him spending in lotteries. At the same time, there were no public robberies in the week before he started spending all the money. People are saying that between the money and Blit's keylice, the Clarences have an Empire official in their house more than once a week."

Brent nodded. "Very well. Send them back a letter saying that we will allow Humbert in with the ten yert per day policy. And keep me updated on what happens with the Clarences."

Three weeks later, the long expected 'new kid' arrived at Naita Academy. He was extremely handsome for an eight-year-old, with smart locks of jet black hair. He had very dark eyes, and was dressed as most of the richer kids at Naita were, in thick grey fabric that covered his whole body. As he walked up the stairs to the academy, Humbert could see many people watching, but he pretended that he didn't notice. He stepped into the room he had been sent to. The woman who greeted him was extremely thin.

"Hello, I'm Ms. Charin, and I'll be your helper for these two weeks. We aren't going to give you a permanent schedule, just in case you don't continue. Instead, you'll get to spend two full days in each of our five major classes; *Space: our Friends and Enemies, History of Neptune, English, Technology,* and *Math.* Does that sound all right?"

Humbert lifted his head up. "Yes, Ms. Charin, that would be very nice. Today do I have the class about space?"

"That's right. I can take you to the room."

From behind her, a voice spoke. "I can take him, Ms. Charin." Humbert turned around and saw a medium sized girl with blond hair, about Humbert's own age. Ms. Charin looked at her for a moment and then said, "Fine, go ahead, Veera." With that, Ms. Charin turned and walked away, leaving the two children standing there.

"Thank you very much," Humbert said to the girl.

"Oh no problem. It's just, you need a friend in Mr. Oxin's class."

"Is he the Space teacher?"

"He is, and he's also the meanest of all the teachers. Come on, you don't want to be late." The two children went running down hallway after hallway, until they got to the room with the post that said, *Rile Oxin, Space: Friends and Enemies.*

Humbert had just walked in when there was a loud rapping noise. Sitting at the table was a man rapping on it with a sharp metal stick. He was young, although there was something old and bitter about him. He had grey eyes, and was dressed in a grey coat. His hair was already greyish, despite his face not having a single wrinkle.

The man stood up and pointed at Humbert with his stick. "You are the new student?"

Humbert stood up and nodded. "Yes sir."

"Well, we'll see in a moment if you're good enough to stay here." Some kids in the class laughed. "Everyone please turn to page 93 in your space books please."

Humbert started to raise his hand, but Mr. Oxin just laughed. "If you're as good as I hear you are, you won't need a book. Now, can somebody tell me what the Unknown Alliance is? I know we haven't learned about this, but information about this is in your books, and I want to see how much you know. Raise your hand if you know."

Humbert raised his hand, as did one other boy. The other boy had thick brown hair, and was a bit chubby. He had been laughing at Humbert the hardest of everyone, though his head had been too far down to see his face. Mr. Oxin gave a curt smile. "Humbert, go ahead."

Humbert stood up, took a deep breath and spoke. "The Unknown Alliance is the alliance of Uranus, Jupiter, and Saturn. It is called the Unknown Alliance because very little is known about those planets and their alliance."

"Very good," Mr. Oxin sneered. "But then what about the other ones?"

Humbert looked at him, his face bright. "Yes sir. They are Earth and Mercury."

By now Mr. Oxin did not look happy and it was clear he wasn't going to back down until Humbert got something wrong. "Tell me about them."

"Mercury is much too hot to live on, and there are no signs of life there. As for Earth, well we know that people live there, although besides that little is known. And of course, there is the rumor that the people on Earth use up all of their space. As in, there is no space on Earth that is unexplored. But that's just a rumor."

"Have we ever been to Earth?"

"No, sir."

Mr. Oxin nodded and gave him a smile. "Very good." He realized he would have to get used to this boy knowing a lot, especially since he was probably going to stay at the school. "So, what you just heard introduces us to our next unit. As you just heard, the Unknown Alliance is the alliance of Uranus, Jupiter, and Saturn. Now, can someone please name all the planets in order from largest to smallest?"

This time a handful of hands rose, including Humbert, the chubby boy who had raised his hand earlier, Veera, and three or four other boys and girls. This time though, Mr. Oxin pointed at the chubby boy. "Go ahead, Trinket," he said.

The chubby boy looked up to reveal his features: a thin nose, shallow brown eyes, and thick dark lips. Despite being only eight years old, he already had the voice of an authority. "Jupiter, Saturn, Uranus, Neptune, Earth, Venus, Mars, and Mercury."

For the first time during this class, Mr. Oxin gave a warm smile. "Excellent job," he said.

Humbert understood this all too well. He would have to work hard to make Mr. Oxin like him, and even harder if he wanted to graduate from Naita, despite being so smart. But he would do it, he would do everything needed to graduate because that would allow him to achieve the one thing he had to: saving his brother.

Two weeks later at the Clarences' house, there was a vigorous knock on the door. Humbert, Blit, and Keileen were the only people at home. "Quickly," hissed Keileen to Blit. "Get into the cupboard." As soon as the door of the cupboard had slammed shut, Keileen opened the door.

Three men entered dressed in black and red Empire uniforms. "How may I help you?" Keileen ushered the men inside.

"We are here for the same reason we were here last week. We would like to take Mr. Blit Clarence away, on the charge of being diagnosed with keylice."

Humbert wandered over next to his mother and looked at the men with her. "And as we told you last week," Keileen said icily, "Blit has run away from us."

"We are well aware of that, madam," the man said. "So in that case, I'm sure you wouldn't mind us conducting a quick search of your 'house'?"

There was a short silence, and the guard was having a hard time keeping his victory smile off his face. Then eight-year-old Humbert spoke up. "Sir," he said politely. "The personal belongings of people are valued on Neptune, and there is no law of the Empire that says that a couple of standard guards have the right to search one's house. In fact, provision nineteen of our Code of Laws explicitly prohibits guards from searching the home of citizens."

All three of the men's mouths fell open, and for a moment Humbert thought they would start tearing the house apart in their search. But they just nodded. "You're a bright kid," one of them said, before they all left.

Two days later, a new law came out stating that any Empire official could search any house on Neptune. The Clarences built a tiny hut in a nearby plot of land, and left Blit there for a week, a week during which guards from the Empire came every day to the house searching for Blit. But finally after a long week of Humbert and his parents sneaking food to the hut, the officials stopped searching. And after a month without any sign of them, Blit returned to the house. Things were far from good, but there was some peace.

Six uneventful years went by, with Humbert working hard at Naita. Blit stayed at home and tried to help as much as he could, but his mental condition had gotten much worse. He was twenty-one years old, but had a hard time remembering anything. Nor could he go outside, because he would instantly be sent away. His only joy was when Humbert came home from school. About twenty minutes before he would come home, Blit would stop doing anything and just wait for him. When his brother arrived, they would hug each other, and the fourteen-year-old would quickly finish his homework and then spend the rest of the day talking with his brother. He would tell him something interesting that he had learned, and then would ask Blit what he thought about it. Usually Blit would just smile and nod, not really understanding any of it, but sometimes he would ask a question about it, or say that one day he would do that.

Humbert would also tell Blit something about the outside world, the markets, the people, the animals, or, best of all, Naita. Humbert would start to say something about Naita, and sometimes it would spark Blit's memory, and he would add on to it, and talk so much about some little detail about the school that Humbert had completely forgotten. And so it would continue all the way until dinner time.

Mars had also turned against Neptune very recently. When Humbert was thirteen, Mars tried to attack Neptune, but Lather Gire, the man in charge of Neptune had responded amazingly well. He had had his men destroy all the Martian ships before they were even four miles into the Empire. He then sent out Neptune's ships to strike back at Mars.

At Naita, it had become time for the last four years of Humbert's education there. This meant it was time for him to choose one main career to study. For Humbert, the choice was easy. He decided to pursue a career in Space Exploration.

He was the best student in his class, but Trinket, the chubby boy, was never far behind. In fact, in skills, they were about the same. The difference was their thinking. While Trinket tended to think about things in a straightforward, governmental type of way, Humbert would ask challenging questions, and wouldn't stop until he was completely certain about how things worked.

After three years in advanced training, it had become clear that either Trinket or Humbert would be the next leader of Neptune. They had both invented extraordinary things. The best thing that Humbert had invented was just an idea, the idea of using the ice outside to cool food, which made it last longer. He had thought of this after spending months pursuing clues about people on Earth. When he had the idea of using ice to store food, it caused a breakthrough in Neptune.

Trinket, meanwhile, had thought of something much more original. He had gotten his hands on one of the fourteen books Mars had sent to Neptune when first forming the alliance. The books had been stolen from astronauts from Earth. One of the books had been a child's book, about something called clones.

No one on Neptune had actually tried to fully understand the book. They had all been reading in amazement, as if they were reading about magic, not even fully processing what they were reading. Trinket read it differently. When he read it, he started actually wondering if it was possible, possible to replicate the thing called DNA. He began thinking about ways this could be done. He told his head teacher, Mr. Raas, and started explaining the idea.

Now, although not many knew this, Kone Raas was more than just the head space exploration teacher for Naita Academy. He also held a senior position in the Empire. Furthermore, it had just been four months earlier when his other top student had spoken to him about the ice box. Kone had dismissed the idea, not realizing the brilliance behind it. And then somehow, Humbert had told the Empire his idea and had become famous for it. If Raas had only listened to him, he would have shared the glory.

So as soon as Raas heard Trinket's idea, he did two things. The first was that he made public what his student had come up with. The second was he took it to the head engineer of the Empire, Lorbit Geisner, who immediately started working on it. And only eighteen weeks later, the Empire created the first clone, all thanks to Trinket.

On one of the first days of Humbert's final year at Naita, Mr. Raas made an announcement to all nine seventeen-year-olds in his Space Exploration class, shortly before class ended. "Like all school years, you have eleven months in your final year at Naita. However, at the end of the tenth month, one and only one of you will be given a scholarship to Dex Academy, which is the best academy on all of Neptune. The Empire only chooses to do this once every five or ten years. Anyone who is not chosen can, of course, apply for Dex, but must obviously be ready to pay the four hundred thousand yert fee."

He paused for a moment, watching the students' reaction. They knew that the chosen person would be Humbert or Trinket, but they didn't know which one.

Trinket jerked his head up, which was something he didn't do very often. At seventeen years old, he had the same alert dark eyes that bore straight into Humbert.

Humbert gave a nod and turned away. He raised his hand in the air. He was dressed in a rumpled white shirt with a black jacket that matched his black hair and eyes. Mr. Raas nodded back at him. "Go ahead, Mr. Clarence."

"Sir, only one boy will be given clearance to Dex?"

Mr. Raas let his gaze hover over him for perhaps a moment too long. "That is correct." He raised his eyebrows at him, as if expecting him to say something else, but of course he didn't. "Any more questions?" When no one else raised their hands, Mr. Raas said, "All right then. Class dismissed."

Humbert got up, stretched his legs, and slung his bag over his shoulder. Despite his small height at birth, he was now as tall as most of the other boys.

He started walking home, and as he did, he thought about what Mr. Raas had said.

He knew that his only choice was to study extra hard. He had thought quite a bit about what he wanted to do when he grew up. There really weren't any jobs on Neptune that interested him. He really wanted to explore other planets, but he had always doubted being able to do that, because every space explorer graduated from Dex. Despite his family having quite a bit of money as a result of his father's bet, he knew they couldn't pay for admission to Dex. But this was an incredible opportunity, and he knew he would have to study at least four or five hours each day all year to beat Trinket.

Of course, there was the enormous problem of Blit. Since Blit was now obese and suffered severely from keylice, his only life was Humbert. How would Humbert break the news to him? He was starting to make a list of ways to tell him, when he stopped for a moment. Something seemed a bit wrong. He looked around the icy landscape, and saw a huge orange box next to him. This had never been here before. And where were the other students who walked home from the academy? He was too far away to actually see Naita, but there were always some students here. And where were his friends?

He climbed an ice stump, and looked back. He saw Veera walking quite a distance away from him. Why was she taking the long way home, when she usually walked with him? He waved at her, but she didn't reply, even though she obviously saw him. Although she was far away, he could see something blue on her cheek, and he could see she was limping. Someone had hurt his first friend at Naita. She was too far away for him to catch up with her, and since she didn't wave to him, he doubted she wanted to see him.

Just then, there was a noise from behind the orange box. He was about to go see what it was, when four burly boys jumped out from behind it. One of them was Trinket.

One of the other boys hurled a large hunk of metal at the ice stump Humbert was standing on. It smashed, and Humbert lost his balance. As soon as he fell, the boys were on top of him. He tried to land a blow on one of them, but another tugged his arm back so hard that he screamed.

Trinket just stood to the side, enjoying himself, while the other three did the work. Humbert started to stand up but one of them kicked him in the groin, and he fell to the ground again. Another boy sat down on his feet, and the third boy sat on his head. Humbert did the only thing he could do. He bit the pants of the boy sitting on his face. The boy gave a yell, and stood up, which let Humbert lift his torso up. The boy sitting on his legs looked dazed, and Humbert smashed his fist into his nose, letting blood run. The boy's eyes closed, and he faded into unconsciousness. Immediately, Humbert felt guilty. What had he done?

He turned to face the third boy, but someone else jammed their iron tipped boot into Humbert's back. "Get down!" Trinket's voice rang out.

"No," Humbert replied weakly, and he felt the load on his back lighten. He no longer felt Trinket's boot on him. But just then, it came flying back down with so much force that Humbert howled. His white shirt was now ripped and ruined. He howled again, and the third boy covered his mouth, with his bare hands. Humbert tried to bite it too, but no sooner had he opened his mouth did the boy's strong grip pull his jaws apart, and no matter how hard he tried to bite, they stayed apart. Then the boy twisted his entire head to the side, and no matter how much Humbert tried to scream, it just came out as a sickening, throaty yell.

"Shut up right now, or I'll have Gormbo snap your head off," Trinket said in his clear voice. Somehow, Humbert managed to stop.

"What did you do to Veera?" Humbert tried to say, but it came out like, "Waa e yu do to Eera?"

Gormbo looked confused, but Trinket understood from behind him. "A few of your closest friends refused to go a different way, so we just had to quickly keep them in check."

"Baa Mehta Ra ally talk about De ow."

Once again, Trinket understood. "Oh, we were going to do this anyway. Just to give you a quick heads up to fall a bit behind this year. But that's enough about me. Let's talk about you, Clarence. I'm afraid it's going to be me that gets the scholarship to Dex this year. Oh, that's me again. Here's where you come in: in order for me to do that, I'll need you to promise me that you're going to back down in your studies. I don't care if you drop out of Naita, or if you stay and just fall behind, or even if you just stay and play with your freak brother."

Humbert's eyes blazed with fury. "Ca yuh let uh ahk norally?"

"Get away from his mouth, Gormbo, and put your foot on his stomach instead." Gormbo deftly let go of Humbert's jaws, and then pressed down onto his stomach.

"Why do you want this?" Humbert asked, through gritted teeth. There was blood everywhere, and he had to make a conscious effort not to start crying. "If you want to get the scholarship, why don't you work to get it?"

Without warning, Gormbo suddenly jabbed his boot deep into Humbert's stomach. Humbert started screaming and choking, and Gormbo was pushing deeper and deeper, and above everything was Trinket's voice.

"I warn you, Clarence, I'm not afraid to kill you. I have big plans. I want to be the next leader of Neptune, and I'm not going to let a scrawny boy like you come between me and my next step to do so." Gormbo's boot was so deep into his stomach that it was practically touching the ground.

Then suddenly it stopped. Trinket's weight was no longer on him, and Gormbo's feet were pulled off. A clear, familiar voice spoke. "Are you okay, Humbert?"

Someone pulled him up. Humbert stood and found himself face to face with Mr. Raas. Despite Mr. Raas having the kindness to break up the fight, it was clear he wasn't going to stay long. "I think you'll be fine, Humbert, just get some rest. I'll excuse you from class tomorrow." He looked around. "This looked like a pretty unfair fight, so expect a decrease in your overall kindness grade, Trinket." Trinket looked around, in a daze. "As for Humbert's torn clothes… let's see, how much did they cost?"

Humbert managed to speak. "About eight hundred yert for all of it, sir."

Mr. Raas quickly took out a handful of coins from his pocket. He counted out eight of them and gave them to him. "That should cover it. I'll be expecting eight hundred yert tomorrow, Trinket, or I'll force your parents to give it to me. Why don't you go home now, boys, and not a word of this in class." And Humbert's savior was gone.

For a second, Humbert thought they would attack him again, but they weren't that stupid. Gormbo, the other boy, and Trinket turned around and went home the way they usually did, without even bothering to wake their unconscious friend.

Humbert was a short distance from his door, limping and bleeding, when it opened from the other side. Two men dressed in Empire uniforms came out. Between them, they were dragging someone. Humbert tried to go forward as fast as he could, straining his eyes to recognize the figure. As it turned out it wasn't necessary. The men dragged him right past Humbert.

It was Blit. "Humbert!" Blit let out a loose scream, but Humbert was just too weak to do anything. The men expected an attack, but Humbert just bowed his head in apology.

"I'll come and get you, Blit," Humbert said weakly, and the guards laughed.

The next day, Humbert and Ward Clarence burst into the keylice slaughterhouse. It was just one large room, with a few doors on the side. Inside the room, there was a large rusty looking machine, which looked a bit too much like a guillotine. There was also a menacing looking man walking around the room.

He had black hair that hung in locks behind his neck, and crystal clear blue eyes. He wore an enormous black rag that wrapped from his waist down to his feet. Besides that, he wore nothing over his chest, and his arms rippled with muscles. "May I help you gentlemen?"

Ward Clarence spoke. "Do you have Blit Clarence in custody here, sir?"

The man casually cracked his knuckles. "Oh yes. He arrived yesterday."

"Where is he?"

"Well, sir, we have a rule here. If the family of the keylice patient is kind enough to hand him or her over to us when we first ask them, then we give the patient a death without pain. If, however, as was the case the Blit, the victim is not handed over at once, then he is tortured for one hour for every day he was held back from us."

Ward stumbled back, and the man stood up a bit taller, his full seven feet. "What kind of torture?" Ward's voice was trembling.

"Oh, we have a variety." The man said unconcernedly. "Peeling off skin, soaking in water and giving electrical shocks, burning flesh, and the like."

Humbert looked the man directly in the eye. "Do you, in your house, have an ice box?"

The man looked a bit confused, but still returned Humbert's stare. "Yes, of course, for plants and meat and whatnot. Who doesn't?"

"Do you know who invented the icing method?"

"I think it was some boy about your age."

"Actually, he is exactly my age. It was me."

For the first time, the man looked away. "What do you want?"

"I am warning you and the rest of Neptune that if you want anything else at all from me, then it's your responsibility to give me back my brother."

"Your brother?"

"That's right. If you do not listen to me, then I will tell the higher ups about this whole conversation. And that will likely put your job on the line."

The man winced. "No need to be rude. I simply do what the Empire tells me to do. You may speak to my boss, if you wish."

"That would be nice," Ward said. "Lead the way."

The man led them to a door, where he knocked. "Come in," a steady voice said.

The muscular man nodded, opened the door, and left. The new man waved in Ward and Humbert. He was dressed in white clothes, and had hazel colored eyes. "May I be of assistance?"

Humbert quietly recounted what had happened since they had arrived. "So we were hoping that you could give Blit back to us."

The man eyed both Humbert and Ward. "I'm afraid there would be many obstacles in the way of us simply letting Blit go. By the time these obstacles have been crossed, your brother, and your son, would be dead. I'm afraid it simply isn't possible."

Humbert could tell that this man was smarter than he might seem at first glance. He was giving them a strong negative answer at first, so that even after they stated all their reasons, the best they could get would be a compromise.

Ward cut in. "Sir, might you mind looking at this from our perspective? If you were a parent, then you would know that the worst thing can ever happen to you is to know that your child is suffering."

"I'm very sorry for your loss, sir, but all parents whose children are diagnosed with keylice must bear this. And you, sir, are in no position to order us around about how we handle our latest keylice patients, especially since you have held him back for so long."

Calmly, but with a determined edge in his voice, Ward said, "Maybe I'm not, but my son definitely is. He is going to create some of the finest things on Neptune. And since I know his relationship with his brother, I know that if Blit dies, the spirit of my son, the smartest baby in the hospital in twenty-three years, will be as dead as his brother. And you have the ability to change that." Ward paused to let that sink in before continuing with his next argument. "Furthermore, the Empire says that those with keylice are killed to prevent them from infecting others. But as you know, my son Blit has been living with us for years now, and none of us show the slightest sign of infection."

The man tilted his head to the side a little, and rested his head on his hands. "I understand what you're saying, but although I am the manager of this facility, I still don't have the power to release prisoners."

"But you have the power to think up excuses. If you tell them that you don't know what happened, they will not lead a lengthy investigation to figure it out."

"But I am not a dishonest man."

Humbert could tell this conversation was going nowhere. "What is your name, sir?"

The man gave a slight smile. "Hart Heelkins."

"Well, I just thought of an idea, Mr. Heelkins. I have a teacher who likes me, named Mr. Kone Raas. As you may be aware, Mr. Raas also happens to have a senior position in the Empire. I think I'll just start to fall behind in my studies. When he asks me why, I'll tell him it was because of a man named Hart Heelkins. And perhaps within forty-eight hours of my telling him that, you'll be a spitter."

Hart nodded, grimacing. "Well, I'm afraid you leave me no choice, then."

Ward shook his head. "No choice but to do what?"

"To give Blit back to you. I'll be right back." He stood up, and walked to the door. "Roclune! Take Blit Clarence out, and bring him here, will you!

"He'll be here shortly. Please, sit down." He pointed at two chairs. Humbert stayed standing. Something didn't seem right. Hart had been far too lenient. Even now, he was smiling, not looking in the least defeated. He had to have a reason for just dropping his entire argument. It could have been the threat of losing his job, but somehow that didn't seem to have scared him very much.

Nevertheless, there was a knock on the door. "Come in!" Hart said, almost laughing.

The door opened and first came the strong man that Humbert had seen at the beginning. And following behind him, was.... Blit.

Humbert pushed his chair away from him, and ran up, wrapping his arms around his twenty-five-year-old brother. And he kept repeating, over and over, "Blit, Blit, Blit." It was then he realized that his brother was not returning the hug. He took a step back, and saw a blank expression on Blit's face.

When Blit saw Humbert's face, he stumbled. "Are-aren't you the-the one who th-threw oil on me when I was burning?" He tilted his head upwards. "Or was that a dream?"

Humbert raced forward and jerked Hart against the wall, his elbow pressing against his throat. Tears were gushing down his cheeks. "What did you do to him?"

Before Hart could answer, someone brought their fist down on Humbert's head. It was Roclune. Then Ward was up. "Don't touch my son!" he bellowed.

The next thing Humbert knew, his father was dragging him out. "Let's go home, Humbert."

It soon became clear that Blit Clarence would never be the same again. Although after a few days he came to recognize that Humbert was not his enemy, he knew next to nothing. Not only that, but he vividly remembered his torture, and would start screaming at random times. The nights were the worst. Not a single night passed without an outburst from him. Sometimes it would be just random sounds, while other times he would shout words. "Get away from me!" "Don't leave me, Humbert!" "Don't hurt me, Daddy!"

It also became clear to Keileen and Ward Clarence that Blit needed something to occupy him during the day, something to keep his mind away from the horrible things that had been done to him. So one day, Keileen introduced him to art. "I'll give you a big task and a small task. Your small task is to make a beautiful painting of me, you, Daddy, and Humbert. Your big task is to master art along the way." She started simple, showing him sketches in the snow, and then slowly led him into scratches on bark.

It didn't take long for Blit to fall in love with art. He would spend the entire day sketching on whatever he could get his hands on. He became so engrossed in art that it would sometimes be Humbert asking Blit to talk instead of vice versa, and sometimes Blit would tell him he was too busy. And on the day that Ward brought home three crisp, fresh pieces of paper, Blit was happier than his parents had ever seen him.

Humbert spent day and night studying, and when the day came that they would decide which boy would be given the scholarship to Dex, he was ready. Although most of the other boys knew that they wouldn't make it, they were extremely eager to meet Lather Gire, who, despite being seventy-four, wanted to come and meet the final geniuses. Only five boys were still in the class. The rest had slowly been weeded out when it became clear that they had no future in space. They had been put in some lesser class where they were learning to become something else. However, the five who were going to be there at the clearance ceremony knew that it would be either Humbert or Trinket. While the other three still studied, they did it only with the incentive of seeing Gire and witnessing the final selection, not with the incentive of getting into Dex.

When the day came, all five boys were seated in a small circle in the small, fancy theater of Naita. They were seated on the stage, with Brent Gaslo standing behind a small stand with some papers and a glass of water. On a nearby chair sat Lather Gire himself. He had short silver hair and intense looking green eyes. His face was wrinkled with time. He was most well-known for his excellent responses to attacks from Mars and Venus. Given his age, it was clear that he would only remain the leader of Neptune for a few more years.

He was already examining the five boys, particularly the two who thought they would be chosen. The one known as Trinket Har did not look happy. His forehead was scrunched up, and his eyes were narrowed. He looked as if he would burst out shouting at any moment. He was sitting across from Humbert Clarence, and would glare at him with such intensity that Humbert would look away.

Even Lather couldn't help but shiver with anticipation to see what the boys' reactions would be when they saw what Lather had proposed.

Sitting in the audience were only thirteen people, the parents and siblings of the five boys.

When everyone had arrived, Brent Gaslo spoke. "Welcome everyone, to the important day where we will decide who will be given a scholarship to the finest academy on Neptune, Dex Academy!" There was cheering from the thirteen people in the audience. "On behalf of Naita Academy, we would like to give a wholehearted thanks to Mr. Lather Gire, who has kindly agreed to announce who will receive this scholarship. Mr. Gire!" There was thunderous applause. Even Blit managed to push his hands together a few times. The five boys were also expected to clap, and they did so. Humbert caught his parents' eyes, and nodded at them.

It was two full minutes until the applause died down. When it did, Brent was standing on the side, and it was Gire who stood behind the stand. "Ladies and gentlemen, in the few times in the past when we provided a scholarship into Dex to a student who attended Naita, we have not needed to spend much time thinking about the decision. There is, in fact, a very simple reason that the scholarship is awarded, and that is because there is one particularly brilliant child." By this point, Gire had made eye contact with every single person in the audience. "But this time is different. For starters, every single child is brilliant." No one said anything, but it was clear that no one believed him. "I'm quite serious. Anyone who showed even a little bit of slacking was immediately kicked out of the advanced class. These five young men are the future of our planet, even if all of them are not admitted into Dex.

"However, if we were forced to choose one person, there is one student who stands out over the rest. Ladies and gentlemen, may I present to you, Humbert Clarence!"

It was too sudden, too immediate. Nobody saw this coming. They thought that Lather would talk for at least another half hour, building up suspense. It was not fitting; it was not right. Almost thirty seconds went by without any actions. Even Humbert didn't move. But finally, finally, Keileen Clarence broke the silence with some clapping.

Then, Humbert got up, and slowly walked over to Gire, who gave him a crisp, hot, fresh paper, the kind that would make Blit jump for joy. It said that Humbert Clarence was now admitted to Dex and provided a full scholarship. At the bottom was Lather Gire's signature, which was written in Mondelf. Humbert took it and, dazed, walked back to his seat. He expected Gire to make a closing speech, however what came out didn't sound like a closing speech. It sounded more like an opening speech.

"I know I said earlier that if I were forced to choose one child, I would choose Humbert, but the thing is, I'm not." Lather was watching the expression on Trinket's face carefully, now. His head had been down, and there had been something horrible in his eyes, but at this, he looked up. "I am in charge of all of Neptune, and there is absolutely no reason at all that I shouldn't let the five smartest youths go to the best school on Neptune. So come on up, all four of you!" He waved certificates around. The boys walked up, some stumbling a bit. They all looked surprised and happy. All except for Trinket. The expression on his face was murderous.

He understood perfectly well what was going on. Gire had understood that he was valuable, and should be let into Dex. He had probably suggested that both he and Humbert be sent to Dex, as it was the obvious solution. Gaslo had probably agreed and was ready to seal the deal, but first asked Raas's view. Raas had probably agreed that he was smart enough, but had told the headmaster how Trinket had unfairly outnumbered and attacked Humbert and been ready to kill him. Gaslo may have related this back to Gire, who said that Trinket obviously shouldn't be rewarded by being given clearance into the school.

They had then arrived at the conclusion that the best option was to have them all let into Dex, but accept Humbert first to give him prominence. They may have gotten wind of Trinket's ambition to become the next leader of Neptune, and they knew that his chances of achieving that would be hurt by being one of four boys that barely made it in after another boy.

Still, Trinket walked up, and accepted the certificate with clenched teeth. Gire pretended as if he didn't understand what was going on, and passed him a pleasant smile as he took it. The other boys, of course, were ecstatic. One was almost laughing, and another had a wild grin on his face, as he murmured, "Thank you so much, Mr. Gaslo." And there was Humbert who was back in his seat with a triumphant smile on his face. Tonight was a night where he had come out on top, when all of his hard work was rewarded.

The first thing that Humbert did when he arrived in Dex was to change his name. The name Humbert Clarence would get him nowhere, especially when he learned about Herida Clarence, a girl who had come to Dex and stolen forty-five million yert. She was caught and stripped of her identity, and had become a spitter. Humbert focused on both the fact that his was a lame name, and that it was almost a replica of a criminal's. He thought that it would be interesting to see what would happen if he took a common name from earth. He debated for a long time, and finally decided that it would only help his cause for exploring planets. He didn't change it legally, because then it would be in the news and all, so he just told his teachers that his name was Jack Keeper.

Things went well in Dex. According to the school rules, he had to stay there for one full year without being able to go back home, but he was very interested in what he was being taught so he did not mind. He was at the top of the class, although Trinket was studying just as hard. Despite not being able to go home, he was able to communicate with his family by writing letters. He sent most of them to Blit, but when he got very vague, random replies, he started writing to his parents instead.

When he went back home after a full year of schooling, he was amazed. His brother had become an incredible artist. When he wasn't drawing, his keylice got the better of him, and he would be screaming and throwing things. But whenever this would happen, someone would give him a pencil and paper, and it would brush across the paper, creating shadows, clothing, creases in skin, details that no one had ever thought to draw. And then there was the painting that Blit was always talking about. He said he was going to make a portrait of their whole family and give it to Humbert. He said it would be so beautiful that everyone would stop and stare at it. He said that Humbert would show it to his teachers at Dex, and they would demand that Blit, himself be brought to Dex. He said that he would be known as the best artist in the universe, and people would come to his house and give him hundreds of yert to watch him draw. He said that it would be his gateway to success. He said he would be more famous than anyone had ever been, all because of this painting he planned to make.

Eight years later, in a small room in the center of the Empire, a young man sat down in a chair across from another young man. Except for the men, the room was bare.

One man had black hair, and black eyes, and a black cloak was wrapped around him. He was known as The Keeper, although his real name was Humbert Clarence. The other man was not a handsome man. His thin nose had a strange part in the middle, where it seemed to curve down and then up again. His mouth was twisted into a snarl, and his eyes were brown and arrogant. He was known as The Governor (based on the English word), though his real name was Trinket Har. He was the leader of Neptune.

The Governor spoke and he did not hide the resentment in his voice. "I understand that you are here, *Mr. Clarence*, to talk about planetary exploration." Everyone knew that the two geniuses did not get along well, and there was nothing either of them hated more than being called by their real name.

"That is correct, Trinket," The Keeper replied coolly. It had become a law that no one was allowed to call The Governor by his real name, but The Keeper knew that he wouldn't be harmed. It would cause an outrage. "I feel that since our alliance with Venus and Mars has ended, we are exposed to risks, greater risks then we have faced in recent years." He took a deep breath. "I think that we should consider heading to Earth to seek, at the very least, more information. We can use what we learn from them to become stronger."

"People of Neptune have debated going to Earth for centuries, Mr. Clarence." He had a gruff, low voice, that went perfectly with the rest of him.

"I know that, but it is time we make a decision." He stood up. "We, Neptune, are a tiny part of our universe. I am tired of the way we live our life. I'm tired of our discrimination, of our cruelty to people with fewer yert. I'm tired of the hazy standard life. I want to go places, to do things. And the perfect place to start is Earth."

The Governor seized his opportunity. "I'm sure that *you* would, Humbert. I'm sure that *you* want to go places, that *you* want to see new planets, to see new places. But unfortunately for you, the entire planet of Neptune does not simply revolve around what you, Humbert Clarence, want to do!"

The Keeper handled the attack with some humor. "You should know that better than anyone." There was confused silence. "The entire planet of Neptune revolves around the sun, Trinket!" Humbert took advantage of Trinket's momentary speechlessness. "But I didn't come here to talk about what I want to do. I have a proposal. You send me to Earth with a few clones and nothing else. I'll try to keep some technological contact with you the whole time. I'll explore for a few months. When I have some sort of grip on what's going on, I'll collect ten or twelve young earthlings who know a lot about life there. I'll have them tell me all that they know. Remember how knowledgeable we were as students? I will find youths like that. Then after I've learned from them I'll just leave and come back, and relay to you what has happened. Then it will be up to you to decide what to do next."

There were a few seconds of silence. "I like your plan more than I thought I would. But there must be a few adjustments. Firstly, you cannot just leave the young earthlings there to tell their parents that a strange man asked them about their world. They must be disposed of."

The Keeper looked like he was going to protest, but he just nodded. "If that is your wish."

"Secondly, you know what Uranus has done, correct?"

"I do." There was life on Uranus, and they had recently started colonies in the empty space of Venus and Mars. The Governor was afraid that Neptune would be next, and had spent a huge amount of money on defenses.

"If news gets out that…" The Governor paused as if it was painful to get out the next words, "…an important man has left, then Uranus might find out and attack. So, my final wish is that you tell no one of your plans before you leave. If you wish, after you leave we can tell your family where you actually are, and have them sworn to an oath of secrecy. If you agree to that, then I will fund your mission."

The Keeper's head was spinning. It was too good to believe, to believe that in just a few months, he could be on Earth. But what would his family think if he just left, without telling them? But he had to. He had to agree. "Very well, then, Trinket. When will I depart? In three weeks?"

The Governor gave a hearty laugh. "You really think we can make preparations on such short notice? It will take a minimum of a year."

This was one thing that Humbert was not ready to back down on, and he knew the Empire could prepare more quickly than this, if there was commitment from the top. "Make it six months then. No more, no less. I'll go to work as normal for the next five months, and then I'll go to my parent's house for the last month. You can tell everyone that I have become seriously ill. Then a year later when I arrive back, you can tell the real story."

"That's fine."

"May I leave now?"

"Just one more thing."

The Keeper was confused now. "What is it?"

The Governor looked seriously at the Keeper. "Did you read the fourteen books from Earth that Mars gave us to seal the alliance?"

"No."

"Typical. But one of those books was titled the hundred most beautiful places on Earth. They are truly beautiful. Some of them are called beaches. Do you know what beaches are?"

"No."

"It is a mass quantity of salt water next to a beautiful substance called sand, which is made of powdered stones. There are many people relaxing on the white beautiful sands. The water is bright blue, and there are waves, which are like walls of water that rise up. It isn't dangerous. It's as though it was made solely for enjoyment. And there are kids, the age we were when we first met. These kids swim in the water and make castles out of the sand, packing it together with water. But it isn't just beaches. There are mountains, which are tall chunks of rock, and trees, and streams that stretch on for miles. Some men climb them for a living.

"For a living, Humbert, a living! Their job is to climb these beautiful mountains. And it is bright. The sun is brighter and warmer there than it ever is here."

"What does that have to do with anything?"

"Nothing. I just want to prepare you."

The Keeper's eyebrows perked up. "May I leave then?"

The Governor stood up. "Go right ahead, Mr. Keeper. It's been a pleasure doing business with you."

No sooner had the Keeper left the building when another man walked into the Governor's room. "Hello, Hart. What brings you here?"

Ten years had not changed Hart Heelkins. Some strands of grey hair had mingled with the brown, but his hazel eyes were as bright as ever, and his face had only become crueler since he left the keylice slaughter house. "Governor! I was listening to your conversation from above, and I realized you forgot something. How do you know that the Keeper won't decide to stay on Earth?"

The governor laughed harshly. "You really are an idiot, aren't you, Hart?" Hart's face flushed. "That's why I was preparing him with descriptions of the beaches and mountains. But I always have a backup plan. If he doesn't return within two years, I'll kill his brother."

Five months later, when Humbert Clarence came for a 'vacation' at his parent's house, his brother said nothing about his painting. The Keeper interpreted the silence sadly. He thought, like so many other things, Blit had given up on art. There was no sign of any artistic materials, not even a sheet of paper.

Humbert had arranged his vacation so that at the end of the month when he left early in the morning, his family thought he was going home. During the month that he was there Humbert began to fear that his thirty-four-year-old brother had gotten worse. Many times, The Keeper would be about to ask Blit to draw something for him, if only to make him stop screaming, but he resisted. Other times he noticed that Blit would look at him and get a faraway look in his eyes.

To make the departure easier, he had arranged to leave at five in the morning on the fifth day of the seventh rotation, before his family would even be awake. Although he told them he was going home, he had arranged to go to straight to the launch center where he would depart for Earth.

> *Day 5, Rotation 7*
> *24, Bridge Street, Sector 45, The Empire*
> *Dear Humby,*
>
> *I had no idea that you were leaving so early. I know this will probably arrive at your house about the same time that you get there, and I hope that your foot is on your doorstep at the same time that a man comes with this very package. I know that you have already seen what is under my letter, and I hope you are in awe of it. I thought that I couldn't keep a secret, but I kept it for a whole month while you were here. Every night, after you were asleep, I was up for hours perfecting my painting. I was going to give it to you on your last day here, but you left so early that I guess you'll get it at your house. Please write back with feedback. Take it to The Governor, keep it in your house, hold it close to your heart. And if you ever remember the Blit yelling from torture, the Blit with keylice, look at this painting and remember this Blit instead. This is the painting that took me nine years to make. Every artistic technique I learned, every shadow I drew, every feeling I tried to express through my paints, it was all practice for this.*

The next time you come, tell me about some more memories from Naita. I still dream about that place sometimes. We'll see who remembers more then.

I love you more than anyone else in the world,

Blit

The Right Thing

TWO PEOPLE WALKED INTO PRIYA market that Sunday. Mr. Peter Lisgard and his thirteen-year-old son Nick, both foreigners from England, were living in India. The first thing you pass in Priya Market when you enter is McDonalds. It occurred to Mr. Lisgard that it was a nice fatherly thing to do, when you pass by a McDonalds, to buy your son an ice cream. It was the right thing to do. So he asked his son, "Nick, would you like an ice cream cone?" And Nick thought that it would be pretty rude to say no, and he did like ice cream and he knew what the right thing to do was.

So he replied, "Yes please."

So Mr. Lisgard bought his son an ice cream and then they strolled down the road where they got money at the bank and oatmeal at the grocery store and were about to leave when Mr. Lisgard remembered that his wife wanted a new charger for her phone. So even though it cost 4,000 rupees, he decided it was the right thing to do, because his wife used her phone a lot and needed a good charger. But then Mr. Lisgard and the shop owner started arguing about the price, and Nick realized that his father was probably uncomfortable talking about money when his son was right there, so he walked outside the shop. After all, since his father had bought him an ice cream cone, he wanted to return the favor. It was the right thing to do.

When Nick came outside, he saw a small beggar boy. His hands were dirty, and he was dressed in greasy rags. His hair was an odd light brown color, probably from being exposed to so much pollution and not getting enough to eat. When he saw the ice cream cone in Nick's hand, his eyes lit up. He reached out his hand with his palm open. Nick was about halfway done with his ice cream cone already. Nick thought that the boy had probably never eaten an ice cream cone before, and it would be the right thing to do to give it to him. So he gave the boy the ice cream. And Mr. Lisgard walked out of the store, just in time to see the whole thing. "Well," he thought, "I want to encourage that kind behavior."

So as they walked out of Priya Market, Mr. Lisgard asked his son again, "Since you gave your ice cream to that boy, would you like another?" Now it occurred to Nick that it wasn't right to eat one and a half ice cream cones in one day. Besides sharing your ice cream cone was the right thing to do.

So he said, "Sure, but only if you share it with me." Now it just so happened that Nick had a cold. Mr. Lisgard didn't want to catch it, but he thought sharing the cone would be the right thing to do, to encourage sharing. So he shared the ice cream, and they finished it as they walked home.

But there was a problem. Some of Nick's germs went from his mouth to the ice cream cone to Mr. Lisgard's mouth. And so it was that Mr. Lisgard got sick.

For some reason, the cold that Mr. Lisgard got was much worse than Nick's had been. It soon turned into a fever and a chest infection.

Mr. Lisgard worked for Hewlett-Packard, the computer company. He had twenty leave days and eight sick days every year. It so happens that the Lisgards had treated themselves to a three-and-a-half-week vacation in South India not so long ago. They had gone to Kerala, Goa, and Tamil Nadu. And so Mr. Lisgard had used all of his leave days on that vacation and had used five of his sick days the month before when he had the flu.

Now Mr. Lisgard immediately used up his final three sick days. On the day that his leave days started going into the negatives, his son decided to see how he was feeling. Nick strolled into the hot room where his father was resting, and sat down next to his father's bed. He wondered for a moment what the right thing was to say to him. Finally, he decided that the right thing was to apologize. So he said, "I'm really sorry for making you get sick, Dad."

At this rather sentimental point in the narrative, someone else entered the room. The family's servant, Ashok, a tall upright man, arrived, holding a tray with two clear glasses of water on it. Nick took one, but as his father got up to take the other, the servant gestured for him to lay back down onto his bed again, and leaned down to give him the water himself. Unfortunately, Ashok's angle was not quite right, and the glass slid off the tray and broke on the floor. Shards of glass flew everywhere, and the hard wood floor soaked up the water. Ashok left in a rush, saying he would be back to clean it up.

Mr. Lisgard glanced at his son, and a smile appeared on his lips. "Well, Nick," Mr. Lisgard said, "I accept your apology. Sometimes we can all do the right thing, but it still leads to a bad outcome."

Nick heaved himself onto the bed, watching Ashok come back in and clean up the mess. "Maybe that's true," Nick said. "But then why should we still do the right thing, if it can cause bad things to happen?"

Mr. Lisgard smiled again but didn't answer, and neither did his son. But their eyes locked for a moment, and as they sat, watching Ashok silently sweep up the glass, they both understood the answer to Nick's question, though neither would have been able to put it into words.

The Four-Dimensional Story

*T*HIS TAXI COMPANY CANNOT BE *trusted. That was my thought as I stepped into the car. It was a small rickety car, with peeling black paint. The driver was dressed in a black shirt that said,* **NO! YOU ARE WRONG! SO JUST SIT IN YOUR WRONGNESS AND BE WRONG!** *He was wearing tattered black jeans, and sunglasses jammed up against his eyes.*

One thing I liked about being in India was that I got to sit in the front seat, and today was one of those occasions. My parents and younger sister got in the back and our driver gunned the engine. It squeaked and then turned off. I peered in the back and saw my mom's eyebrows lift in concern. The driver tried again and this time it turned on. With that, we started off.

Our driver was talking on the phone faster than he was driving. He was speaking so rapidly, it was hard to understand him, despite the fact that I knew quite a bit of Hindi.

Just when I was starting to relax and think that we would get to our friend's house and everything would be fine, I heard a little bit of what the driver was saying. "I'll be there in five minutes. Five minutes, sweetheart."

Now, who am I to be nosy, but we wouldn't be at our friend's house for at least another half hour. I peered in the back again and saw that my dad was leaning forward like he was about to say something, but then he leaned back again, although I could tell that he was still tense.

By now we were speeding up quite a bit. I looked ahead, and saw an enormous sixteen wheeler truck in our lane. Well, not exactly in our lane. To the right of our lane was another lane, and to the right of that lane was a tall wall. The truck was partly in our lane and partly in the lane next to ours. I expected the driver to stay behind the truck, but no. At the same time, the truck was moving over into the right lane, leaving less and less space between it and the wall. But instead of slowing down, the taxi driver sped up to try to squeeze in the shrinking space. Our driver was trying to pinch between the truck and the wall.

There was a screeching and crunching noise as I realized with horror that we were stuck between the truck and the wall. My sister was crying, and my parents did not look happy.

I looked out my window, and saw the truck driver, an enormous laid back man eating something or other. Our driver wound down my window, tossed his cell phone under my feet, and leaned across me. He was yelling at the truck driver, and although I didn't understand the words, it was clearly nothing good. I didn't like having this man so close to me, and there was something odd on his breath, something I had once smelled at a dinner party. It was the smell of alcohol.

The truck veered to the left, releasing our taxi and drove off. Our driver took off after the truck driver.

He was swerving between lanes, squeezing between cars, and saying what he would do to the truck driver when he caught him. My dad leaned forward and looked angrier then I had ever seen him. His face was bright red, and he was screaming at the driver. "I noted down the truck's license plate, now stop! Stop!"

The driver just shook his head. "I'm gonna get him," he murmured.

"Stop! STOP! I HAVE KIDS WITH ME! Are you going to endanger their lives for the sake of your stupid truck driver? IT'S YOUR FAULT, YOU KNOW! IT'S YOUR FAULT! WHAT WERE YOU THINKING, TRYING TO SQUEEZE BETWEEN THAT TRUCK AND THE WALL?"

The driver seemed to be in a daze. I glanced at the speedometer and saw we were going more than 100 kilometers an hour. "I'm going to call the police!" My father yelled, with his head stuck all the way into the front seat. "Just stop your craziness and take us where we're going!" It was hard to believe he was the same man *who had showed me how to use the queen's gambit on a chess board this morning.*

I thought this would never end: the screaming, the crying, the speeding, and the bright screen of the cell phone still lying on the floor. But finally, after what seemed like forever, the taxi broke down. My family sat there, panting, and thinking about how lucky we had been.

I think that now, as a family, we are more careful. We think a little bit more about the choices we make, because we remember how close we were to losing our lives.

"So what do you think, Ms. Keys?" I was sitting next to my friends, Stefano and Rahul, and Ms. Keys, my assistant English teacher, was reading the drafts of our personal narratives. She had long red hair, and her blue eyes were outlined with black eyeliner.

"Well, Matthew," she said, and she seemed to be choosing her words carefully. She had just moved to India and joined the school a month ago, and had taken the place of Mr. Rafael, whom she could never replace. "I like your style of language, but I'm afraid that your story doesn't meet the criteria. You were supposed to write about an event that changed you. I don't quite see how this drunk driver incident changed you as a person."

"But, Ms. Keys," I said, remembering last night when I had been up until eleven o'clock writing this, "it changed me because, well...."

"Exactly my point. It isn't too late to start over with a new idea. What is an incident that changed your ideals?"

And just like that, my entire draft had been thrown away. "Well, there was this time I went on a roller coaster when I didn't listen to my parents and I regretted it."

"Excellent idea, Matthew." And with that she was gone, praising Stefano's story about going to the Fourth of July fireworks alone.

I sighed and took out a fresh piece of paper. I titled it The Coaster.

Three English classes later, I had finished my piece.

The Coaster

I had been on enough rides to last me a lifetime. Hershey Park was amazing! I had gone on bumper cars that bumped into each other about ten times a minute, a Ferris wheel that took us high over the hill, and tons of other cool rides. Now we were going to the roller coaster section of the park. In the distance I could see the huge loops that the coasters made. I gritted my teeth and started walking toward the roller coasters.

When we got to the roller coaster section I looked at all the roller coasters with awe. Some of them were steep, some weren't. All of them had height or weight limitations. I looked at all of them for a while until I found the biggest one I could ride, for which I just barely made the height limitations because I was tall for my age. I immediately started begging my parents to let me go on it.

Now before you ask "Why would you do that Matthew?" I'll tell you that I wouldn't have done it if this were happening right now. But back then I was a six-year-old with absolutely no experience with roller coasters and I had no idea that they were evil things that make you choke and fear for your life.

My parents warned me not to go on it. They said it was way too big for me and urged me to go on another smaller one. My mother was especially worried. She said I might throw up because it had so many ups and downs. But I persisted.

We were at Hershey Park with some friends, and my friend's older sister went on the same roller coaster that I really wanted to go on. She reported back that it was super scary and she was not going to go on any other roller coasters again at this park.

My parents said, "See? If Anam, who's two years older than you, goes on it, and comes back so scared, you definitely shouldn't go on it." Still I persisted. I told them that other kids were going on it and I was tall enough to be allowed, so why were they not letting me have fun?

At last my parents gave in.

"Don't blame us if it's too scary," they said.

My dad came with me on the ride. We sat down and buckled up our seat belts. We slowly started going up. I started feeling a little bit bored, but I still felt a bit of tingly excitement creeping into my stomach. I remembered Anam's face of fright as she stepped off the roller coaster, and my heartbeat started racing.

We inched up and up and then, just like that, we stopped going up. I tried to get up to see where we were going, just as we lurched down. We were falling, plummeting, and I knew we were going to crash. I was screaming and grabbing on to my dad and starting to choke. Then I realized we were going up again! I didn't know what to do. I just wanted to jump out of the whole ride! I could hear my dad trying to comfort me but it was like his voice was in the background.

I realized that my parents had been right. It wasn't that they wanted to stop me from having fun. They wanted me to have fun. And right now I was not having fun. I was lurched out of my thoughts by the roller coaster going down again. And then it happened again! And again! And again! My throat was parched, and I was feeling very dizzy. I wanted to be anywhere but where I was right now. I wanted to be with my friends, laughing and talking, or be at home, playing ping-pong. Most of all, I wanted to be with my mother. To feel her arms wrapped around me.

When it finally stopped, I unbuckled my seatbelt and sprinted as fast as I could away from the ride as if it were a hungry monster that would grab me and throw me back onto those horrible ups and downs.

The whole rest of the day I was too scared to go on any more rides. Whenever I saw a ride that looked like fun, that image of the roller coaster going down would come into my head and I would politely say, "No thank you."

When we were back in our hotel room, I told my parents how right they were about the roller coaster and apologized for not listening to them. I also said that I was never going to go on a roller coaster again as long as I live. And so far at least, that has been true. That was my first and last roller coaster.

I personally liked my first piece much better, but too bad for me.

The way our English classes work is that our teacher helps us through one piece of writing in the genre we are learning. Then, at the end of the unit, we have an hour in class to write our own piece in that genre to show what we have learned. We are graded on this second piece.

The day of the assessment came, and I knew what I was going to write. I was not over Ms. Keys making me start over, for I knew that if my main English teacher, Mr. Roger had looked at the story about the taxi, he would've understood. I had already brainstormed at home what I was going to write. When the time started, I began scribbling quickly on the paper. When the time ended, I had just written the last word. As Mr. Roger was picking up our papers, I quickly ran through the story in my head.

The Painting

I looked at my final painting. It was a sharp and vivid picture of my family and me in a taxi squeezed between a wall and a truck. The taxi driver could be seen chatting on his cell phone in the window.

"Hi Matthew," came a voice next to me. I turned and saw my art teacher, Ms. Lees.

"Hi Ms. Lees," I said. "Do you like my painting?"

Ms. Lees looked at my painting and sighed. She put her hand into her blond hair and ruffled it. This was her first year at our school and she wasn't as supportive as the rest of the teachers. When she spoke, her voice was heavy, as if she was tired.

"Matthew, this was not the assignment. What you were supposed to do was to paint a picture of an experience that means a lot to you. This is a good picture but looking at this crazy driver, I don't understand what it means to you. Please start over with a painting of something from which I can easily learn something about you."

I wanted to say, "You know what, Ms. Lees, this does mean a lot to me and it was the scariest thing I ever experienced in my lifetime!" Or "You know what? If you had been there you would know how scary it was. So don't speak for me!" But I didn't say any of those things because I knew that I would get in trouble if I said anything like that.

Then I watched as Ms. Lees praised my two friends sitting next to me, Stefan and Ahul, for their pictures of fireworks and a lemonade stand.

I slowly started over, drawing a picture of myself in a meadow with sheep and birds and a beautiful pond.

From this experience I learned that life is sometimes not fair. I also learned that what might mean a lot to one person may be meaningless to someone else. Even though that painting meant a lot to me and depicted one of the scariest times in my life, to Ms. Lees it was just a depressing picture. Also I learned that adults are always the boss so even if I want to say something to them, I have to be careful because they are not my friends. They are teachers and I have to always agree with them.

I nodded and handed my story to Mr. Roger, who winked as he took it. I was glad that it wasn't Ms. Keys who would read and grade it. I wasn't sure if I had done the right thing, but it was too late now.

Time went by, and I started my fantasy unit in English. One day, right before lunch, we got fifteen minutes to read whatever we wanted to. I grabbed a horror story book, called *Double Dare to be Scared*, opened up to a story called The Principal's Office, and began to read.

The story was long and dull, without the author's usual fun, gory style. It was more like realistic fiction, about some boy who had been suspended one too many times, and was sent to the principal's office to be lectured. Soon I felt distracted and I was glad that the story would be over in just another page, and so would this class, when I couldn't believe what I read. The principal had pressed a button on his desk, which caused laser beams to shoot and kill the boy. His remains had been burned, and then collected with a vacuum.

I reread the last page twice, then walked out to lunch, still dazed, as I remembered the last line in the story: "Send in the next student."

I had lunch, and then went to math, which I was happy about. Not only because I liked math, but also because it would hopefully help me forget the story I had read.

In the middle of math, the classroom phone rang. The math teacher, Ms. Pan, answered, "Yes, he's here." Pause. "You want him in your office." Pause. "Sure." She put the phone down and looked directly at me. "Matthew, Ms. Polly would like you in her office."

"Am I in trouble?" I asked.

"I don't think we send you to the counselor's office if you are in trouble," she said.

I walked slowly down the hallway, as if each heavy step took effort. I could see the laser beams jutting out and killing the boy, and the vacuum cleaning up his remains. I wondered if that would be me soon, if the smiling face of Ms. Polly would brighten with joy as she arranged for my demise.

Nevertheless, I got to her office, and tapped timidly on the door. It opened and you beckoned me inside with a smile on your face.

"And here I am," I said to Ms. Polly.

"Wow, Matthew, that's quite a story." I had once read a book that said you can tell if a smile is real by looking at a person's eyes. Right now, Ms. Polly's eyes were crinkling up and seemed to be laughing, so I knew her smile must be real. "Well, I'm really sorry about your experience with Ms. Keys, but I hope that you've generally had a good experience with teachers here at the BFT school?"

"Definitely," I said. "It's a great school and I'm really happy to be here, I just felt hurt when, like I said, Ms. Keys just turned my writing away." When I had first come into her office, Ms. Polly had given me some putty and told me to twist it if I ever felt nervous. Right now, I twisted it until there were creases all over it.

"Of course," Ms. Polly said. "Now my question for you is what do you want to do about it?"

I stretched the putty out until it was so thin you could see through the strands. How was I supposed to answer this? I would feel selfish in a way, if I said I wanted her to get Ms. Keys in trouble. "I don't know," I said, so quietly someone else might not have heard me. But I knew Ms. Polly heard me.

"Can I tell you a secret?" Ms. Polly said, her eyes looking at me warmly.

Under normal circumstances, I would have thought she was treating me like a baby, asking me these cheesy questions, but the thing was, it didn't feel that way. It felt genuine. "Yes," I said.

"Ms. Keys is only staying in your class for another week. After that she'll be joining the high school."

Relief filled me, and suddenly my words were straightforward and clear. "Then I don't think we need to do anything. I mean, I'm not sure I completely forgive her, but if she's leaving, then it's fine." I plopped the putty on the table in front of me.

Ms. Polly beamed at me. "All right then. Is there anything else you want to talk about?"

"I don't think so."

"Think?"

I grinned. "I don't need to talk to you about anything."

"Well then, why don't you return to class?"

I finish typing and reread what I have written, making a few corrections and edits. Then I sit and think. I have been waiting all year to enter the school writing contest. Today the contest was announced, and I want to submit the story I just wrote that is titled "The Three-Dimensional Story." It is what you have just read. I call it three-dimensional because at the end of each piece of the story, the reader realizes it is actually a story within a bigger story.

I debate with myself for a long time whether or not to submit it.

It is my best story, but I am afraid that I might get in trouble or that Ms. Keys will feel sad if she finds out about it. I think about changing some of the names by spelling them backwards or using names that rhymed with the real names, but that seems silly. Finally, I decide that it would be best to submit it as it is. I print it out, put it in an envelope, and send it to my school.

The way the contest works is that after reading all of submissions, the judges pick the top ten pieces, and the authors names are posted outside the school office. Then there is a big show on a Saturday in the auditorium with three judges. The judges read each piece of writing aloud, and each judge ranks each piece between one and ten. The average rating for each writer is posted on the wall. Then the three students with the highest ratings get gold, silver, and bronze trophies.

The day the top ten names are posted, I am on fire with excitement. I ask my mom to drop me off early, and I'm at the list twenty minutes before school starts. Since my last name is Wesner and the names are written in alphabetical order by last name, my eyes immediately go straight to the bottom. And there it is, the last name on the list, Matthew Wesner.

I somehow last the week before the final event on Saturday, but finally I am there, sitting in the semicircle of chairs around the judges. I look over each judge.

The first is Mr. Hannon. He is a really friendly eighth grade English teacher, and I want to have him next year. He is smiling pleasantly at the audience, and already knows me from the chess club. He winks at me when he sees me looking at him.

The second is Mrs. Verma. She is a first grade teacher, and she must also be good at writing. She has short black hair, and greenish eyes that somehow remind me of a cat's.

The third judge is - I stop and rub my eyes to make sure I am seeing correctly, but I know I am. I close my eyes, and slowly massage my temples. The third judge is Ms. Keys.

The judges take turns reading the pieces. Mr. Hannon reads the first girl's piece, and I can't help but think how good it is, and how I am going to lose, especially because Ms. Keys will probably give my piece a one. The judges rate the girl's story, and the average score is seven. Then Mrs. Verma reads, and so forth, until finally Ms. Keys reads the story of the boy sitting right next to me. The stories are read in alphabetical order, so my piece is last.

I do the math after the boy's piece is finished and rated. If I get more than an average seven, then I'll be in third place. If I get more than an average seven point five, then I'll be in second. I have to get an eight point five to be in first place.

Mr. Hannon starts reading, and things are okay until it gets to the second dimension. As soon as Ms. Keys' name is read out, I can see the alarm in her face, and I know I am going to lose. A murmur goes through the audience, and even Mr. Hannon's face starts to get red. As I watch Ms. Keys, I suddenly feel sorry for her. I feel bad for sending the story to the contest. I decide that this is worse than what she did to me during class. I clench the sides of my chair while the story continues. I fantasize about there being a fire alarm, or better yet a real fire so everyone will have to leave and forget about my story.

After what feels like forever, Mr. Hannon reads the scene in Ms. Polly's class and finishes the story. I feel the tension building up in the room.

"An interesting story by Matthew Wesner," Mr. Hannon says. "As always, the judges will have two minutes to think about the story before they rank it."

The two minutes seem to take forever, and I watch Ms. Keys' face the whole time. It is a bit pale, and her eyes seem to be avoiding my gaze.

"All right then," Mr. Hannon's voice booms. "I'll start by giving it a solid seven." My heart sinks. A seven. To get a trophy, Ms. Keys' and Mrs. Verma's scores have to average seven point five or more.

Mrs. Verma looks directly at me. "I rank it eight point five." There's some light applause from the audience. It is now completely up to Ms. Keys. If she gives me a five point five, then I will be tied for third, and I didn't know what would happen then. If she gave anything more than that, I would get a trophy. But I know I shouldn't be thinking about getting a trophy. I should never have submitted a story about her. I'll be lucky if she ranks it more than three.

Ms. Keys pushes her red hair behind her head, clears her throat, and says firmly, "I give it a ten."

The audience applauds loudly, as the two other winners and I walk slowly up to accept our prizes. On the marble base of my gold trophy these words are engraved: **1st Place in 2016 Middle School Writing Contest.** As I pass the judges, I look Ms. Keys in the eyes for the first time since arriving in the auditorium.

She looks me straight in the eye, winks at me, and pulls down on the lobes of her ears, which is the Indian sign for an apology. I don't think anyone notices except for me, but I look back at her and nod, with a smile of thanks. She has been forgiven. And oddly I also feel like I have been forgiven by Ms. Keys – forgiven for writing the story about her, for submitting it to the school contest, for having it read out in front of everyone. Yes, somehow we are both forgiven.

Mother Dairy

I N INDIA YOU DON'T BUY all of your groceries from one store and then leave. Here you go into town and buy vegetables from the vegetable man on the street and fruits from the fruit man on the street and so forth. Everyone in town knows that for dairy products the best (and only) place to go is Mother Dairy. Mother Dairy is a dairy company that has small stores all over India that sell any dairy product you can imagine.

You can get white plastic bags filled with milk, and you can choose how much fat you want, only here they don't say 1% or 2%; they say single-toned or double-toned. You get paneer (something like cottage cheese) to make dinner with, you get yoghurt in three sizes, and you can get ice cream. You can even get milk cakes, which aren't really cakes at all. They are very sweet Indian sweets made from milk and sugar that taste delicious. You can also get frozen peas at Mother Dairy. (Don't ask why.)

Anyway, the Mother Dairy near our house is run by a father and son named Rajesh and Sanjeev Shindari. The funny thing is that the father always seems to be grumpy and the son is always smiling.

Eventually Sanjeev and I became friends. Even though he isn't very old, Sanjeev often reminds me of a jolly grandfather. He has short black hair, always wears a black t-shirt and has a big tummy that falls over his waist. Whenever anyone gets anything from Mother Dairy when Sanjeev is on shift, they get to talk about the local gossip and hear some friendly jokes.

It is a whole different story, though, if Rajesh Shindari is on duty. His hair is bright white, and I have never seen him smile, much less laugh. If he is on shift, the line goes through much, much faster. He never says anything and sometimes you think he hasn't heard you, until half a second later he has your order in his hand and you are expected to leave immediately.

Anyway, when I became friends with Sanjeev, I would go to the shop whenever I could to hang out and talk with him. Soon he started telling me their story, which helped me understand why he was always happy and his dad always grumpy. He told it to me in bits and pieces, but I'll try to pull it all together to tell it to you.

After Sanjeev Shindari graduated from college, his father, a small Mother Dairy shop owner in Lucknow, urged him to join him in the shop.

"A father-son business, what could be nicer?" However, Sanjeev had always dreamed of having a more exciting job and life than running a small Mother Dairy in a city like Lucknow. So, ignoring his father's pleas, he headed off to busy Mumbai.

His father angrily returned to his shop. For years Mr. Rajesh Shindari had hoped that after his son graduated he would join him in his lonely shop, but now his plans had been crushed. He had seen himself spending the days playing Ludo and chess with his son, while customers slowly trickled in and out.

When he got to his shop, Rajesh hurled himself onto his chair angrily. Business was terrible. At least one thing that might be better with his son seeking his fortune in Mumbai is they would have more money.

For the next few days hardly anyone came to his shop. Apparently another company called Amul Milk had come to Lucknow and now everyone was going there. Most of Rajesh's milk soured, and the paneer spoiled. At least the frozen peas were still okay. He put in a tiny order for products to replace the ruined ones. He sure hoped his son was doing better than he was.

And Sanjeev was doing much better than his father. As soon as he arrived in Mumbai he was offered a job as a driver. Mr. William Benton, a rich London businessman had come to India for two years with his family "to explore international business prospects and to give his family a wonderful experience."

Mr. Benton and Sanjeev arrived in Mumbai at the same time. They soon became close friends. When Sanjeev heard that William needed a driver, he said that he would love to work for him. When he heard how much money Mr. Benton would pay him, he was even happier. He thought to himself that this was the first step to making his fortune. Moreover, he had heard how badly his father's business was doing.

After about two months everyone was happy. Mr. Benton and his family were happy because they had a good driver who knew the ins and outs of Indian driving. Sanjeev was happy because he was pursuing his dream in Mumbai and making more money than he ever thought he would make. Even Rajesh was happier than he thought he would be from his son's rash decision, because even though his business was still not going well, they had enough money from his son's job.

Then one spring morning, about four months after the Bentons had moved to Mumbai, something terrible happened. Sanjeev was driving Mr. Benton to work, and he drove fast, easily mastering the twists and turns of Indian traffic. Sanjeev turned around in his seat as he told Mr. Benton a story of something funny that had happened to him. But as Sanjeev turned around, driving the same path he drove every day, he didn't notice the begging children as he skimmed the curb.

Sanjeev swerved to avoid the children and ran right into a newly built lamp post. The lamppost fell over, smashing the roof of the car, and crushing William Benton's skull, instantly killing him.

Sanjeev was unhurt and immediately called the police.

Mrs. Kate Benton had a quick funeral before immediately taking the next plane that she could find back to London with her children.

But it wasn't over. The Bentons filed a case against Sanjeev Shindari. To avoid going to prison, Sanjeev had to pay back to the Bentons the entire cost of the car, and damages expenses from the death of William Benton.

When Sanjeev broke the news to his father back at the Mother Dairy shop, Rajesh Shindari was furious. All of the savings that he had (which was almost nothing) would have to be given to the Bentons, and a large loan would have to be taken.

Sanjeev fled to Lucknow to work with his father, but word soon got around that Sanjeev had been in trouble in Mumbai and had been involved in the death of his employer. Although it had been an accident, rumors started to swirl around town. The few people who still came to their shop stopped coming. In desperation the Shindaris fled to a quiet neighborhood in Delhi, near some relatives of theirs. They reopened their shop there, the father still furious at Sanjeev. Business went much better than it had ever gone in Lucknow, and soon they had started to pay back their debts.

They are still there right now, and my family goes and buys milk from them. And if you go there, depending on who's minding the store when you arrive, you will either be greeted by Sanjeev Shindari, smiling and trying to make a good impression on customers, or by grumpy old Rajesh Shindari, never happy, and still angry at what life handed him.

Meenakshi

M Y NAME IS LOGAN CONNAHAN. I'm thirteen years old and live in Boston, Massachusetts. My father's name is Ivan Connahan. He's half Irish, and half American. My mother's name is Romina Connahan. She's one fourth American, one fourth French, and half Indian. Interesting background, right? I have sandy blond hair and brown eyes. I've been to Ireland and France, and I live in America. But I've never been to India.

Right now I'm sitting on a plane heading to India, so I guess that won't be true for long. The light of the mini TV is shining in my tired eyes, and I turn it off after seeing that there are still nine hours left in the ride. I try to fall asleep, but it's hard with the turbulence shaking the plane.

One day about seven months ago, my seven-year-old sister Maya and I were eating breakfast. It was a Saturday morning, and the sun was shining. The TV was on with some Bugs Bunny cartoons showing, and everyone was enjoying the lazy start to our weekend. We were sitting at the table with my parents, eating waffles and talking about which countries we had been to.

"I've been to Paraguay, Uruguay, Ireland, America, France, India, and Canada," my father said.

"I've been to India, France, England, Germany, and America," my mother said.

"I've been to Ireland, France, and America," seven-year-old Maya said smugly.

"I've been to Ireland, France, America, *and* Thailand," I said even more smugly. "That's one more then you, Maya."

Maya sniffed. "It's not my fault that you got to go on a vacation to Thailand with Mom and Dad before I was born."

"But Thailand is the best of all those countries," I said, smiling.

"Enough, Logan," my Mom said, looking at me.

"Sorry, Mom," I said, and then gave a cough that sounded a lot like "*Jacuzzi.*" I'd told Maya many times about our Jacuzzi in the five-star hotel we had stayed at in Thailand. I could tell neither of my parents had noticed, but Maya was giving me the evil eye. I winked at her, and then took a bite of waffle.

"Anyway," Dad said. "The point is, your mother and I were thinking about going to another country."

Maya sucked in her breath. "Thailand?"

"Well," Dad said. "Maya, you're three eighths American, and a quarter Irish, and an eighth French. And you've –"

"Wait a minute," I interrupted. "I'm also a quarter Indian, Dad."

"I was just getting to that, Logan. You've been to Ireland, and you've been to America, and you've been to France. But you haven't been to India."

"So we're going to India?"

"That's what we were thinking about," my Mom said.

"Can we stay at a hotel with a Jacuzzi?" Maya asked.

"We'll stay at several hotels, Maya. We will go to seven or eight different places, and at most of them we'll stay at hotels, unless we're staying with relatives."

I had to admit, I was getting pretty excited. I loved planning vacations, and with eight or nine places to find hotels and activities for, I would be very busy. "So we'll go during the summer?" I asked.

"Yes," my Mom said. "Dad and I hope to stay at each place for about a week."

"Will it be more like a vacation, or more like just seeing relatives?" I asked, taking another waffle.

"Both," my Dad said. "In some places, like Kerala, it'll be like a vacation. You'll get to stay at a nice hotel and relax for a few days on the beach. In other places, like Uttarakhand, where your mother is from, we would see her family. You would be amazed at how differently they live than we do."

"Just one more question," I said. "Can I plan the trip?"

Dad smiled. "This is the part that we thought you'd be most excited about, Logan. Mom and I know how much you love planning vacations, so we thought we'd let you book all the hotels and planes. We'll give you a budget for all the places, just like a real travel agent. Then we'll check everything before finalizing and making the bookings."

So that was how my four busy months had started. I spent almost all of my time after school working, and finally I'd come up with a nine-week trip. And now I was on my way to India for the first time.

The Delhi airport was different from any airport I'd ever seen. It was huge for one thing, but I'd seen huge airports before. I guess the best way to describe it is bustling. There were so many people there, busy with what they were doing and where they were going. I saw one man pushing a trolley that was so loaded up with suitcases I couldn't see his face. I thought it would definitely topple over, but he somehow was managing to move it along.

When we got outside, there were hundreds of people holding signs with different people's names on them. One said Mr. Rakesh Sharma. Another said Madame Aucleir De Vinu. We searched until we found one that said Mr. Ivan Connahan. It was the middle of the night, probably about one in the morning, but I felt awake. It was jet lag, that strange feeling that comes inside of me during international trips. It would take about a week until I was on India time. As we stepped into the car, Dad greeted the driver.

"Hello sir. How are you, sir?" The driver asked.

"I'm good. And you?"

"Oh, I am top class sir."

"And what is your name?"

"My name is Sahil, sir."

"Okay. So, Sahil, we're going to The Oberoi tonight."

"Oberoi?"

"Yes, do you know where it is?"

"Oh yes, Oberoi is very nice hotel. Top class." The Oberoi was probably the fanciest hotel I had chosen. We weren't rich, but we had all agreed that since we were arriving in Delhi in the middle of the night and since we would be jetlagged it would be nice to stay at a nice hotel. Delhi was also the only place where we would just be staying at one hotel the whole week we were there.

I was amazed at how many people were driving in the middle of the night. There was probably more traffic now, at 1:00 in the morning, then there was on a normal day at noon in Boston.

When we finally got to our hotel, Maya asked me, "Hey Logan?"

"Yeah Maya?"

"Do you think there's a Jacuzzi at this hotel?"

"I think that there probably will be. It's a pretty fancy hotel."

"As fancy as your hotel in Thailand?"

"I hope so."

When we got inside the hotel, we were greeted with glasses of mango juice. I took a glass but was disappointed. The first drink that I tasted in India was very sweet. It tasted a little bit like mango, but much more like sugar. Maya, on the other hand gulped it all down.

"Do you want mine?" I whispered to her.

"Really?"

"Sure. I don't like it."

Maya looked at me like I was crazy, then took the glass and gulped all of it down without so much as a thank you.

By the time we got to our hotel room, it was three in the morning. Maya sprinted to our bathroom and then squealed with surprise. I trudged in and saw her leaning over the bathtub, with an expression of delight on her face.

I wanted to just stay up until the next morning, but my parents both insisted that we should try to sleep. I lay in bed, tossing and turning and not falling asleep.

But I guess eventually I did fall asleep, because when I woke up, sunlight was streaming in, and my watch that I had set to India time said 11:00.

That day we went to the India Gate. I guess it was pretty cool to see all the names of soldiers that were written on the memorial. Then we went to dinner at a great restaurant. It was my first time eating real Indian food. Sure, I had eaten at Indian restaurants in Boston. But it tasted so different from this restaurant. There was thick naan with paneer, a kind of cheese that I immediately fell in love with. For dessert was gulab jamun, some kind of spongy chunk of dough floating in syrup. During the day, I was practically falling asleep, but by night time I was wide awake. Maya took a bath in the Jacuzzi and loved it. Once again, I tossed and turned, not falling asleep, but eventually I did.

The next morning, I got up at 9:00. I was improving.

That day we went to Delhi Haat. Basically it was a place where people from all over the country came and sold crafts. At least, that's what my Mom said it was. Actually, it was just a bunch of stalls selling cloth. I found it a bit boring, but Maya surprisingly liked it. We ate lunch there, and the food was as good as yesterday. Were all Indian restaurants this good?

Since we were all really tired, we went back to the hotel and went swimming in the pool. Well, not swimming. More like relaxing in the cool water since it was so hot outside. Then Maya and I played ping-pong, while my parents worked out in the gym. At about six o'clock in the afternoon, when my friends in Boston were waking up, we went to a nice market called Khan Market. We ate some very good authentic Chinese food at a place called Mama something or other.

The next morning, I got up at 9:30. My Mom was in the room with me, but Dad and Maya had gotten up early

and were swimming. I pulled my bathing suit on and went downstairs. I wasn't a great swimmer, but I still swam a little, and then played Marco Polo with Dad and Maya. Then Maya dared me to go into the sauna for five minutes, and then jump in the cold pool. I thought that Dad would say no, but he just shrugged and said I could do it if I wanted to.

"Come on Logan, don't be a sissy," Maya said.

"I'll do it if you do it, Maya."

"Sure. Dad, can you time us?"

"Okay," Dad said. "But if it gets too hot, don't be afraid to come out."

He started the timer on his watch, and Maya and I walked inside the sauna and sat on the wooden benches. After about thirty seconds, my whole body was soaked with sweat. The same seemed to be the case for Maya, but her eyes also seemed teary. Neither of us spoke to each other, we just sat there, watching each other. A minute ago, I had been soaking wet with pool water, but now my whole body was wet with sweat.

After about two minutes, I noticed Maya was crying. "I don't like it, Logan. I want to leave." Under normal circumstances, I would've teased her, except I felt the same way.

I was about to answer her, when something amazing happened. A voice started speaking in my mind, a strong clear voice. It was just a girl's voice, but it was powerful. It was not in English, but in a language of its own that I seemed to be able to understand. I'll translate it to English. *I know you're coming. I have heard so much about you. Your name - Logan.* I looked at Maya, who was still watching me, with tears in her eyes.

"I don't like it, Logan -"

"I don't like it either, but -" But I stopped when the girl's voice spoke again. *Surely you can stay in the heat a little longer. Just look at what I face.* Suddenly, my sight started to change, as if an extra eyelid had been pulled over my eyes. I could open it, and see Maya again, and feel the heat, but it was more interesting to close it. I was standing in a dark, hot house. I saw the girl who had been speaking. She was no older than three, not old enough to speak the way she had been. She was holding a rag and wiping the floor. The rag was filthy and looked like it smelled disgusting.

I opened the extra eyelid in my mind and saw that Maya had left. She was probably telling Dad that I was going crazy. Dad flashed me two fingers from outside. Two minutes left. I wouldn't have made it, except for my curiosity about the girl. I closed my eyes, and I could see her scrubbing the floor again. I tried to talk to her, and my voice rang out in my mind, clear and strong as if I was an adult. *What is your name?* The girl heard me, and looked straight at me. *My name is Meenakshi. You will see me soon.* One minute left. I closed my eyes again, and spoke in my mind.

How are we doing this? The girl looked at me and smiled. She shrugged, and laughed. Then she put her hand on her forehead and concentrated hard. All went black. It looked how it normally looked when my eyes were closed. I opened my eyes and saw Dad looking at his watch.

"Time," he mouthed. I got up and started walking to the door. As I did, I briefly closed my eyes again and saw nothing.

For the rest of my time in Delhi, Meenakshi kept popping up in my mind. When she did she could see where I was. She saw the Red Fort, and she loved the Taj Mahal when we took a trip to Agra. She told me that her parents were making her work hard because I was coming. She said that it was going to be a surprise when she saw me, but she was going to see me soon. I learned the ins and outs of mind communication. I knew how to shut her off, just like she had done to me in the sauna. I knew how to briefly flash an image, or to show her what I was thinking and who my family was. The only thing I didn't know was why and how this was happening.

After Delhi we went to Uttarakhand, where I apparently had cousins I'd never met. This was where my Mom was from. We started in Nainital, which I guess was pretty, but all it seemed to have was lakes. We stayed there for a couple of nights, and the best part of being there was buying a golden deck of playing cards. After that, we went to Ranikhet, which was where I would meet my cousins. The whole three-hour drive, Meenakshi kept telling me about how I was getting closer to her, until I finally shut her off.

We spent the whole day meeting distant relatives in Ranikhet who I couldn't communicate with, and who didn't seem that interested in me.

The next morning, we got up early and drove from Ranikhet up a steep mountain to a village where my mother's cousins lived. Mom told us this was the village where her father had lived when he was very young. The roads curved around the steep mountain. It made Maya feel carsick and we had to stop a few times for her to walk around to get some fresh air.

Finally, we reached the village and I saw a young man carrying a small girl. There was no doubt about it. This was Meenakshi. I walked over to her, and I saw the recognition spark in her eyes. She clasped my finger.

"Iska naam Meenakshi hai," her father said. Using the little bit of Hindi I knew, I understood that he was telling me what her name was.

"Hello, Meenakshi," I said.

Meenakshi got down from her father and walked toward me. *We meet at last, Logan.*

She could use mind communication if she wanted, but I wanted to talk to her. Then I realized that Meenakshi probably didn't understand English. I could use some bits and pieces of Hindi, but mind communication was much easier.

You look just like you did in my head. I said, half joking.

Meenakshi laughed. *Come with me and I'll show you the farm.*

Sure, let me just tell my father. I walked back to where my father was going through the formalities with Meenakshi's parents. "I'm going to be playing with Meenakshi," I said to him.

He nodded, although he seemed to only be half listening. I bounded back to Meenakshi. *Did he say you could come?*

Yup.

Those two cows over there are where we get our milk from. Their names are Raju and Robin.

Interesting names.

My big brother, Raju, told me the story of Robin Hood, who stole from the rich and gave to the poor. He had read the story in his school.

Meenakshi's brother was big and beefy, with thick black glasses. *Can you mind communicate with your brother?*

Nope. Once, when I was two, my parents took me to a dance. One of the young women who was dancing started speaking in my head. I was amazed. Since then I tried to mind communicate with everyone I met. It didn't work. I usually only tried with people who I met, but the moment my mother told me your name, I knew there was something different about you. Then I started talking to you, and it worked.

What about the dancer?

I talked to her for many months, but then eventually I guess she got tired of me and shut me off every time I talked to her. I didn't talk to her for a long time, and when I tried again it didn't work at all, as if I had never been able to talk to her.

Now I don't want to start that whole classic thing in all the books and movies where I was just a normal kid, and then suddenly I have superpowers. But to me, that's how it felt. I mean, I'm not your average American kid, because I'm part Irish, part French, and part Indian. But I wasn't extraordinary, that's for sure. I remember the summer before sixth grade, when I got so into Harry Potter I was practically waiting for the letter from Hogwarts to come and invite me. I remember when I was seven, and had read the book *The Wishing Chair*, and spent months thinking about how much

I wanted to fly on the magical rocking chair. During those times I had felt ordinary. But now, now I felt like I was the least ordinary person on Earth.

Over there are our mango trees. You've tried mangoes in India, right?

Sure. They're the best mangoes I've ever tasted.

Well, the freshly grown ones are ten times better. Meenakshi showed me how to climb up and pick the low hanging mangoes. For a three-year-old, she was very good at climbing trees. She was right – the mangoes were absolutely delectable. They were bright orange, and it was impossible to suck one without juice falling onto the ground.

Then Meenakshi took me up a hill. When I reached the top, I gasped. The view was amazing. I could see snowy mountain peaks in the distance, even though it was hot here. I thought I had seen nice views in Boston and other places I had traveled, but they were nowhere near as good as this.

She started taking me to show me something else, but my Mom called me to come to her. "You seem to like Meenakshi, Logan."

"She's great. You don't think……" My voice trailed off. I was going to suggest that we take her home, but then I realized how stupid that was.

"I don't think what, Logan?"

"That we could come back here later, as a family?"

My mother looked at me oddly, and I wondered if I had said too much. "It's unlikely that we'll come to India again, as a family. You should know, as our travel agent, how expensive it is."

I nodded, but in my head I vowed that I would come back, and see Meenakshi again.

Meenakshi's family gave us some biscuits, and milk that was fresh from Robin, and then it was time to go. Sahil said it would be dangerous to be driving in the mountains late at night. Meenakshi's entire family came out to say goodbye. After saying the formal goodbyes to Meenakshi's family, I picked up Meenakshi and swung her in the air.

Logan, will you come back here? Her expression was so innocent that I felt like I had to tell her the truth.

My parents said it would be too expensive, but I'll come alone if I have to. I'll see you again.

I know you will, Logan.

How?

How what?

How do you know I will?

I know you Logan. Despite being only three, her eyes had a certain astute feeling to them, as if she knew more than me.

I put her back onto the ground, and whispered into her ear, "Goodbye, Meenakshi."

The rest of our vacation flew by, but I enjoyed it. My favorite part was Meenakshi, but I loved the beaches in Kerala as well. I communicated with her strongly the whole trip and I showed her all the places we visited. I could see and hear her as clearly as I had when we were together.

When I started eighth grade, talking with Meenakshi was an enormous succor through all the homework and fights. I lost some friends and made some new ones. But I always had Meenakshi. It was a parallel world for me, someone to talk to when I was tired or troubled. The time difference didn't seem to be a problem. When I was up, she was up. I would talk to her in class, whenever I wanted to. And every night, as I lay in bed, I would tell her all about my life, and she would tell me about hers. And I never told anyone about her.

But then one day, things started to change. I was at my friend Theo's sleepover birthday party. It was a blast. I had just started high school and had many classes with Theo, who was my best friend. We lay in sleeping bags that night, talking about homework and girls and teachers and parents and cars and lots of other stuff. That day I hadn't talked to Meenakshi at all and for the first time since I had met her, I didn't think about her as I lay in bed. The next day, as my Dad was driving me home from Theo's, I went back to Meenakshi. It didn't work the first four times I tried to reach her. The fifth time I tried, she replied, but her voice seemed faint. *Meenakshi*! I said. *What happened? Why didn't you answer?*

Why didn't you answer? she replied. She was five years old now. *Last night, I tried so much, and you never answered.* She flashed me an image, but it was blurry. I could tell that she was crying in bed. *I can't lose you, Logan. I can't.* Her voice was trembling. And then her picture became very blurry, as if lots of sand had been blown all over it.

Meenakshi! What's happening? Why is your picture so bad?

No Logan! I don't want you to become like the dancer who left me. She seemed to be getting hysterical, and I didn't have the heart to tell her that I could hardly hear her now.

Meenakshi, I have to go now. I'll talk to you again tonight before I go to bed.

Logan, don't forget. Please, don't forget.

I didn't forget, and we talked for a long time that evening. But her voice was buzzing, and her scenes were fuzzy. She didn't say anything about me, so I figured my voice was strong. But then again, maybe she just wasn't saying anything.

From then on, she was always fuzzy, and sometimes we couldn't communicate at all. I tried to talk to her every day, but the truth was sometimes I was just too busy or didn't feel like it. I had more homework than I could handle, and friends to hang out with, so I had a hard time doing everything I needed to each day even without Meenakshi. Then one day, in tenth grade, I couldn't talk to her at all. For the next four months, I couldn't reach her.

I had pretty much stopped trying when one day I heard her voice in my head. She was crying.

Logan, what's happening? Why didn't you listen to me?

Meenakshi, I can't! I've tried every day.

Logan, listen to me, we have to talk every two minutes to keep our connection strong.

I was straining to hear her. *No, Meenakshi, you don't understand. I can't talk to you that often. I don't even know if I can reach you again.* I was tearing up now, and was glad I was alone in my room.

Logan, I want to see you again.

I want to too, Meenakshi. And I will. I'll find you.

I'll come and meet you on the hills of......... her voice faded out...... 43.......

Meenakshi, I can't hear you!

There was silence, followed by a scream. I tried to communicate, but it didn't work. "No," I said aloud. I was sobbing now. "Come back, Meenakshi. Please, come back."

There was no reply.

I never heard her voice again.

After getting a degree in journalism, I became a newspaper reporter. I traveled all over the world and wrote about everything. I was based in San Francisco, and I wrote mostly for *The Chronicle*. When I was twenty-six years old, *The Chronicle* said that they wanted an article about the migrating population of Ranikhet, Uttarakhand. I immediately volunteered for the job.

When I was thirteen, our driver Sahil had driven us to Uttarakhand. I still remembered the taxi company. So when my plane landed in Delhi, I found the company and asked for Sahil. The manager checked and told me that Sahil was 75 years old and only went on short drives. I asked to see him.

Sahil was sitting in a beaten up green armchair, drinking a huge mug of tea. He was much older, but some of his features were the same. As soon he saw me, his eyes widened. "Ivan sir?"

I grinned. "His son."

"Logan?"

"Yes indeed."

"Logan, you have become reporter?" he asked, pointing at the badge on my shirt.

I nodded. "And how are you?"

"Oh I am top class, Logan sir."

I laughed and ran a hand through my hair. "I was wondering, could you drive me to Uttarakhand, to the place where I met my family?"

Sahil's warm smile melted into a frown. "I would love to drive you to Ranikhet. However, the company's rules are that once you're over seventy years old, you cannot drive outside of Delhi. This was established when seventy-year-old driver drove straight off the side of a mountain."

I nodded, grimacing. "But do you remember where exactly you took my family that day?"

Sahil looked genuinely surprised. "Of course. A good driver must never forget where he takes his customers."

Relief washed over me. "So do you think you could tell the driver who will take me exactly where to go?"

"That I could do, Logan sir."

The arrangements were made for a different driver named Kabir to take me to Ranikhet. Sahil gave him the directions and we started off. It was a long drive, and I was very excited. I kept wondering what Meenakshi would look like and how her personality had become. Many times I had to restrain myself from telling Kabir to drive faster. Soon the city melted into farmland and some hours later the hills came into view. I looked out, scanning for familiar landscape. Sahil had advised Kabir well, and we soon reached the village that we had visited thirteen years ago. I got out of the car and walked hurriedly toward the land where their house was.

But when I got to the rolling hills where the house and warm, happy family had been, all that was there was an abandoned house. No Raju and Robin, and no people. I ran into the house and started looking around, but it was completely empty. They had taken everything with them when they moved. I searched every room, but found no sign of the sixteen-year-old Meenakshi or her family. I sat down in the room where Meenakshi and her brother had slept. All there was to see was an empty room, with the walls peeling and crumbling. I sat there for almost a full hour thinking about Meenakshi. I thought about the hundreds of families migrating from the hills, and the article I would write started to come into focus.

Finally, I stood up, wiped my eyes with a handkerchief, and walked outside. I told Kabir to drive me to the hotel where I was staying in Ranikhet.

As we drove out of the village, I saw a teenage girl with long black hair getting into an auto rickshaw. I saw her face for just a moment, but her eyes looked familiar. Before I could see her clearly, the auto rickshaw left, heading away from me. It soon mingled with five other identical three wheelers on the road.

Battle of Brothers

I

A MAN WALKED ACROSS A DUSTY backstage and turned into a dark, gloomy hallway. He glanced at his watch, knowing that there was still an hour until the show started. No one was there besides him, the backstage man. He walked over to the prop table, when he suddenly stopped and gasped in shock.

Lying on the floor was a dead woman. If you just looked at her face, you might not realize she was dead. She was rather pretty, with smooth black hair and pale skin. Her lips were smudged with lipstick, and her eyes were closed in a way that you could almost believe she was sleeping. But, if you looked at her chest, you knew she wasn't sleeping. Her chest was soaked with blood, and there was a knife sticking in it, the blade about halfway concealed. The man, whose name was Devin Benzene, panicked.

He sprinted straight to the phone in the corner of the backstage. He snatched it off the hook, sweating madly now, and, his fingers trembling, dialed 9-1-1.

"Hello, this is Sergeant Henry Welver speaking, NYPD. How may I help you?"

"I'm calling to report a murder."

"A murder, eh? Who's speaking?" The man had a heavy southern accent, so heavy that it made it hard to understand what he was saying.

"My name is Devin Benzene; I'm working as backstage boy as my summer job. I just arrived here, and I found a

dead woman, and I don't know what to make of it, and...."
Devin's voice trailed off.

"Where are you?"

"Broadhurst Theater, New York City."

"Please stay right there. We'll be there within ten minutes."

"Thank you." There was a faint click at the other end of the receiver, and Devin placed the phone back, and then picked it up again. Almost in a daze, Devin spun the dial a few times, and then held the phone to his ear.

"Hello, this is Robert the Incredible speaking, who is this?"

"I'm Devin, your backstage boy. I'm calling to tell you that tonight's show has been cancelled."

Robert's smooth voice sounded anxious, although by the end of the conversation, Devin expected him to be much more than anxious. "Cancelled? Why?"

"I discovered a dead body in the theater."

"And so the whole show is called off?"

"Well, the police are on the way and I assume they'll investigate for any trace of the murderer."

"You fool! You called the police?"

"Well what was I supposed to do? I couldn't just -" There it was again, the faint click at the other end of the line. He had been cut off. But even as he put the phone back, the door to the theater opened. The police had arrived. They had come in much less than ten minutes.

Devin walked to the door, and halfway there, met the two policemen and the detective who had come.

"Are you Devin Benzene?" one of the policemen asked.

"I am. I called a few minutes ago to report a -"

"Murder. Yes, I know. After you show me the body, you can leave."

"Actually..." the detective said. "I'm afraid we must take your fingerprints."

Devin's eyes widened. "Surely you know that I didn't do it?"

"Well, of course, but it is a formality to take the fingerprints of individuals who find and report murders. I know you don't have a problem with that?"

Devin stumbled backwards. "Of course not." He hadn't done it, so why was he nervous? "Let's go."

Devin led the way to where he had found the body. "Do you recognize her?" he asked the detective.

"I do. This is Dorothy Stevenson." the detective said simply.

"Is she rich?"

"No, she's not, and I don't know why someone would murder her. The only reason I can think of is her husband. Jack Stevenson is quite controversial."

"Why?"

The detective rubbed his eyes and yawned. He was a short muscular man who wore a heavy brown coat. "I'm not sure. Something about a magician named Leonardo robbing him. When Stevenson took the case to court, he found that what he had interpreted as robbery was actually an investment that the magician was making for him. He tried to sue Leonardo, but lost the case. In his anger, he shot Leonardo. It didn't come close to killing him, but he was put in jail for the attempt. It was only for a few years, but when he came out he was very angry. People say he's been part of organized crime, but there's no proof. Or something like that," he added, grinning. "Come on," he said to the policeman, after they had taken photographs from every angle of the dead body. "Load the body into the car, but only touch the blade of the knife. We don't want to disturb the fingerprints."

The policemen grunted, and hoisted the mangled body up into the car.

"Do I have to come?" Devin asked. The police station was the last place he wanted to go to.

"I'm afraid so, but don't worry. After you're done, I'll send someone to take you home, and you can forget all of this ever happened." Like that was going to happen,

Devin thought. "You're staying with your parents for the summer?" Devin nodded.

They walked out of the theater. The policemen and the body were going in the police car, and Devin and the detective were going in the detective's car. The ride was mostly silent, and soon they had arrived at police headquarters. The detective led the way into the building. The room that Devin was taken to was brightly lit, and the man who was there seemed to be waiting for Devin. Devin pressed his fingers onto the inkpad, then pressed them onto the paper.

"Thank you very much," the detective said, "and I apologize for any inconvenience."

"No problem," Devin said. "If someone can just take me to the theater, then I can drive home."

As a burly policeman was driving Devin to the theater, the policeman's phone rang, cutting through the silent night like a dagger.

"Hello," he answered. "I see, yes, yes. Okay, that's fine. Goodbye."

"Is something wrong?" Devin asked.

"Oh no," the policeman said smiling. "Everything is perfectly okay, Mr. Benzene." Devin leaned forward, then quietly gasped. The policeman had one hand on the steering wheel that he was using to maneuver the car. His other hand was clutching a revolver. Had he gone crazy? It was then that Devin noticed that the policeman had made a U turn. Within minutes they had arrived back at the police station.

The policeman jumped out of the car, and with his hand still on his revolver, he barked at Devin, who was still sitting in the car. "You're under arrest for the murder of Dorothy Stevenson!"

"What?" Devin shouted angrily. "I didn't kill her!" He was starting to feel dizzy now. Why would someone frame him? What had he done?

"Your fingerprints matched perfectly those on the knife. Now get out of the car. We'll show you the match if you want, once you are in jail."

"I've been framed!"

"Explain it to the judge, Mr. Benzene, explain it to the judge."

II

Two years later, thousands of people gathered to see two of the Benzene triplets perform in Las Vegas. The theater was completely full, as people gathered to see Benjamin and Trip Benzene perform for a paying audience for the first time in their lives. Finally, the lights came up to reveal two young men who looked exactly the same. One was sitting on a stool, the other was standing up. They had the same short black hair, and pleasant dark eyes. They were dressed in matching black collared shirts, and black dress pants.

The man standing up spoke first. "Thank you, thank you everyone." There was cheering from the crowd. "My name is Trip Benzene and this is my brother Benjamin." More cheering. "Benjamin specializes in possible impossible feats, and I specialize in sleight of hand. I know that most magicians don't say what they specialize in, but we think the more the audience understands, the better. Unless they understand *everything* – in which case the show is ruined." There were some chuckles from the audience.

At this point, Trip took out five slips of paper. He showed them to the crowd. Each paper had a letter on it from A to E. There were five seating sections in the theater – A to E. Trip walked up to the front row and asked someone to pick a random strip. They picked D. "In section D," Trip continued, "There are fifteen rows. We will call the first three rows A, then next three rows B, and so on." Trip then asked someone else to pick another strip. This one was C. "Rows seven to nine," Trip announced and put strips D and

E in his pocket. He walked a little bit downstage to another audience member. "What's your name, sir?"

"Jonas."

"A round of applause for Jonas please!" Trip said, and the audience clapped. "Now Jonas, you can pick any strip you want, and please hold it up to the crowd. If you pick A, it means row seven. B means row eight, and C means row nine." He spread the strips out face down. Jonas picked one and held it up. "C! Very well!" Trip walked down to row nine in section D. He strolled down the row, and then walked back down to the stage. "Can everyone in that row please take out their wallets and hold them up in the air? Thank you." The eyes of everyone in the theater were intently watching everyone in the row, as they looked into their purses and backpacks and back pockets. Soon there were some cries of anguish and yelling.

"Is there a problem?" Trip asked calmly.

One man in the row stood up. "I can't find my wallet." There were cries of "Me too!" and anxious nodding.

"I see," Trip said quite calmly. "Can everyone in that row please come up to the stage?"

People started moving fast, and it was obvious that they were not enjoying themselves. Trip had to resist the urge to just give them back their wallets. He wanted the audience to be happy. When they leave, they'll be happy, Trip assured himself.

When everyone finally arrived, Trip spoke again. "Can everyone on stage please pick someone from the audience. You go first," he said, pointing to the first person. "Pick anyone from the audience."

The person, who was a girl in her early twenties, raised her hand and, trembling, pointed at an elderly man in the audience. "You," she said in a barely audible whisper.

"Excellent," Trip said. "Can you please come to the stage?" he said to the man.

While the man walked up, Trip asked the next person to pick a someone from the audience. He too pointed at someone, who was then invited on stage. When everyone in the row who had lost their wallets had picked a person from the audience, Trip arranged them so that the people who had lost their wallets were standing in a line, and the people whom they had picked from the audience were standing in a line in front of them, each in front of the person who had picked them.

"Now," Trip said, as if he was chatting about the weather and not fifteen people who had just been robbed, "Can everyone who does not have their wallets reach into the back pocket of the person they chose?"

First there was silence, as everyone jerked their hands into their partner's pockets. Then, like a stone's ripples through the water, there was a ripple of murmurs and applause, starting from the stage, then going to the front rows, and ending at the outskirts of the seats. Every person who had been robbed joyfully held up their wallet, which they had found in the pocket of the person they had picked from. Their faces displayed pure amazement, and they looked at Trip as if he had supernatural power.

As all of the bewildered, smiling people started walking off the stage, Trip noticed a pack of standard playing cards sticking out of the elderly man's pocket.

"Wait one moment," he said to the man. "Can I have your cards?"

The man nodded, and gave him the deck.

"Ladies and gentlemen," Trip yelled out to the audience, and the people who were leaving stopped. "Sir," he said to the man. "The deck is obviously in no order, because it was in your pocket. Correct?"

"Yes, I think so."

"Would you like to shuffle it?" Trip asked holding out the deck.

"No, it's fine."

"Then please pick a card." Trip fanned the cards out in a circle. The man picked a card. "Please show it to the audience." He did. It was the King of Hearts. "Sign it." Trip gave him a permanent marker. "Now put it back in the deck." The man did. Trip handed him the deck back. "Please confirm that your card is in the deck.

"It is," the man said, showing the audience that it was.

"Now look up," Trip said.

The audience looked up and gasped. On the ceiling, were the letters K of H. That would have been amazing enough, but the letters were made out of playing cards, and if you looked closely, you saw that each card was actually a king of hearts.

On top of all that, Trip said, "I think if you look in the deck, your card will have disappeared." The man looked through the deck, then looked up at Trip as if he were seeing him for the first time, then dazedly walked back to his seat.

"Thank you, everyone!" Trip shouted, as people started to get up. "Please come back after intermission to see my brother perform!"

III

After the fifteen-minute intermission, everyone came back. If anything, they looked more excited to see Benjamin perform than they had for Trip. The stage had changed a lot. In the center of the stage was a five by five grid of open fireplaces, small iron plates with newspaper and wood stacked inside, surrounded by iron grates. There were also two life-size dummies sitting in armchairs on one side of the fireplaces. One was a figure of a woman, one of a man.

Benjamin's eyes ran over the crowd like water, watching everyone, and sucking everything in. Although his eyes were identical to Trip's, they looked deeper, as if he had experienced more than his brother.

"When I was seven years old," Benjamin began, "my other brother, not Trip but Devin, who currently lives in jail, lit fire to our house. I was only seven years old of course, and all I could do was wait while my father called the fire department. But now, I often think about what I should have done." Benjamin waved his hand, and three men dressed in black came up to the stage and lit fire to each of the fireplaces.

"Since my parents could not be here tonight, I will use these dummies instead to represent them." There was some laughing in the crowd, but Benjamin's expression was quite serious.

"Can I have a volunteer from the audience?" Hands shot up everywhere. "You, sir," Benjamin said, pointing to a trim little man with a small beard. "Will you please come up to the stage?"

The man walked up, combing his hair with his hand as he did so. "Sir," Benjamin said, "Will you please try to pick up my father?"

The man walked up to the dummy and put one hand underneath it, and one hand on the side of it. He pulled with all his might, but it hardly budged. His face was red and sweaty, and a vein bulged on his forehead. Finally, the man lowered his head and looked down at the floor, and he slowly walked back to his seat, his feet shuffling on the floor.

"No surprise there," said someone in the audience.

"Well then perhaps you, sir," Benjamin said to the man who had made the comment.

"Me? Well…. I'm not sure."

"Oh, look at those bulging muscles of yours. I'm sure you can do it." The audience was roaring with laughter.

"Oh, okay." The man looked to be about twenty, and he did have bulging muscles. He jumped onto to the stage, and used the same grip the other man had used. He lifted the dummy about an inch above the ground for about four seconds, and then dropped it to the ground, panting madly.

"Not bad," Benjamin said. He waved the person back to his seat. "If the fire were to happen today, then I would have first rescued my mother."

He removed his shoes and socks, hoisted the female dummy up and put her on his back. There was some murmuring in the crowd. Benjamin then started walking through the fire. With each step he made, he lifted his foot high up, so that the audience could see his smoldering feet. "Then perhaps I would be halfway across when I would hear my father calling out for me. I would look back and see that the flames were getting taller." Benjamin waved his hands, and suddenly the flames were twice as tall. The audience watched, enthralled, as Benjamin continued.

"Perhaps my heart would not let me do such a horrible thing as leave my father to die." Benjamin walked back over the fireplaces, his feet smoking. He was still hunched over, because his "mother" was on his back. When he got to where his "father" sat, he rolled his mother onto the left side of his back, picked up his father, and put him on the right side of his back. There were lots of "ooooh"s and "aaaah"s from the audience. He started walking through the fireplaces again, and one of his feet caught on fire.

"I would see that the end was close, and then I would hear a noise." He cocked his head. Even the audience could hear something. Then they saw Trip yelling on his stool.

Benjamin stopped. "Surely my conscience wouldn't let me leave my brother behind." For the second time, Benjamin returned through the fire. When he got to the end, he took one hand off his shoulder, where he was holding the dummies, and used it to pick Trip up and put him on his back with the dummies. Then he walked back through the fireplaces, carrying Trip and the two dummies. When he got to the other side, his feet were scorched, but he was smiling.

"I would of course leave Devin behind, because he created the problem in the first place." Benjamin's face was not in the least sad as he spoke these words.

If the audience had heard him, they didn't respond, because they were still applauding.

As had happened at the end of his brother's act, the audience started to leave, but Benjamin raised his hands to stop them. "You, sir," he said to the elderly man whose card had been abbreviated on the ceiling, "perhaps you wouldn't mind looking in your back pocket. Trembling with anxiety, the man reached into his back pocket and removed the King of Hearts. He held it up in the air and, to the applause of the audience, showed them his signature in black marker on the card.

Trip stood up and walked over to stand next to his brother. "Please put it back in your pocket." The man did so. Then Trip reached into his own pocket, and pulled out the signed card. "Look in your pocket." The man did so, and although he pulled the pocket inside out, there was no card there. His eyes widened, and he briskly walked out of the theater.

The applause was wild, and Trip and Benjamin held hands as they bowed. Then the lights went out.

IV

The next night at about eight o'clock, two men entered a coffee shop. They spoke to each other in low voices. Soon another man came in. Unlike the other two men, who were young, this man was at least sixty years old. He was dressed in a black and white fur overcoat and grey pants. He had a large nose, with lots of pimples on it, and wore thick glasses with black plastic frames. He looked very different than he had when he had been at the Benzenes' performance the day before. The other two men were dressed identically in button up white shirts, and dress pants, with smart brown belts. They had matching short black hair and pleasant dark eyes.

One of the identical men spoke first. "I heard there was a problem, Evans." He said this coldly to the older man.

The older man rubbed his nose and adjusted his glasses. "I don't think so, Benjamin. I'm quite sure that you said I would get fifty percent of the profits. Unless you expect me to believe that we only made a hundred dollars yesterday, I don't see why my check says fifty dollars."

Benjamin laughed. "You thought we would give you half the profits? For doing your puny part?"

The man's brow furrowed. "Puny? Without me, the whole show would've collapsed."

Benjamin snorted. "Perhaps so, but the only thing you had to do that required any effort was removing a card from your pants pocket, and moving it to your coat pocket in a matter of ten seconds. I had to burn my feet, and my brother had to put several complicated tricks in place before the show. And you expect fifty percent of the profits? We said we would give you fifty dollars."

"Fifty dollars! Each ticket cost fifty dollars."

Benjamin shrugged. "Maybe we could have negotiated, but you just agreed. I'm sorry if there was a misunderstanding, but a deal is a deal. If you want, we can give you a few twenties."

"Twenties? I want at least ten percent of the dough."

At this point, Trip intervened. "I also remember fifty dollars, but I understand why Evans may be concerned. I agree with him that he may deserve more. After all, without him, I wouldn't have been able to do my card trick, and you wouldn't have been able to "move" the card to the stage. Evans, would you be happy with eight percent?"

Evans seemed to be a bit happier. "That seems fair."

"I think we can do that, right Benjamin?"

Benjamin's fists clenched. "Do you want us to go broke?" He said through gritted teeth.

Trip leaned back in his seat. "What do you mean? You saw what a big crowd we had."

"That crowd is nothing compared to what it could have been. Not to mention that we have to rent rooms in Las Vegas, which is expensive enough. On top of all that, we rented out the nicest theater in Las Vegas for the show. And now, we have one plant, and he demands ten percent of the profits?"

Trip sat up straight in his seat. "Listen here Benjamin. If you want to leave and go start your own magic business, where you starve your plants and try to get as much money as you can, then leave. But if we're doing this together, then you have to give me a say too."

Suddenly, Benjamin jumped out of his seat, and knocked over his chair. A waitress started walking over, but he waved her away. His face was contorted with rage. "If I left right now, you realize that you would be nowhere. I manage all of our finances alone. If you knew how hard it was..."

"You act is if I'm a baby, Benjamin." Trip spat his words out. "As if I had nothing better to do than to watch you fake walk on fire. As if I know nothing about finances. I'm your twin, not your baby brother. You're just the same as you were when you were younger. Always bragging to Devin and me how you were born three hours before us. Now what, you think you learned finance in those three hours?"

Evans looked as if he really didn't want to be there. His nose had gotten extremely red. "Perhaps -" But Benjamin interrupted him.

"You shut up. You're just a rich retired twerp who tries to squeeze money out of us young men who work hard for our dough."

"You know what, Benjamin? I'm not sure I want to work with you at all. I could be a lot more successful with a solo act." Trip said, watching the waitress walk over to their table.

"Well, we'll see about that!" Benjamin shouted. And with that, he started walking towards the door. "The next time I see you, brother, it will not be on a happy note." He opened the door and left, letting the cool November wind fly into the cozy coffee shop.

Trip sat up straight and rigid in his seat. He shook his head, as if trying to get a bad image out of his head. Evans started pushing his chair out as if he were going to leave, but Trip held up his hand. "Without Benjamin helping me with my finances, I won't be lingering around in Las Vegas. I'll be traveling the country, going to different cities, and performing. If you want to join me as a plant, Evans, I'm all for it."

Evans shook his head, and gave a tired smile. "I would enjoy it, Trip, but I'm much too old to be traveling around the country. But I wish you luck on your journey and in your life of magic."

Trip nodded, and the two started walking out of the room. Neither mentioned Evans' share of the profits.

V

In San Francisco four months later, many people had arrived to see Trip Benzene's first performance without his brother. Many people had heard about their Las Vegas performance, and about the ugly split up that had followed. A few people had come from Vegas to see it, but most of the audience were San Francisco locals. Near the middle of the audience sat a young man about Trip's age. He was dressed in a black overcoat and had slightly overgrown black hair. His beard was ragged, and his eyes were fixed only on Trip and nothing else. From out of his coat pocket, he removed a small notebook and a pen. He opened up the notebook, and titled the page *Trip Benzene's performance*. Then, resting his head on his chin, he fixed his eyes on the stage where the lights were coming up. Oh boy, was this going to be fun.

The lights came up on Trip Benzene. He was seated on the same wooden stool that he had sat on in his earlier performance. The spotlight fell on him, and he gave a warm smile to the crowd. He spread his hands out and nodded. "Thank you for coming, everyone. I was very happy to hear that there is a full house tonight." The stranger in the middle of the audience scowled. He scribbled into his notebook, *Bare stage except for stool and table with wheels. Some red envelopes on the table. Could be compartment in table.*

Trip jumped off the stool, and enthusiastically came to the front of the stage. "Can I have a few volunteers? Please just come up here. Come on up! I don't need to call on you. If you want to be a volunteer, just come up here!" People started coming up from all parts of the audience.

The stranger frowned, and wrote, *Anyone can come up. Can't all be plants.*

Trip handed a few of them envelopes. "Pass these around. Confirm that they're just envelopes." After they had been passed around, Trip took them back and then continued. "Thank you, now can you please get into a line?" They did so. "Now the first person in line is you, sir."

Probably a plant, the man scribbled. *Easy to get to the front of the line.*

Trip clapped his hands, and an assistant came to the stage, holding a huge yellow rubber die. "Since you're the first person, can you please roll the die?" He handed the die to the man in the front of the line, and the man shook it and tossed it onto the stage. It landed on a six.

"Thank you very much, now please come forward to the edge of the stage. Now you, madam," he said to a woman who had volunteered. "Since you are the sixth person in line, you will get to roll the next die." Trip clapped his hands again, and a big red die was tossed onto the stage. The woman rolled a four. "Great. Now you can come forward, and the person fourth in line from you will roll." This continued, while Trip put the envelopes in a drawer in the table. Then he shrugged, as if wondering what was the point of doing that, and took them out again. Finally, after four rolls there were four people standing at the edge of the stage.

The stranger was writing madly, so much so that he didn't look at parts of the show. *Doesn't seem like plants, everyone is truly rolling the die. What other way is there to make the die land on a particular number?* Then he paused, as if realizing something. *Maybe not plants. Maybe remote controlled die? Who knows?*

"Thank you very much," Trip continued. "Now, you can all leave, except for you four. You guys stay here. Thank you very much! Please let's have a hand for our volunteers!" Everyone clapped, and Trip beamed. Everything was going perfectly. First the full house, then the volunteers, now the clapping. Then he noticed something odd. One man wasn't clapping. He was jotting something down in a notebook.

The stranger glanced behind him, and Trip saw his eyes for the first time. He knew who this man was. It was Benjamin! Trip knew why he was here. Benjamin was taking notes on how the tricks were being done. Trip wanted to sprint down and grab Benjamin, but the applause was dying out, and he had to continue.

He gave the audience a convincing smile, and nodded. He took the envelopes back. "These envelopes all say something on them."

He faced the first one toward the audience. It said **Nothing**. "This envelope is nothing," Trip said. Some people in the audience laughed. He put the envelope on the table.

The next envelope said **Money**. "This envelope is money. And this one is mine." He held up one that said **Mine** on it.

"This one is yours." The envelope said **Yours**.

"And this last one is, um," he flipped the envelope around, and everyone started laughing. It said **A Beautiful Single Woman** on it.

"Inside one of these envelopes is a hundred-dollar bill." Trip said. Then he brought one of the four people to the front. "Can you please choose one of the envelopes? Once you choose it, it's yours to keep, and if it has the hundred-dollar bill in it, then it's still yours. Choose any one you want."

"I'll take mine," the volunteer said. He was no older than twenty and he had a lopsided grin.

Trip played right along with it. "Are you taking mine?" he thundered. The audience was laughing.

"No," the boy said, leaning his head backwards. "You can have yours."

"Oh yeah?" Trip said, laughing himself. "Well these are all mine, so I'll take mine, yours, the money, and definitely a beautiful single woman. Don't worry, I'll still give you nothing." Everyone was roaring with laughter.

"Fine then, you can have mine, you just see what you get!" Trip continued, and he held up the envelope labeled **Mine**, tore it open and ripped it into tiny pieces. It was clearly empty. "Go back to your seat now please," he said to the man.

Trip then turned to the next person, a young woman in her early thirties. "And which envelope would you like?" Trip said, smiling. The woman looked at him shyly.

"I'll take the money."

"Well, I'm sure you would, but you need to choose an envelope, not the contents of it."

"No, no, the envelope labeled money."

"Okay," Trip said. "Unfortunately, the lesson for you to remember is that my job is to lie." He twirled the envelope around, showed everyone that it was labeled **Money**, and then tore it up. It also was empty.

"Go back to your seat, ma'am. Let's see, who's next?" An elderly man was next. He had thick grey hair, and eyes that were opened in slits. He was dressed in a grey suit. "I'll take the woman," he said in a hoarse voice. The crowd laughed, and Trip twirled an envelope, showed that it said **A Beautiful Single Woman,** and ripped it to shreds, so it was clear to the audience that it too was empty.

"Too bad she wasn't there," Trip said, smiling.

When Trip saw the last person, he stifled a laugh. "You need the woman," he said when he saw the handsome muscular man step up. "Too bad she's already taken."

"What's left?"

"Nothing of mine," Trip said. "There's yours and there's nothing. It's a free choice."

"I want nothing," the man said.

"Finally!" Trip said, and the crowd laughed. "A man who isn't greedy. Everyone else wants money, women, even mine, but you, you want nothing in this world."

Trip took the envelope, and smiled as he opened it up with a grin. He put his hand inside, as if feeling for something, then took his hand out and grinned. "And since it was nothing that you wanted, it is nothing that you will get." He shook it upside down to show that the envelope had nothing in it. "Thank you, you can return to your seat."

Trip ran a hand through his hair, straightened himself, and smiled. "Well ladies and gentlemen, there's only one envelope left. That's right, everybody. It's yours!" Then, working slowly to build suspense, he opened up the final envelope and showed that inside of it, was a hundred-dollar bill. The crowd was cheering, all except for Benjamin, who scribbled his final note, and got up to leave.

VI

The lights went down, and immediately Trip dashed down the aisle amidst the audience. At first the audience thought this was part of the show, but Trip knocked down a boy and had only one objective in mind: his brother. He saw Benjamin running toward the exit up ahead. Trip's face was damp with sweat, and he took off his jacket and tossed it onto a seat. He was gaining on Benjamin, but nearly tripped on a man carrying a small video camera coming out of his seat. He regained his footing, pushed past the man and continued his pursuit of his brother.

Benjamin was sprinting, and out of the corner of his eye he could see other members of the audience watching him. He was almost out the door now. Just when he could see the red Exit sign, a huge snack cart crossed in his way.

"Popcorn, candy, chips, buy what you want!"

"Excuse me sir," Benjamin said hurriedly. He could see Trip gaining on him. The snack cart moved on, and Benjamin had made it to the door that exits the theater when he realized he no longer had his notebook. He turned around and saw people walking over his precious navy blue notebook in which he had written down what Trip had done. Somehow, he had dropped it. Benjamin grimaced. Now he had a choice. He could either run outside, where his taxi was waiting and get in and get away. Or he could run back and try to get his notebook before Trip got there.

Benjamin saw members of the audience watching him and saw Trip notice the notebook on the ground.

Making a split second decision, Benjamin turned around and started running full speed forward the notebook. He saw the determination in Trip's dark eyes, and thought to himself how just a few months ago he and Trip had been performing together. And before that, they had always been good friends. And now they were running head on towards each other, each trying to beat the other to the notebook. Then he realized that it had to happen this way and that it wasn't his fault and that...... He was getting distracted. It seemed as if he and his triplet brother were going to get to the notebook at the exact same time.

Thinking about this made him remember once when they were twelve years old and had a long footrace. Devin had claimed he was the fastest runner of the three of them, while Trip had thought he was the fastest swimmer. Benjamin had taken up football as his main sport, but he still thought that the three of them would tie in all three things since they were identical. But Benjamin had been wrong. Devin had crossed the finish line over three seconds before Benjamin had, and Benjamin had crossed it four seconds before Trip. And the next day at the pool Trip had made it to the end of the pool three seconds before either of the other brothers. And Benjamin had clearly been in the best of the three at football. Benjamin had been proven wrong – just because they were triplets, it didn't mean one couldn't be better at something than the others.

But now, now it seemed that Benjamin's original idea was being proved right. He and Trip collided next to the notebook at the same time. Trip leaned down to get it, but Benjamin hit his knee onto Trip's forehead. Trip let out a yell, but held on to the notebook. Benjamin tried to grab it from his hands, but Trip pulled it behind his back.

A crowd was gathering around watching them fight, and Benjamin heard someone exclaim that this was the great magician who had just performed. Knowing they were referring to Trip, it only made Benjamin fight harder.

But Trip had a firm hold on the notebook. Benjamin made a final attempt at a distraction, and said, "Devin! How did you get out?"

Even though it was a lame attempt, it worked perfectly. Trip started to turn around, and Benjamin jabbed his hand into his brother's stomach and grabbed the book, which fell loosely to the ground. Benjamin leaned down and picked it up, and started running toward the door, which was less than ten meters away, with Trip chasing close behind.

Benjamin flung open the door, letting the cool San Francisco air blow into the theater. His taxi was waiting outside for him, and Benjamin tried to open the door, then muttered a curse. It was locked. He banged on the window, and the cab driver unlocked it, but by now Trip had caught up. He sank his fingernails into the notebook, which made it fall into the street. Benjamin snatched it, then climbed into the car. It sped off, leaving fumes behind it.

Without missing a beat, Trip fished his keys out of his pocket, letting a lint coated peppermint fall into the street. With his magician's hands, he deftly unlocked his own car, and got in. Benjamin's taxi rounded a corner, and Trip followed it. For about ten minutes, he followed the taxi until it parked at the Ritz-Carlton, one of the fanciest hotels in the city.

Trip was surprised that Benjamin could pay for something like the Ritz-Carlton, since Benjamin hadn't performed any shows recently.

Benjamin slipped his taxi driver a twenty, and then sprinted up the steps, his brother close behind. But when Trip entered the hotel, there was no sight of Benjamin.

He found himself in a huge lobby, with leather couches, and TVs. There were enormous windows, which looked out onto the city street.

He walked up to the reception, out of breath, and leaned on the counter. The woman at reception was a thin woman with blond hair and a sleeveless turquoise shirt. Her eyes were the same color as her shirt. She looked like she should be a model instead of a hotel receptionist.

"Ma'am," Trip began. "Can I have Benjamin Benzene's room number please?"

"I'm sorry sir, but Mr. Benzene wants to have his room number kept private."

Trip sighed. He reached into his pocket and took out a twenty-dollar bill. "If I give you this, will you leave me at his room?"

The woman looked down somewhat scornfully at the twenty, as though Trip had offered her a dirty Kleenex.

She tilted her head up ever so slightly so Trip could see her nostrils that were as perfectly formed as the rest of her, and she said "We are not in the habit of giving out our guests' room numbers to..." her eyes went up and down Trip's rumpled shirt, sweaty face, and desperate eyes, "... any man who runs into the hotel."

Trip was too desperate too worried about what this beautiful creature thought of him. "Can you at least tell me the floor?"

The woman leaned forward and said abruptly, "I'm sorry, sir." She clearly wasn't. Trip turned to leave.

VII

Two days later, a new DVD was released and widely circulated among magicians, show business people, and fans of magic. It was called **THE TRICK OF A MAGIC TRICK.** It was produced by a man named Benjamin Benzene. Within a week, over ten thousand copies had been sold, and one of them was purchased by Trip Benzene.

He had purchased it at a local video store in Chicago, where he was preparing for his next show. Walking by the store, he had noticed the DVD in the window because his own face was on the cover. He took it to his apartment and turned it on.

In the first scene, there was a black hat spinning around with music playing in the background, and then a snow white rabbit emerged from the hat. There was the sound of applause, and then a dagger flew down and jabbed the rabbit straight in the stomach; from the inside came only cotton. Then in fancy black print, the title of the video appeared: **The Trick of a Magic Trick.**

Then Trip saw his brother on the screen. He was sitting at a table with a standard pack of playing cards on it. The back of the video had said that the whole thing was forty minutes, and Trip was ready for anything.

"What is magic?" Trip's brother spoke on the TV. "Nothing but purposeful deception. It begins with an idea, usually an idea of how to trick someone else into believing one thing has happened, when in reality a completely different thing has happened. Here is an example."

The camera zoomed out, until you could see a girl in it. She had blond hair, and dark blue eyes. Benjamin opened the deck of cards to reveal a blue deck of Bicycle playing cards. He gave it to the girl saying, "Shuffle this as much as you want, Magenta." The girl did a perfect riffle shuffle, then another, and then gave it back to Benjamin.

Benjamin took the deck back, shuffled it one last time, and then fanned it out. "Pick a card, any card."

Magenta removed a card, and showed it to the camera. It was the four of diamonds. Then Benjamin put his hands about two feet away from each other horizontally, and said, "Say stop whenever you want."

He started dribbling through the cards, until Magenta said stop. There, Benjamin made a break and motioned for the girl to put her card in the deck where she had stopped it. After she did so, he gave the deck a few cuts, even a shuffle, and then started riffling through the corner of the deck. "Say stop whenever you want."

Magenta stopped Benjamin, and Benjamin showed that where she had stopped was where her card was, the four of diamonds.

Trip rolled his eyes. The trick was so simple, and it was still not clear why his name and picture were on the cover of the DVD. He turned back to the screen. "This trick is a perfect example of misdirection. When Magenta put her card in where she wanted to, I actually held a break with my finger." The camera flipped around so you could see the break, then flipped back. "Then, when I cut, I cut straight to that break, which pulled Magenta's card to the top."

Trip groaned. Obviously. "When I shuffled, I was keeping her card on top. This was a classic case of misdirection, because while I was talking the audience didn't notice that I was controlling the card to the top. From there, I did what is known as a riffle stop. Wherever Magenta said stop, I pulled down the top card." He showed the move in slow motion, then took a bow.

The screen shifted, and then Benjamin was leaning on a blue couch with his elbow. He was dressed in a two-piece suit with a navy blue tie. He had a martini in his hand. He took a drink, then faced the camera head on. "The latest hit in magic is Trip Benzene, who also happens to be my brother. So let's have a behind-the-scenes look at Trip Benzene's latest performance." He took another sip of his martini.

The screen shifted so Trip could see himself asking for volunteers. "Please just come up here. Come on up! I don't need to call on you. If you want to be a volunteer, just come up here!"

Then Benjamin's voice spoke while the volunteers walked to the stage. "The number of volunteers, as you realize, could be unlimited. And if you think about it, you'll realize that the volunteers serve only one purpose. That is to inspect the envelopes."

Trip was seen speaking to the volunteers. "Pass these around. Confirm that they're just envelopes." The scene shifted again to Benjamin leaning on the couch. His martini now was only about three quarters full. "After the envelopes had been inspected, the whole dice rolling thing happened. And no one, no one in the audience had been watching Trip Benzene, they had only been paying attention to the dice. And what was Trip doing?"

The scene shifted back to the theater and zoomed straight onto Trip, while you could hear the dice rolling in the background. Trip put the envelopes in a drawer in the table, then shrugged and took them out again. In reality, this had only happened once, but on the screen, it happened again in slow motion. It happened three more times in slow motion, and while it did, Benjamin's voice continued to drift through. "What's really happening here? It seems as if Trip had a change of heart after he put the envelopes in, but why would that happen? He decides to put some envelopes in a drawer and then changes his mind? The answer is quite simple: he did it for a reason. There were other envelopes inside that he was clearly switching with."

The scene shifted back to Benjamin, whose martini was now half finished. "What was different about these new envelopes, you ask? They had words on both sides. You may have noticed that Trip twirled the envelopes around before he flashed them. This is because the words on both sides let him always choose an envelope that didn't have the money in it and show the side with the word the audience member picked. He ripped up the envelopes instead of letting the volunteer open it so they wouldn't see the word on the other side. Of course there would still only be a one in two chance that the right envelope would be left at the end. But he took care of that as well. The second to last envelope that was chosen by the volunteer actually had the money in it. Perhaps you remember..." The scene shifted back to the performance, and one could see Trip putting his hand inside the envelope, "searching" for the money. "Actually he was just sliding the bill down his sleeve." The video showed the move in slow motion.

Trip got up from his couch and turned off the TV. He murmured something incomprehensible, and then smiled a secretive smile, as though already picturing his revenge.

VIII

Outside of a theater in Boston at about seven o'clock at night, Trip Benzene stood in the wind, greeting everyone who was coming to see his show. Or at least so it would have seemed. People walked up, flashed their tickets, and then if they wanted to, they got to shake hands with a smiling Trip Benzene.

A man who had a buzz cut, and eyes very similar to Trip's showed his ticket and started walking past. He was wearing a black cloak, as well as a black bowler hat. He looked like one of the French gentlemen you sometimes see in the park.

As soon as Trip saw him, his eyes lit up. "May I see your ticket please, sir? The man frowned, and shoved a crumpled bit of paper toward Trip.

Trip looked at the ticket for moment, studying it. "Sir, I'm sorry to tell you that this is counterfeit."

"What! I bought it through your own website, Mr. Benzene!"

"I'm afraid there are many fake websites that charge money for fake tickets."

"No, I'm quite sure this is real. I was at your last show in San Francisco, and I bought the tickets through the same website."

"Well, I'm sorry to say that you're wrong, sir. I won't let you into my show with fake tickets." People were bustling about, and Trip had stopped greeting anyone. He was only fixed on one man. The bowler hat man. If you had looked closely at Trip, you would have seen that his face shone with excitement, as if he had won a million-dollar lottery, although he was trying to keep it contained.

The man with the bowler hat frowned deepened. "Fine then," he said in a defeated tone of voice. "I'll buy new tickets."

"I'm afraid it's a full house tonight, Mr. uh, what's your name?"

"My name is Simon Badeaux."

"Really? Well then, Mr. Badeaux, perhaps I could see some identification?" Trip glanced at his watch and frowned. The show was starting in ten minutes.

The man looked Trip right in the eye and said in a heavy French accent, "I don't see why that's necessary, Mr. Benzene."

Most people had entered the theatre, but a few remained outside watching this unusual conversation. Trip gave the stranger a queer smile. "Come now, Benjamin, surely you knew that you couldn't fool me with that horrible disguise."

The man looked surprised. "Benjamin? I said my name was Simon."

"If that's really true, then why can't you show me any identification?"

"I suggest a deal, Mr. Benzene. I'll show you some identification, if you'll then let me in with my ticket."

Trip looked a bit confused. "Fine, that's fine," he said airily.

Simon rummaged through his bag, until he found a worn out wallet with the words *Étienne Products,* printed on it and underneath in smaller letters, *Made in France.* Trip's mind was whirring.

Simon rummaged through some cards, then finally took out his driver's license. It had a photo of a younger, unsmiling Frenchman, but Trip could see that his eyes were the same, and he happened to be wearing the same suit he was wearing now. But, most convincing of all, was the name written on the bottom of it. It said, in fancy letters, *Simon Badeaux.*

Trip thought about all the people who had entered the theater while he was interrogating Simon, and how many of them he hadn't taken a look at. He sighed. His brother must have made it through while he was distracted by the Frenchman.

Simon looked at him. "May I leave now, Mr. Benzene?"

Trip looked at him, his buzz cut, his dark eyes, the creases in his forehead. Had he really thought this man was his brother? In a small voice, he said "Yes Mr. Badeaux, you may leave."

Simon shuffled off, murmuring something about how this was the last magic show of Trip's he was ever going to attend.

Trip looked at his watch, and let out a curse. The show was going to start in three minutes. He flung open the door to the theater, and started briskly walking down the aisle. He knew how unprofessional it was for everyone to see him walking to the stage, but he didn't have a choice. He wondered whether Benjamin was in sea of faces he was walking quickly by. Benjamin had made over ten thousand dollars from his previous DVD, and Trip realized that most of the audience had probably come to see if Benjamin could ruin his show again.

He slipped backstage, and his backstage boy approached him. "Where were you, Mr. Benzene?"

"I'm sorry, Jim. You know how my brother ruined my last show?"

Jim's face reddened. He was no older than twenty. He wiped a mop of his straw colored hair behind his head. "Yes, Mr. Benzene?"

"Well, I was trying to see if I could catch him coming inside."

"Oh."

Trip slipped a comb out of his pocket, and combed his hair up. He started walking away, when Jim spoke again. "Mr. Benzene?"

Trip turned around and looked the boy straight in the eye. "Yes Jim?"

"Did you catch him?"

"No. I thought I did, but the guy who I thought was Benjamin turned out to be someone else."

"Oh," Jim said again. "I'm sorry, Mr. Benzene."

"No need for you to be sorry, Jim. I just hope he decided not to come."

Jim nodded vigorously. "Me too."

Trip could hear the announcer, announcing his act in a booming voice. He could feel the audience's excitement. Then, after the cue from his announcer, he strode onto the stage.

IX

In the center of the stage was a medium sized table. It was covered with a thick purple velvet blanket. The audience's attention was clearly focused on the table, but they applauded politely when Trip entered the stage and the announcer left. On the left side of the stage sat three other items, each one covered with a purple blanket.

Trip flashed his audience a smile, but he was really scanning the crowd for his brother. He didn't see anyone, but he did see a man filming his performance. *The theater owner had not told him that his show was being videoed.* He tried to get a better look at the man, but because of where he was sitting, his head was mostly in the shadow of a pillar.

Trip walked to the center of the stage and pulled off the velvet blanket. He placed it on the floor. It was lumpy, with bumps in the fabric that made it seem like it wasn't such good quality. As he yanked off the blanket, there were some murmurs from the audience, which then turned into laughter. Under the blanket was a nest with three pigeons inside. One was wearing a football helmet, while another wore miniature goggles on his face. The third one was the funniest, though, wearing tiny white sneakers with laces on them.

"Today's show will be a story about three brothers who lived together in harmony." Trip gestured to the three pigeons. "But before I begin the story, I just want somebody to quickly come up and confirm there's nothing else in this nest or on the table. How about you, young man." A boy about thirteen years old came up. "Do you see anything here?"

The boy hopped on stage, studied the area for some time, then shook his head. "Great. You may return to your seat." The boy slowly walked back, with a proud grin on his face.

"There's just one step left before I begin the story. I'll need three volunteers." Hands shot up everywhere, until everyone in the whole room except for Trip and the man with the video camera had his or her hand up. "Um, why don't you come up," Trip said, pointing to an old lady with snow white hair and wrinkles.

"Actually, on second thought, why don't you just stay there? I'll come to you." From the folds of his jacket, Trip removed three name tags. They were mini index cards with loose pieces of string attached to them. He then removed a blue marker and asked the woman to sign it. She did so, and Trip walked back to the stage. He grinned at the audience and then pretended to rip it. It made a loud ripping noise, and the audience looked ready to see it in two pieces. But Trip shook his head and showed proudly that it was in one piece. There was some modest applauding in the audience.

"Okay, one down, two to go. Two more volunteers please." Hands went up everywhere. "You and you." Trip said, pointing at a tall, shady man with locks of dark hair, and a young woman with bright red lipstick applied unevenly. "I think you can come up to the stage if you don't mind."

The two came to the stage and Trip gave them each an identical name tag card. Once they had signed their names, they returned to their seat, and Trip did the same ripping trick with the other two name tags. He then hung a name tag on each pigeon's neck. The pigeons didn't seem to mind the tags, as they hung loosely around their necks.

"Now," Trip said, smiling. "I will start the story. Like all stories, this story has a villain in it." Trip waved his hand and a big black crow swooped in and landed on the stage. There was some polite applause. "And a pretty girl." A smaller pigeon came flying in. It had fake eyelashes attached to it, as well as some lipstick. "Like many love stories, our villain," he pointed to the crow, "fell in love with our girl." He gestured to the pretty pigeon.

Trip snapped his fingers and the eyelash pigeon and the crow started clicking their beaks together. There was some laughing in the crowd. "Unfortunately, things went wrong for our villain, and he decided to take out his anger on his dear girlfriend." Trip clapped his hands, and the lights went crazy, flashing every color in the spectrum. Music started playing, loud enough that a few people covered their ears. And, when the music stopped, and the spotlight turned on the stage again, the eyelash pigeon had blood streaming out of her side. Her eyes fluttered one last time, before they closed for the last time. Nobody spoke, and there were looks of disapproval on several faces in the audience. This was taking the trick a bit too far.

"It was only after the villain had done this vicious sin that he realized truly what a villain he was. As it happens, our villain was very powerful. So he decided to commit one last wicked deed. He decided to frame one of the brothers." There was some dramatic music. "One of our pigeon friends was put in jail." Trip snatched the pigeon with running shoes and carried him to the side of the stage where the three other mysterious objects were covered with purple velvet blankets. Trip whipped off one of them and revealed a small wire cage. It had no floor, just more wire on the bottom. And there was no food or water, just filthy rust on some of the wires. It truly looked like a bird jail.

Trip tossed the pigeon into the cage, slammed the door shut, and put the purple blanket back on top. "The other two pigeons were so terribly upset, that they started a life of seclusion." Trip took off the blankets from the other two items.

They were identical bird cages but in better condition than the "jail". Each had some birdseeds, as well as some hay to walk on, and a little water bottle to drink from. He picked up the goggles pigeon in one hand and football helmet in the other, and put one in each cage. Trip put the blankets back on top of the two cages and put the blanket back on the nest on the table. He then started walking slowly around the stage.

"Everyone thought that the three brothers' friendship had come to a close, until one day something amazing happened."

Trip circled back to the center of the stage, and whipped the blanket off the table. Sitting there were the three pigeons again, one with the goggles, one with the football helmet, and one with the running shoes. The cocked their heads at the audience, looking like nothing had happened.

Hanging around their necks were the three loose name tags. He called the three people who had signed the cards back up to the stage. "Tell me, are these your signatures?"

The young woman with lipstick nodded slowly. "That's amazing!"

The shady man with locks of dark hair eyes simply nodded, as if deep in thought.

The woman with snow white hair enthusiastically said, "Indeed, it is."

Trip walked to the center of the stage, right next to the center table. "Thank you very much, ladies and gentlemen. I am Trip Benzene, and good night!"

X

"Ladies, and gentlemen, welcome to my second episode of THE TRICK OF A MAGIC TRICK. Once again, I will be revealing the amateur tricks my brother, Trip Benzene, has tried to pass off on his audience. I'm sure that many of you enjoyed his recent trick with the pigeons, and if you would like to continue to enjoy it and keep your childish belief in magic, I would advise you to stop playing this DVD at once. But, if you enjoyed it so much that you are curious how it was done, then please keep watching."

Trip smiled as he relaxed on his couch, watching the TV. He knew his trick had gone perfectly. He had bought the DVD just a couple of hours ago, and had turned it on as soon as he returned home.

Benjamin was sitting with the girl from his other show, Magenta was her name. They were sitting across from each other on a wooden table. "Last time we saw how Trip used misdirection to carry out his trick. This trick uses a concept slightly different than misdirection. I don't think there's a name for it, but let me explain it to you. It's doing something that the audience thinks is fancy to hide what is in in fact simple sleight of hand. I'll do an example with Magenta." He removed his Bicycle playing cards from his pocket, and fanned them out in a circle, his thumb being in the middle of it. "Magenta, my friend, pick a card, any card."

Magenta took a card out between her thumb and index finger. She showed the audience that it was the Ace of Diamonds. Benjamin let her place her card back in the deck wherever she wanted to, and even gave it a shuffle. He then spread his hands out, one on the far left side, one on the far right side, with the deck in his left hand. He bent the cards in a way that sent the cards flying from his left hand to his right hand. When he held them in his right hand, he flipped over the top card, and showed that it was the Ace of Diamonds. Trip clapped mockingly. His brother wasn't good at card tricks, and they both knew it.

"How is this not-so-good trick done? When I was letting the cards fly from one hand to the other, I was actually maneuvering Magenta's card to the top. Quite simply, you may have thought I flew the cards from one hand to the other just to make it look fancy, but it was actually the base of the whole trick. This is the same concept in my brother's trick."

The scene changed to the theater where Trip had performed, and showed him ripping the paper. "Why did he do this? I mean once it was sort of neat, but why do it with each and every signature? The camera kept repeating

Trip "ripping" the paper in slow motion. As this happened, Benjamin's voice continued to float in.

"When you send an email to someone else, you CC others. Not many of us know what CC stands for. Carbon copy. It's an old technology where carbon paper is used to make a copy underneath an original. My dear brother has always scoffed at modern technology. So he was using a good old fashioned carbon copy. The ripping was actually peeling off the copy. Once he did that, it was simple. He put the name tags on the pigeons, while actually holding the carbon copies in his palm. Then while the audience was distracted with the flashing lights and music nobody saw what he was actually doing."

The camera shifted to the flashing lights scene when the bird murder had supposedly occurred. The camera froze in the middle of the scene, and Trip's figure could be seen leaning over the cloth.

Benjamin's voice continued. "He had obviously kept a few identical pigeons underneath the cloth in the middle of the stage and he places the signature copies under their necks. You'll notice that in the end, although the pigeons were back in the middle with the signatures on them, he never showed that they were no longer in the little cages where we saw him put them.

"He then compared the signatures, which of course were the same, because they were copies. And that, very simply, is how the trick was done. Thank you very much for watching! Stay tuned for the next TRICK OF A MAGIC TRICK video."

Trip lay down on the couch sleepily. Now it was time to step up his game.

XI

One evening a few weeks later in a small dingy area of New York City, two young men were talking in a small crumbling house. The only part of the house that wasn't completely ruined was a small, round wooden table where the two men were sitting across from each other. The first man was Benjamin Benzene, who was earning quite a name – and quite a bit of money – for himself as a ruiner of magic shows. The other man was massive. He took up half of the table, and his beefy elbows resting on the table seemed to have added several cracks to the table. His blue eyes were illuminated like a cat's by a small lantern in the corner. He was dressed in an enormous black overcoat, and if you had looked underneath the coat, you would have seen a pistol, already loaded. You also would have found a midnight blue whistle in his shirt pocket, which when blown by him, would call in seven more men half his size, all holding unlicensed rifles, ready to attack whomever they were called to attack.

The man's name was Jack Stevenson.

"I'm talking big money here, Stevenson," Benjamin said coldly. "It might be easy to do for you, but with the money you get, well you could buy …."

"I'm not stupid," Jack interrupted in a husky voice. "I know you're trying to tempt me with talk of big money. Tell me what I have to do. And since you know how much I hate magicians, you better give me twice as much money as you planned. I don't work for magicians unless there's some real money involved."

"Do you know what I do for a living, Jack? I'm not a magician. My job is to ruin other magicians' lives. I've already messed up all my brother's shows ever since he stopped working with me."

"So tell me what I have to do?"

"I'm performing in a show tomorrow, right here in New York City-"

"I thought you said you weren't a magician."

"Not as my main job."

"So then why're you performing?"

"Beside the point. Anyhow, I-"

"In fact, I don't see how it's beside the point at all."

"Look, I like magic tricks. And I especially enjoy debunking modern shows. But I like performing also." He waited for Jack to say something, but he didn't, so Benjamin continued. "I know my brother is going to come. I advertise my shows, and I know he'll see an ad and be eager for revenge. I won't personally be there to make sure he doesn't get in. I could just hire someone cheap, but just in case, I thought I'd take some extra protection. That's where you come in."

"So all you want is for me to make sure your bro doesn't get in."

"Sort of. If he does come, I want you to tell him to leave. Think up whatever excuse you want. If he says fine, then great, let him get out, and you can leave. But, knowing my brother, it's unlikely that he'll just leave because some random man told him to."

"So that's what I'll be? Just a random man?"

"Sure. Just tell him that you know who he is, and that I don't want him there. Anyway, he'll probably stay, and that's when the real task starts. I want you to show him who's boss."

For the first time since the conversation began, Jack Stevenson grinned. "Now you're talking. I get to beat up a magician?"

Benjamin shrugged. "Beat him up, mug him, shoot him, whatever you want. Just make sure he doesn't show up at my show. My only rule is no killing. That would be a bit too punitive."

"And how will I be paid?"

"I will come back here one week after my show. If my brother didn't get in to ruin my show, then I'll give you the payment. I was thinking four grand flat, plus ten percent of the profits of my show."

Jack coughed. "Four grand?" he asked, his eyes widening.

"That's what I was thinking. I suppose I could make it five if you want, but no more than that."

"It's a deal." Jack's face was bright with excitement. "Four grand, plus ten percent of your profits if I can stop him from ruining your show." He stuck his hand out, and Benjamin clasped it, in the light of the lantern in the corner.

Six blocks away, in the police station of the NYPD, two different people were discussing something not so different.

Trip's eyes were firm, and his tone was icy. "I've helped you with whatever you wanted, Anderson. When you needed a witness for a suit, it was me who came to court with you. When you wanted me to tell your girlfriend about your hike to the base camp, I told it to her without a trace of doubt. And now for the first time, I'm asking you for something, and you're hesitating. What kind of friend are you? Without me, you would be nowhere. I was the one who helped your father get used to the fact that you were becoming a police officer in New York City. What have you done for me, Anderson? When I made this plan, I was counting on you, and now you won't even carry out a simple task for me?"

William Anderson had long dark hair, and stormy, intense, eyes. The traces of scars on his face showed that he had sorted out some of the not-so-pretty fights in the alleyways of the city. "I never said I wouldn't do it, Trip. I never said anything the whole time you explained your devilish plot. But look at me, Trip. I'm the senior officer here." The thick creases in his forehead deepened. "Everybody trusts me. But if I was caught, well I don't want to spend the rest of my life in jail."

Trip frowned. "I don't understand. You're not doing anything wrong. You're helping out your friend."

"First of all, that's putting it lightly. Why wait here trying to get the police involved? You could just drop your whole stupid plan, and let me live my life in peace. This crazy feud between you and your brother has been in the papers – and not just the entertainment pages. A reporter saw you fighting and interviewed several witnesses about it and watched your brother's videos. Lots of people are talking about it."

Trip had a strange look on his face. "Yeah, I've seen the trash they printed in the papers. Look, Anderson, this plan has taken me months of work." Trip's face softened. "You must understand. If you don't help me, I might be dead by next week. You know the mob better than anyone else. They're merciless. If you're a police officer and my friend...."

Anderson held up his hand to cut off Trip. He stood up. "All right, I'll help you, Trip. You're right, you have helped me a lot, and it's my turn to return the favor. You can go, and count on seeing me soon."

XII

Outside of a small theater in New York City, as people showed their tickets and walked inside amidst the smell of fumes and grilling hot dogs, Jack Stevenson lurked in the shadows. It was dusk, and long shadows were cast along the sidewalk. That made it all the easier for him to blend in and not attract notice. Although it might have appeared that Jack was simply lurking around, his eyes kept flitting past the wide open double doors, scanning for a particular person to walk in.

It was then that he noticed the sleek convertible pull up and park by the theater, its exhaust dissolving into the air. The person who stepped out was the person Jack had been watching for. Trip Benzene left the car, with a spring in his step. He had been very easy to spot, for he wasn't in any disguise at all. Now came the fun, Jack thought. He had found Trip; now he had to make him leave.

Jack approached, making sure his timing was perfect. He didn't want to wait until Trip reached the doors, for then he could run inside, which might attract the notice of the theater staff. Instead, when Trip was about ten meters away from the door, Jack approached him. "Excuse me sir. You wouldn't mind coming with me for a moment, would you?"

"No, not at all." Trip said, smiling. "As long as I'm back here by six-fifteen."

This was getting easier and easier. Jack led him to a side alley, where he cornered him against a dirty wall. "I'm afraid your brother doesn't want you entering his show." The sun had set, and in the alley it had suddenly become rather dark.

"I don't think so," Trip replied, trying to keep his voice calm. "You think you can tell me what to do? Let me leave, please."

Jack smiled, revealing his yellowish teeth. He gripped the pistol beneath his coat. "If I were you, I'd get out right now."

"I'm sure you would, but the thing is, you're not me." Trip smiled, and tried to duck underneath Jack's arms, but Jack was much too fast. He knocked Trip to the ground with the back of his arm, then whipped his pistol out, and aimed it directly at Trip's forehead. "Get out of here."

Trip just shook his head. "I know you won't shoot me," he said, his jaw jutting out, but he didn't seem very sure.

Jack leaned forward, and put the end of the revolver at Trip's forehead. "I'll leave," Trip said, his voice shaking. "Please. I'll leave, and I swear I won't ruin any of Benjamin's shows. And I'll even give you -"

That was when it happened. Someone shoved Jack onto the street, the pistol went flying to the ground, and in a whir of blue, Jack had been handcuffed. Jack kicked the person in the knee, but the man just grimaced.

He picked up Jack's gun and aimed it at him. "If you make one more move, I'll shoot! I'm NYPD and you're under the arrest," he said, fingering a badge. "I want you to walk into the car and sit down. If you make any other move, I promise you I'll pull the trigger of your gun, which just happens to already be loaded."

Jack Stevenson walked into the car, and the officer's stormy eyes looked straight ahead, never once turning back.

XIII

Inside the theater, Benjamin Benzene stood on stage in front of a gargantuan tank, which was filled with water and some large fish.

"Thank you very much for coming!" Benjamin said to the audience, "This is the first solo show I have ever done in my entire life in a real theater for a paying audience. I hope you enjoy yourself. And, I'm warning you right here and now that if you are sensitive to gruesomeness, then you should leave right away." There were some murmurs in the audience but nobody left.

"Glad to see you are up for this - let's begin the show!"

"We're going to start by classifying the four animals inside this tank. This might be a bit boring, but if you like life science, then you'll like this." A projector lit up, displaying an already prepared slideshow. The first slide showed a photo of a strange looking shark with black holes for eyes and razor sharp teeth.

"This is a shortfin mako," Benjamin said calmly. "For those of you who don't know, this animal is responsible for many reported human deaths. It is also the fastest shark in the world. And, it is also right here." Trip walked over to the tank, and pressed his fingertip to the glass, pointing to a shark that looked identical to the one in the photograph. "Say hello to Mako, everybody!" There was cheering from the audience.

Benjamin clapped his hand, and the projector went on to the next slide. This one had a different photo. It was what you would picture when you think of a shark. It had a single fin, and was both white and grayish. "This is the great white shark, officially the most dangerous shark. Being hit by this monster is like being hit by a freight train, and each of his teeth are three inches long. Here it is." He pointed tentatively to the shark, which was easily the largest in the tank. "It is also very easily angered," he said slowly. "Next slide please."

On the next slide was an enormous fish. It was similar to the great white shark, except it looked about twice the size. It was a light blue color. The whole body was the same shade exactly, and it didn't look very smart. Its name suited it perfectly. "This is the bull shark," Benjamin said, which caused some laughing. "Many people think that in fact, the bull shark is the most dangerous shark. It has 69 recorded attacks, but experts think there have been many more that were not recorded. It is also one of the only sharks that swims in both freshwater and saltwater. I won't even point to it in the tank, because I'm sure you've already noticed where the bull shark is." It was not very hard to miss, that was true.

"And our final shark is responsible for more human deaths then all of the other three put together. It is extremely vicious." On the projected image it was black, blue, and white. It looked identical in the tank. It was the smallest in the tank, but it was the most mean looking as well. "Ladies and gentlemen, let me introduce... the oceanic white tip shark!" There was a bit of applause, but mostly people were starting to get bored, and Benjamin knew it.

"Okay, I know this might have been a bit boring, so we'll get to the real show, which I hope will be worth the wait." Suddenly, Benjamin pulled his pants down. There was a murmur, but he was wearing a bathing suit underneath. He whipped off his shirt, and smiled at the audience. "That's right everyone, I'm going swimming!" There was a little platform above the tank, and that was where Benjamin seemed to be heading. He climbed to the top and spoke from there.

"For the record, these sharks haven't been fed for six hours. This isn't animal cruelty; it is simply enough time to make them..." he paused for effect, peering down into the tank, "...hungry."

A few people in the audience started to speak loudly, as if they thought they should prevent what was about to happen. "Okay, so what I need you to do is to please count down from ten. When you get to zero, I'm going to go swimming with the sharks."

The audience slowly started a chant. And, if you had walked into the theater at that time, you would have felt the tension in the room, building higher and higher as the numbers got lower. As the tension grew, the voices of the audience got softer. By the time they had reached two, it was barely a whisper, and the one was hardly audible.

But, nevertheless, Benjamin did jump. A panel opened at the top of the tank, Benjamin jumped in, and then it closed just as fast.

Many people turned away, but those who managed to watch saw all four sharks attack Benjamin Benzene. Of course, it was very blurry, which made it hard to see, but it was hard not to notice all the blood in the tank. Some of the people who had turned away, kept glancing back at the tank, seeing the blood, and then quickly turning away again. Soon, you couldn't even see Benjamin, all you could see was blood.

After the audience had been just watching the blood for several seconds and growing more and more anxious, there was a faint knock on the door of the theater. If it hadn't been so quiet in the room, the audience would've missed it. But it was so quiet, so quiet that you could hear your own blood throbbing in your ears.

A young man who was seated closest to the door slowly walked to the door and opened it and then gasped. The door flung open, and in walked......... Benjamin Benzene. People looked back at the tank, which was still filled with blood, with the great white shark that was slowly swimming through it. Benjamin was dressed in a black cloak, but his eyes looked sunken and weary. He tousled his hair with his hand, and then sat down on a chair on the stage, as if he was suddenly exhausted.

"Thank you very much," he said weakly. "Goodnight, everyone." And with that, the lights went out.

XIV

Three days later the following article was published in *Magic Magazine*.

A Brother's Revenge
By Trip Benzene

For those who don't know me, I'm Trip Benzene, the brother of Benjamin Benzene. As many of you know, my brother has done many things to me that cannot be justified, most recent being that he ruined my magic shows by making a video that showed how I did my tricks.

Now, one of the first lessons that our parents taught us was that two wrongs do not make a right. So even though my brother ruined all the shows that I've done without him, and even though I know how he did this trick with the sharks, I would never stoop so low as to write in a public article how he did it.

There are, however, a few more things I want to bring attention to.

First of all, it's just as easy to put a trapdoor on the bottom of a tank as it is to put one on top.

Second of all, to release something resembling blood is not a very difficult thing to do. Even kids' magic kits have fake blood.

Thirdly, glass walls are not very visible inside water.

Lastly, imagine a glass cylinder running from (trap) floor to (trap) ceiling inside a tank.

Think about that, and be sure to come to my next show!

XV

The news was released in the entertainment pages of all the local papers, and everyone was excited about it. It was first released in New York City, but gradually word spread to other parts of the country, until it seemed that no two theaters in New York City would be big enough to hold the audience. That's right, two. Benjamin and Trip Benzene were each having a show the same night. Both in New York City and both for a very short time - from eight o' clock to eight thirty. Local news shows on TV and the radio were talking about it. They interviewed people who had seen them fighting, and invited other magicians to comment on their mastery of magic and on their rivalry. It was being called "Battle of Brothers". No one knows who first started using that term, but it caught on.

There was more. Both of the theaters where they were performing in had been specially built. Nobody knew where the money had come from to build the theaters so quickly, but they were built.

At Trip Benzene's show, in the center of the stage was a large, boxy looking machine. It was made of metal, and was very rusty with splattered paint. On top of the box was a place where you could step inside, with a swinging door. Trip stood in the middle of the stage, looking out at the audience, which completely filled the theater. All the seats were filled, and people were sitting near the stage, as well as standing in little nooks and alleys.

"I know that this is my shortest show yet, but I did that on purpose. It is not because I wanted to match the timings of my brother, whose show I am pleased that so many of you have chosen to skip, but because I wanted to have a little examination of time.

"I doubt that anyone in this room has actually considered the question of what is time? Or why does time pass in the way it does? Why can't it go by faster?" He removed a pen from his pocket and tossed it in the air. "We all know that it's gravity that's pulling the pen down, but why does it take the time that it does to fall down? I repeat, why does time go by in the way it does? Great scientists don't know the answer to these questions, and I'm certainly not one to claim that I do. Rather, I would like to prove something. We think that on Earth, time always goes at the same pace. That's what I'm about to prove wrong.

"Every day, I shave," Trip said, pointing to his jaw. "But, were I not to shave for one day, I would not grow a beard. I would have to wait maybe three days to get a decent stubble. But to get a beard that was, say, four inches long, it would take at least a year. We are about to have an intermission. Intermission is ten minutes, and when you come back, in ten minutes, I will have a beard. Any questions?"

A young man raised his hand. He didn't seem very impressed. In fact, he looked upset. "How do we know that you won't just plop on a fake beard?"

Trip shrugged. "You can pull it if you want." There was some laughing in the audience. "Now, this rusty looking box will be the key to this magic. It is also what I have spent a large fraction of my life working on. It is a time machine." A murmur went through the crowd, and there was some frowning. This wasn't the usual quality of Trip's tricks.

"Before the intermission begins, I will step into the time machine, and exactly when intermission ends, I will step out with a beard. Also," he added, almost as an afterthought, "I'd like to announce that this is my last magic show."

There was lots of shouting in the crowd, and several people seemed very upset. Trip waved his hand for silence, and then continued. "I have decided that I don't want to pursue magic as my profession. I plan to get a medical degree and become a doctor. Nevertheless, I hope you enjoy my final show."

The shouting seemed to turn into applause, which grew and echoed in the new theater, which seemed to cause more applause, until the room was a crescendo of clapping. As the applause slowly died down, Trip stepped into the box. As he did so, the lights came on, and some people started to leave for intermission so they could come back quickly and see a bearded Trip Benzene. Other people remained in their seats with their eyes glued to the machine.

XVI

Trip stepped inside the box, and closed the top, letting the darkness slowly engulf him. He snatched a key from his pocket and opened the trapdoor on the floor. It flung open, which resulted in him falling straight down. He cursed as he fell underground. How had they made this tunnel? He took a flashlight out of his pocket, and flipped the switch to turn on the bright light. He shielded his eyes as it came on, for they had already adjusted to the dark. When he had adjusted again to the new light, he started looking around. The tunnel had been poorly built, for it was crumbling dirt. It stretched out a long way, but Trip had expected that. He glanced at his watch. He had only eight more minutes left until intermission ended, and he'd need to show up with a beard.

He started jogging down the tunnel, his shiny black shoes causing an outburst of dust with every step. Finally, the tunnel ended, and there was the small iron trapdoor. He tapped softly on the door. He knew the signal. Two taps back meant come in, one tap meant try again later, and no taps meant he needed to tap harder. On the other side of the door there were two faint taps. Trip quietly opened the small door and squeezed his body through it.

He had entered a jail cell. It was small and bare, with a dirty toilet in the corner. Sitting by the trapdoor, was a man the same age and size as Trip. In fact, he looked very similar to him, except that he was a bit thinner and frailer, was dressed in old dirty jeans, and, of course, he had a beard.

The man got up immediately, and wrapped his arms around Trip who did the same to him. There were tears in both men's eyes.

"Trip, I, I, thought I would never see you again."

"Devin, I'm very happy to see you also, but we must hurry. My show starts in about four minutes."

"Of course, but you're coming to Rehoboth?"

"I would never forget."

"And what about -"

"He'll be coming soon. Just be patient."

"Should I wait for him?"

"Of course not. You must go immediately."

The two men quickly took off their clothes, and put on the other's. Then Devin went down the tunnel, making sure to lock it from the inside and cover it with dirt. Trip pulled on his brother's dirty gray T-shirt, reached into his pocket and pulled out a fake beard, which he clipped to his chin. He hoped he looked enough like Devin so that the guards wouldn't suspect him.

Devin sprinted down the tunnel. It had been years since he had sprinted anywhere, so it took a while for his legs to get used to it but it felt wonderful to run again, and he ran like anything, despite the fact that he was wearing Trip's dress shoes. Two minutes later he was in the box that was the time machine, and he could already hear the audience getting impatient. He took a deep breath and jumped out of the box. There was such loud cheering and applause that when Devin tapped his foot as a nervous habit, he couldn't hear it. He beamed at the audience. He realized that they were cheering for him, and that, along with the fact that he was out of prison, made this the best day of his life.

He stepped off the stage, and took another bow. "I'm sure many of you are doubting that I actually grew a beard in this short period of time. So, I will take three volunteers to come up and pull my beard, as long as it's not too hard."

He picked three random volunteers from the audience, and had them in turn pull the beard. Not only did it not come off, but better than that was the fact that they felt like the bristles of a bear.

People started filing out of the theater, talking about what a wonderful show Trip's last performance had been. For Devin, it would be easy now. He would check into a nice hotel in Manhattan, with Trip's passport and credit card that he had given him. He would spend the night there, and then head out. He would be free.

In Devin Benzene's cell, Trip lay on the ground, slumped over, with a hint of a smile playing on his lips. He was extremely tired and he knew that it would be many hours before he slept again. A guard passed his cell, and out of caution he turned his head to face the wall, so the guard would know he was there but wouldn't see his face. There was still much more to do.

XVII

At Benjamin's show, the crowd was as big as his brother's. He was sitting on a stool in the middle of the stage. The only other equipment on the stage was the same tank of water with the ladder that had been in his last show, only without the sharks, and a very official looking box. It was metal and had a door on top. Besides that, it looked quite ordinary.

Benjamin was wearing a tuxedo, and his deep brown eyes looked straight down, as if he were a statue until his show began. Finally, the show started, and Benjamin stood up and walked to the center of the stage.

"Before I begin this show," he said, speaking so quietly that the audience had to strain to hear him. "I have an announcement to make. This will be," his voice was hardly audible now. "This will be my final magic performance." There was gasping in the audience, and Benjamin looked down again, as if ashamed of his choice. When he spoke again, his voice was firmer, as if he was starting to approve of his own decision. "I hope to get a degree in transcendental meditation." By now everyone had heard what he had said, and was listening attentively. "However, I do hope you enjoy my final show. It took me a lot of time to plan. I'm also very happy that you came to my show instead of my amateur brother's.

"Now may I introduce Howard, an assistant of mine who works at Boxie company." A man walked down from the back of the audience. He was dressed in a collared blue shirt with a name tag on it that said: Hi, I'm Howard. His shirt said: Boxie Co. We sell boxes.

"Howard made this box that you see here. Howard, could you please tell the crowd about this box?"

Howard gave a gleaming smile that only salespeople have, and said, "Sure. This box is made out of good quality stainless iron, about one inch thick. To demonstrate the durability of the box, we have a large hammer here." A robed assistant appeared with a huge hammer that he slammed against the side of the box. It made a great clang, but the box wasn't even dented. The robed assistant left.

"As you can see, this box would be very hard to break out of or into, unless of course, you had the key.

"This leads us to our next point: the key." From his pocket, Howard took out a steel key. It was old fashioned, and had spikes along the side of it. "This is the only key to the box, and it works from both the outside and the inside." Howard slammed the door of the box down, and then easily unlocked it with the key. He left the door open.

"Now there's only one feature left to mention. I'm sure some of you noticed the holes, but for those of you who didn't, I'll tell you about it." Howard walked next to the box, and put his fingers in the two holes that were on all six sides of the box. "There are twelve holes in this box; two on each side. These go all the way through the box, so if the box was dropped in water, it would soon be filled with water. And if there was a person inside, without the key, within a few minutes they would drown." He paused to let his words sink in.

At this point Howard stepped back and Benjamin stepped forward. "To make sure everyone believes Howard, we will have a demonstration. Benjamin clapped his hands and the robed assistant came up to the stage again, picked up the box, climbed up the ladder to the tank, and dropped the box in the water.

There were a few moments of silence, and then the assistant tossed in a grappling hook, which caught on to a hook on top of the box and was then pulled back up. The assistant took the box down the ladder again, set it on the edge of the stage and left.

"You can now clearly see that the box is filled with water, and that took less than five minutes," Benjamin said. "So what is going to happen is this. I will be thrown into the tank of water inside the box and remain there for the fifteen-minute intermission. You can go buy drinks if you want, or you can stay. Either way, after the intermission, the box will come up with me inside, hopefully alive." He gave the audience a smile.

"However, before the intermission, there is one more piece of business to take care of. The key." Howard gave him the iron key, and Benjamin clapped his hands. The robed assistant appeared for the third time, this time wheeling a small stove.

Benjamin nodded, and said, "I'm going to need five witnesses to make sure that what I say I'm doing, I'm actually doing." He called up five random people to the stage, and then brought up one more person, a seven-year-old boy, who said, "Pleeeeease, Mr. Benzene?"

Benjamin gave the key to one of the people, and asked him to put it in the pot that was on the stove, and make sure it stayed there. The man did so, and then Benjamin asked a woman to turn the heat on high.

Not even a minute later, Benjamin held up the pot and showed the audience that it was nothing but grey glop. He then dumped the glop onto the front of the stage. He looked at the audience for a moment.

"Now, as I'm sure you remember," he said, "Howard unlocked the box before the key was melted. So, if we lock it now, it will never open again. And," here his eyes looked wild, with the reflection of the flames in the stove on them, "if we locked it with someone inside it, they would never come out."

He paused for just a second, so what he said could sink into the audience. Then he suddenly burst into action. He sprinted across the room, jumped into the box, and slammed it shut with a click.

Then Howard walked back to the center of the stage, and said, "I can promise you that the door to the box is locked. But, just in case you don't believe me, anyone who wants to can come and pull." Dozens of people dashed up and tried to pull it open, but to no avail. For about five minutes they pulled and pulled, like a scene from the Sword in the Stone, shoving each other for a turn to tug. Then, slowly, they started walking back. Finally, the last of them gave up and returned to their seats.

As soon as the last audience member had returned to his seat, the robed man came for the last time, picked up the box, and let it plunge to the bottom of the tank.

Howard announced that intermission had begun, and that when the show started again, the box would be taken out of the tank, and Benjamin would come out. "And, also, if you don't need to leave, feel free to stay through intermission.

Some people left for the intermission, and many more stayed and watched the box closely. What didn't occur to any of them was that Benjamin Benzene was already leaving.

XVIII

As soon as he got in the box, Benjamin grabbed one of the two tiny blue kits that were hidden, stuck to the bottom of it. It had cost him over a thousand dollars to buy these from the black market. For a second, Benjamin felt a wave of doubt if he was doing the right thing. He had lied to a lot of people. But when he remembered the reason, his doubt left him.

It had all started with one event, just one thing. The moment Trip told him who had actually killed Dorothy Stevenson, the two brothers had started plotting their elaborate plan to put the real murderer in jail and help Devin to escape.

Benjamin had been sitting in his dormitory in his college, when his cell phone had rung. He quickly answered it, not wanting to wake anyone up. "Hello, is that you, Benjamin?" Trip's smooth voice echoed in the phone.

"Yes it's me, but what's the big idea calling me at one in the morning?"

"You answered on the first ring, so I don't think I awoke you. Anyway, it's important."

"I was up with homework. What's the news?"

"I figured it out."

"Figured what out?" Despite the fact that it was so late, a note of excitement had crept into Benjamin's voice.

"Who murdered Dorothy Stevenson." Benjamin said nothing, so Trip continued. "I did some investigating, and I figured it out. You know Jack Stevenson? That guy who sued Leonardo Sinket?"

"You mean Dorothy's husband? He murdered her?"

"A friend of mine is good at checking on these kinds of things so he's been helping me. He heard that Jack had been in with the New York City mob. I checked around and figured out it was true. After getting some more information, I realized something else. A few weeks before the murder, Jack had invested an enormous amount of money in some company that was doing very well. He had lost a lot of money before the investment in parties and gambling, so he was excited to make this investment. Unfortunately, the company collapsed, and within a week later, the whole thing was shut down. Now Jack was truly almost bankrupt. What happened next took a while for my friend to uncover. Jack Stevenson had placed a three hundred-thousand-dollar insurance policy on his wife exactly a week before the murder. Not only that, but Devin confirmed that a heavyset man who sounded a lot like Jack had bumped into him earlier that day with some sort of inkpad. He had disappeared before he could do anything about it. Of course, the police had no reason to investigate any further, since Devin's fingerprints had already matched. Jack got the insurance money, took it quietly, and managed to become himself again. There were rumors that Jack and Dorothy, who had married when they were quite young, had grown apart. People had seen them fighting at parties and even arriving and leaving separately."

"By now, Benjamin's face had gone white, but that didn't stop the anger in his voice. "So what are we going to do? We could kill him, you know."

"Kill who?"

"Stevenson."

"We must be careful, Benjamin. By the end of this, I hope he's in prison, but we can't let ourselves get arrested in the process."

"What do you mean the end of *this*? What's this?"

"I've already started a plan. We'll work on it until we're completely satisfied. Remember, what we're aiming for is for Jack to be in jail, Devin to be out of jail, and you and I to both be alive."

That had been the start of months of planning, starting with the decision to drop out of college, followed by hours and hours of practicing magic every day. Every other Sunday during visiting hours, they would visit Devin, and give him hushed updates on their progress.

Now, looking back on it, Benjamin was amazed at how much of the plan they had managed to pull off. In fact.... if the rest of the plan worked out, then as soon as two days from now... no he couldn't think like that. He just had to finish his job, for there was already an inch of water in the box.

It was pitch dark, so Benjamin removed his flashlight from his pocket, and switched it on. The whole place lit up, and Benjamin stood the flashlight up in a corner. He then opened up his kit. There were two things in the kit: a metal stick and a very thick gel. Benjamin quickly stuffed the gel into the keyhole. He then dropped the kit on the ground with a clatter, and snatched the other one. He stuffed the other kit in his pocket, grabbed the flashlight, and then stuck his fingers through the two holes on the bottom of the box where the water was coming in. He smiled to himself. It had worked. The magnets on the bottom of the tank had attracted the magnets at the bottom of the box, putting the box in the perfect position. There were two holes of the same size on the bottom of the tank right underneath the two holes on the bottom of the box. He ran his long fingers through the holes at the bottom of the tank, which connected with holes going through the floor and unlatched the small lock underneath the floor. At the exact same time, he turned the lock of the small trapdoor in the box.

The audience wouldn't notice any of this because the trapdoor was in the middle of the box. The audience couldn't see what was happening on the floor underneath the tank.

The door flung open, and Benjamin fell down a bit, along with all the water that had gathered. He put the trapdoor back on above him, and then locked it. It was hard to reach because it was so high, and he stumbled a little, but he soon regained his balance and walked downhill through the underground tunnel.

After about three minutes of walking he had reached the bottom. There was a small iron door in front of him.

He tapped once, quietly, and wasn't surprised when the door opened. Standing there was a man who looked a lot like Benjamin except he had a beard. "Devin! You weren't supposed to open the door, just tap twice."

The other man had a hint of mischief in his eyes as he spoke. "First of all, that wasn't necessary, seeing that I was right next to the door. And second of all, I'm not Devin, I'm Trip."

Benjamin ran his eyes over the man in front of him, then gave a stiff nod. "Right. Sorry. Devin already left?"

"About two minutes ago."

"Okay." Suddenly Benjamin felt disappointed. He had been looking forward to seeing Devin in the midst of their plan. Nevertheless, he opened the second kit, and jammed the thick goo into the keyhole, and tossed the iron stick onto the floor. "So wait ten minutes until this is dry, then you'll see there will be a small hole in it. Stick the stick into the hole, and then pull it out. That will be the cue to get out of here. Remember, the drunk guard has duty from ten to two, and he doesn't come by during the eleven to eleven-thirty gap, so that's when you leave."

"I know, I know. We've reviewed this dozens of times. Are you okay, Benjamin?"

"Yeah, I'm fine. I had just been looking forward to seeing Devin again."

"But you saw him two weeks ago."

"I know, just, just like to see him leave."

"You'll see him in a week."

"I know. Well, bye Trip. Good luck."

"Bye Benjamin. Don't forget to lock the door on your way out."

Benjamin slipped out, locking and covering the door behind him. It was hard to climb back up, but he was fit and did it within five minutes. He unlocked the trapdoor, took a deep breath and climbed up, locking the door beneath him. The box was filled with water but as soon he was in the box, Howard's voice rang across the theater, and he knew he had just had a very close call. "Thank you very much for returning. And now, I present to you, Benjamin Benzene." Howard didn't realize how risky it was, announcing like that, for if it had taken Benjamin but a moment longer the timing would have been wrong and the show would've been ruined.

But that hadn't happened, so Benjamin jabbed the stick in the hole, and twisted. The door popped open, but Benjamin made sure to first grab the key and put it in his pocket. Then he swam up, his lungs bursting, to the cheering of the audience. Everyone applauded as Benjamin took a bow, still panting, and then the lights went out.

XIX

Trip lay down on the dusty bench that had served as Devin's cell for so long. He was extremely tired, but he wasn't going to let himself fall asleep. He didn't know what would happen if he woke up to see that it was nine in the morning. It wouldn't take long for the guard to realize that he wasn't Devin.

A guard passed by the cell again, but this time Trip forced himself to look straight at the guard. The guard's gaze didn't linger, and he soon passed onto the next cell. Trip felt relieved, but he tried to force himself not to be. He had to be relaxed when the guard passed. He doubted that the guard would notice, but there was no harm in trying to play the part.

He soon got used to the steady movements of the guard. *Back. Forth. Back. Forth. Back. Forth.* With every movement of the guard, Trip's eyelids moved down a bit until finally his eyes were completely closed.

His head started to feel heavier and heavier, until he drifted off to sleep.

He was sitting in the jail cell, the guards pacing back and forth. Suddenly one of them burst open the door and aimed his gun at him. "I know you're not Devin," he said. The man turned into Jack Stevenson.

The scene changed and they were on the streets of New York again, as Jack put his pistol to Trip's forehead. Trip examined the rusty thing jutting into his skin, that if one little button was pressed, he would be lying in the city, with blood pooling out. "You're not going to shoot me," Trip said. The whir of blue came, signifying Officer Anderson, but it was too late. Jack pulled the trigger, and the shot echoed through Trip's head, and when he touched it, it was just wet blood. He screamed and screamed as the blood soaked into the sidewalk, and Anderson just stood at a distance and watched, while Jack kept pulling the trigger.

He jolted awake, his head still feeling sore. How could he have let himself fall asleep? He looked at his watch, and saw that it was only 9:45.

The next hour and a half was probably the worst in Trip's life. He would keep telling himself not to fall asleep, but then he would, and would be engulfed in nightmares. When he would wake up, he would still be aching from his dreams, and then he would be afraid he had missed his time slot. Not only that, but while he was awake, for some reason he kept thinking about sad things that had really happened, the biggest one being dropping out of college. He had been at the top of his class and would have been in medical school right now, if he hadn't started working on this plan. The two years of his life that he had used for his brother would be two years of his life he would never get back. And it would also be hard to get back into college, since he had already dropped out. He suddenly felt angry at Devin for letting this happen to him. Sure, he had been framed, but then both Trip and Benjamin had dropped out for him, had risked a lot for him, and now Devin was at some hotel, while Trip was enduring the worst hours of his life. Then the image of Devin's thin body and grateful face popped into his head, and the anger drained away.

Finally, after an eternity of waiting, Trip stood up, stretching his legs. It was 11:08, which was the perfect time to sneak out. Both his brothers had locked and covered the trapdoors so they wouldn't be discovered, so Trip had to leave through the main door. But, like everything else, this had already been planned. He picked up the metal stick that had been lying on the ground and jammed it in the small hole that had appeared in the goo. He paused for a moment, just thinking about the consequences of his getting caught.

It would only be a short period of time after they had caught him that they would realize that he wasn't Devin. They would realize that a jailbreak had taken place, and Trip and Devin would both be put in a much higher security prison. He remembered how hard it had been to spend just an hour and a half in jail. But years? How could Devin have lasted over a year in jail?

When they had been kids, Devin had always been the happiest, the jokiest, and, of course, the best at magic.

He twisted the key defiantly, then moved back, as the key made a loud clicking noise. Surely the guard had heard that. No, he couldn't be paranoid like that. The guard hadn't noticed anything. Trip slipped out, shutting the door so it looked like it was locked. He then started walking down the hallway.

When he was about twenty meters past the cell, he heard footsteps behind him. Trip was lurking in the shadows, so he looked back and saw the drunk guard walking again. The guard was almost at Devin's cell, so Trip couldn't turn around. He had to keep going. But why was the guard coming this early? Devin had told him he came by at 11:35.

The guard passed the cell, barely glancing in. How had he not noticed that no one was inside? Trip started moving much faster, filled with fear of the guard. Even if he was drunk, there was no way he wouldn't see Trip walking.

He was almost there now. He just had to turn left, walk down the hallway, and he would reach his destination. Sticking to the wall, he made the turn, and took a deep breath. Another man was walking ahead of him. He was very big, and was pushing a trash cart in front of him. Trip shook his head. They had messed up. According to Devin, the garbage man was supposed to come in five minutes. Trip thought quickly. He removed a playing card from his pocket and held it so tightly his knuckles turned white.

The guard would be here in a few seconds. Just when he was about to run, he heard the big man speak.

"Oh not again! I need a goddamn key!"

It was now or never. Trip tiptoed forward and slid the playing card through the legs of the man who was pushing a trash cart. The man leaned down to pick it up, and immediately Trip slipped through the hole of the legs of the trash cart. He could hear the footsteps of the guard behind him. He cleanly pulled himself up, and pushed himself inside the trash bag, shoveling trash on top of him with his hands. What was supposed to have happened was that only the trash cart would be there, and Trip could burrow himself inside safely, but since the janitor was there too, he had had to improvise. But it seemed to work.

The man picked up the playing card, barely glanced at it, and put it in his own pocket, then turned around to face the guard.

"Sorry, Carlos," came the guard's voice. "Here's the key."

"This has got to be the fourth week in a row this has happened," Carlos said, with a heavy Spanish accent. "I tell you leave the blooming key in my office, but no! Every single bloody week you have to screw up my schedule, by swaggering up behind me, so drunk that you, why you wouldn't even know if somebody had left the jail!" Trip heart stopped beating for a moment. What had he said about the leaving the jail? Had he seen Trip?

The guard walked up, still tilting side by side. Devin had been right about one thing: the guard was drunk.

The guard unchained a key from his belt. He walked closer and closer to the janitor, until even in the trash bag, Trip could smell the alcohol on his breath. "Look, I'm sorry. What else do you want me to say?" the guard asked, laughing.

"I don't want you say anything! I want you to leave the key in my office!" The guard nodded, and pressed the key into the Carlos's hand. Trip had to resist the urge to jump out, grab the key that was sitting loosely in Carlos's hand, open the door and leave.

"This is not funny." Carlos said. "If this happens again, I will personally go and report to the warden that you are drinking on the job." Trip was getting more and more anxious. Stop the small talk, he thought.

The guard stopped laughing. "Look, I'm sorry, all right? It won't happen again."

"It better not."

Finally, Carlos walked to the end of the hall, pushing the cart with Trip inside. When he got to the end, he opened the door, letting the cool night air enter in gusts. The guard turned around behind him and continued on his round.

Carlos pushed the trash outside, then turned back toward the jail to close the outer doors. As soon as he did so, Trip jumped out of the trash cart and bolted around the corner. When Carlos turned back, Trip was nowhere in sight. Carlos returned inside, and Trip jogged carefully away.

For the first time in two years, Trip was free.

XX

One week later, at Rehoboth Beach, three separate cars pulled up. One was a Chrysler 200, spitting out gas and fumes. It was a start for Devin Benzene, for he couldn't afford a nice car right out of jail. The second was a Honda Accord. Trip stepped out of it, and there was no way he could hide the smile on his face. There was no place he liked more than the beach. He grinned at Devin and gave him a warm wholehearted hug, just as the third car pulled up. It was a bright red convertible. The roof was off, and the salty air was blowing in, making the driver's hair fly.

Benjamin stepped out and wrapped his arms around Devin. "We did it, Devin. We did it." When they pulled apart from their embrace, they saw Trip was already in his bathing suit.

"What're we waiting for?" he exclaimed. "Let's go!"

The others changed, and then they went down to the beach, with Trip running ahead, and Benjamin and Devin walking behind, talking to each other. It was a perfect day to be at the beach. The sun was bright, the air was warm, and the wind kept pulling the wonderful salty air from the water onto the people. The water was bright green, and the waves seemed to be getting bigger and bigger. Hundreds of people were in the ocean.

After about an hour of swimming, Devin and Benjamin got themselves each a beer, while Trip kept on swimming.

They waited for a table, and when one turned up they grabbed it before the previous people's food had been removed.

"So what do you want to do with your life?" Benjamin asked Devin. "Trip wants to become a doctor, and I want to try and get a degree in transcendental meditation. But we haven't talked about what you want to do."

Devin looked at him incredulously. "Really? I want to become a magician."

Benjamin looked out, and saw Trip riding on a wave. Trip pointed at the table where Benjamin and Devin were sitting. Benjamin brought his gaze back to Devin. "After all this, you want to pursue that as your profession?"

Devin looked him straight in the eye and nodded. "Yes, I do. I like doing it, I'm good at it, and I can get good money for it."

"How do you know you'll get good money? The best magicians do, but not all of them. And it's a tough life."

"I will be one of the best magicians," Devin said quietly and firmly. Benjamin looked closely at Devin for a moment and saw a determination he had never seen in his brother before.

Trip walked up, beads of water falling from his skin, and was starting to sit down, when Benjamin said, "Why don't we go back into the water? The temperature is perfect."

The three brothers got up and went back in, splashing, and laughing and swimming much farther out than everyone else. Benjamin and Devin could ride the waves almost as well as Trip.

They had their whole lives ahead of them to do whatever they wanted.

Notes

The trick with the envelopes is adapted from a trick by John Archer as shown on Penn and Teller.

The trick with the sharks and the idea of videoing and ruining magic tricks are drawn from the 2013 film, Now You See Me.

Slide

PARKER STEPPED ONTO THE TOP of the water slide, the cold October wind freezing him in his short bathing suit. His hair was being pulled back and he pushed it away from his forehead before going down the water slide. Water County was an amazing water park, but he had the feeling that he would like this slide more than any others.

The slide was in a tunnel so it was dark inside, but sunlight still streamed in from outside. The slide was very slippery, so he went fast, but after two full minutes he was still sliding. Parker had a feeling that this wasn't supposed to go on for so long. His stomach was beginning to hurt and he was feeling slightly dizzy. He was speeding so fast now that his thighs were stinging. He could only barely hear the kids laughing in the park outside.

Ten minutes later the slide finally came to an end. Parker anxiously stepped out, expecting to see more slides, but found he was in a new place. He turned around, ready to climb back up the water slide if he had to, but found that the slide was gone.

Parker looked around. He was in the middle of a huge cornfield that stretched out for miles around him. The brown-gold corn seemed to go on forever and the deadly silence made him uncomfortable. His throat was already parched from the unbearable heat. He had barely been there for a few seconds, though, when someone grabbed him. He turned around to see a tall skinny man dressed in some sort of red uniform covered with badges.

"I've got one! I've got one!" The man in uniform shouted. Right behind him another man came over. This one was also in uniform but was much shorter and stockier, and his uniform didn't have any badges.

"Now see here Malbono," the shorter man said. "It's my turn." The taller man grunted but let go of Parker. Malbono walked away dejectedly. The stockier man now grabbed Parker and they started walking briskly in the direction that the water slide had been.

"Excuse me, but where am I, ple-"

"You are in Herrin, my name is Chock and I'm supposed to be taking you to be executed."

"Executed? But what did I do?"

"No time to explain. If Malbono ever finds out I let you go, well......" the man sighed. "Just run into the forest and try to stay alive. Good luck."

Parker didn't know what was going on, but he knew that this was not a good place. He realized that this guard, or whatever he was, had just risked a lot to help him. And he also knew that he had to stay alive. He started running toward the forest. Why was he supposed to be executed? What had he done? His thoughts were interrupted by a voice yelling behind him.

"You there! Stop in the name of King Jecker!" Parker turned around to see the tall man, Malbono, running toward him. Parker remembered what Chock had said: If Malbono ever finds out I let you go...

Parker started to run faster. However, Malbono was clearly much faster than he was. Within a few minutes, he had caught him. Now that he was caught he decided to play it friendly.

"Hi, I'm Parker Worth, I was wonderi-" Parker stopped. Malbono had a hand behind Parker's neck and a knife at his throat.

"No talking! Walk back this way, I don't know what Chock was thinki, OWWW!" Malbono let go of Parker and clutched his knee, which was bleeding, an arrow stuck in it. Suddenly, a scrawny boy holding a bow came running out of the bushes.

"Come on, run!" The boy yelled. Parker didn't wait. He was on his school track and field team and he ran fast, faster than the boy. Soon they were in the forest, but since the boy was still running, so was Parker. Finally, after half an hour of running they stopped in a clearing. Parker was panting, but not nearly as much as the boy, who was doubled over, coughing and hoarse. When Parker got him calmed down, the boy introduced himself.

"My name is Puck." Parker smiled. Puck was a small boy, with short blond hair and dark eyes.

"You are the first person I've met here who has a somewhat normal name. I mean seriously? Malbono and Chock?"

Puck laughed. "Well, thank my parents for that." As soon as the words came out of Puck's mouth, his face instantly darkened.

"What's wrong?" Parker asked, clutching Puck's shoulder.

"My father is a captain in King Jecker's army. When I turned thirteen a few weeks ago, he wanted me to join Jecker's army also. I told him I wouldn't but he insisted. Finally, I ran away with just my bow and some arrows. I've been running around Herrin shooting animals for food. When I saw you, I thought it was some sort of turn in fate."

"What makes you say that?"

"Boy, you really are clueless. There is a prophecy that a cestovatel will kill King Jecker. When Jecker found out, he ordered that all places where cestovatels come in from should be heavily guarded. That's why as soon as you came, guards found you. However, lucky for you, you got out of it. Now if I start training you, you could become the cestovatel of the prophecy!"

"Okay, wait a second. I'm not ready to commit to this. First of all, what's a cestovatel?" It was pronounced like *sestovatal*. Puck gave an exaggerated groan.

"You are a cestovatel. A cestovatel is someone who comes from another world. Of course, in the case of Herrin, cestovatels are only from Earth."

"You know about Earth! What do you know about it?"

"That it's a place where cestovatels come from and no one from Herrin has been smart enough to figure out how to get there."

"Do, uh, cestovatels ever get back to Earth?"

"Well nowadays, they all get killed. Before Jecker was king, the king was King Kuff. But that was way before I was born, so I don't know what happened to them then. Anyway, enough questions. Tomorrow, we will go to the market and buy you a weapon. With any luck, we'll get through your training without Jecker finding us."

That night as Parker lay on the hard ground, he thought about how excited Puck had been. But the thing was, Parker wasn't a hero. He was just a normal kid in Einstein middle school. He had two best friends, Will and Sam. He had a crush on Lizzy Samson. He had a dog that it had taken him a year to convince his parents to buy for him. His Mom was his favorite person in the world. His parents weren't really rich or poor. He liked math and science and hated Latin. He wasn't someone from a prophecy in an alternative universe destined to kill some evil king. He was just normal old Parker Worth.

Yet he liked Puck. In fact, Puck reminded him of Will, - the mysterious smile, the little jokes, the enthusiasm. If they ever got back to Earth, Parker could picture Puck joining them in the slumber parties with his friends. As he dwelled on these thoughts, his eyelids started slowly closing. Within a few minutes, he was fast asleep.

The next morning the alarm clock on his digital watch woke Parker up. He thought that was a shame, because at least one good thing about being in a different world was that he could sleep in. Puck was still sleeping a few meters away.

The bushes rustled. Parker shouted and grabbed the first weapon he could find, a thick wood stick.

Into the clearing stepped a man holding a lumpy bag. He was tall, with a withered, stark white beard. His hair was tied in a ponytail. He had the saddest eyes Parker had ever seen. Just by looking at them, Parker could tell that they had once been a brilliant blue. Now they seemed dull, with soft grey streaks running through them. Someone could have painted a picture of his eyes that could make you cry.

"Is it you?" The man asked in a hoarse voice that sounded the way Albus Dumbledore sounded in the movies.

"Pardon?"

"Are you the cestovatel that will kill the evil King Jecker?" Parker was saved from his response, however, when Puck got up.

"Can't you talk a little quieter to yourself, Ma-" he stopped when he saw the stranger. "Wait a second! I know you! You work for King Jecker! Your name is Zrádce!" He said Zrádce in an Italian accent, sort of like *Zah-rah-dah-say-ah*. "So you think you can just show up and kill Parker? You'll have to fight me first!" And just like that, Puck had an arrow notched, pointed toward Zrádce. Zrádce didn't look at all scared.

"Relax, young one. I have run away from Jecker's palace when I heard about this youth." Puck's eyes narrowed into slits.

"You expect me to believe this? What are you doing here anyway?"

Parker spoke up. "Puck, lower the bow. If this man was going to kill me, he would have done so already. Zrádce, explain from the beginning."

Zrádce sighed. "My father died soon after I was born. My mother, who had no money left, realized she was dying too. Father had worked in King Kuff's army, so mother turned me over to him. Kuff gladly accepted. My mother died in peace. Kuff raised me up well, and soon I was a general in his army. When I was thirty-six, Kuff died of old age. Amid all the chaos after the death of Kuff, Jecker did a few favors for people, consolidated some power, killed two rivals, and before we knew it, he was king. Jecker had his own army that was much stronger than mine, but none of his soldiers were as smart as me. So soon I had become Jecker's advisor.

"When I first knew him, he was not so bad. But as he got more and more powerful, he got greedier too. Soon he became completely corrupt. He demanded large tributes from people around him, he tortured and killed those he thought were threats, and he cleverly divided the knights and lords to prevent them from rising against him. I kept working for Jecker. I rarely actually helped him but I got enough food, a fancy room, and some power over how things went in the kingdom. What more could an aging advisor ask for? Inside, I knew what Jecker was doing was wrong. But I also knew that no one could do anything. Jecker had become too strong. Then I heard the prophecy. Right then, I swore that if there was any clue at all that the prophecy might come true, I would turn against Jecker. A decade passed and I was sure that the prophecy was a fake. Then you came along. A hunter saw you escape from the guards and word spread of your arrival. I thought that you might have a chance, but I was not brave enough to leave yet. Then yesterday something else happened and I realized it must be part of the prophecy. Yesterday...." he lowered his voice.

"King Jecker has been severely wounded in an accident. No one outside of the palace knows. If there is a time to challenge him to a duel it is now. There is a rule that if someone wants to challenge the king to a duel, they must be allowed through the castle gates to fight. It's the only rule that is keeping the people's hopes alive. That's my story."

Puck and Parker exchanged glances. Zrádce's story sounded true enough. Parker started to say something, but Zrádce spoke first. "So here is what I propose. Tomorrow morning, we leave for the palace. I will pretend to have caught you, Parker, and will bring you to the palace. When you are in front of the king you will whip out your sword and start fighting. Jecker is still a skilled fighter, but he is hurt. The ribs on his left side are where he is wounded the most. If you hit him there it will get you much time. For now, well, I brought you a sword to practice with. It's called Farthadonos. Today we will practice."

From out of his bag, he pulled out a thin, light brown sword. "It was the best I could steal from the armory. It isn't perfect, but it will do." He handed it over to Parker. It was surprisingly light. Parker whipped it through the air and it made the loud sound of whooshing air. He already loved it!

The rest of the day went by fast with Puck and Parker dueling. Zrádce had let Puck borrow his own sword, called something so long that neither boy could pronounce it. It was much heavier than Parker's, but also much more powerful. Yet Puck seemed uncomfortable with the sword. Twice, when Zrádce wasn't there, he had whispered to Parker that they shouldn't trust him.

The boys were about equal, but no matter how many times Parker would try to feel proud of himself, Zrádce would say, "Do not get cocky. If you cannot even beat this boy every time, then how will you beat King Jecker?"

"But you said he was wounde-"

"If he wasn't wounded it would be impossible. Don't forget that Jecker is the best sword fighter in Herrin. If the circumstances were different, I would give you months, even years to train. But Jecker will get better soon. He has the best healers there are."

That night three people sat around the campfire, cooking two rabbits that Zrádce had shot while the boys were practicing. Parker was feeling more scared than he had ever felt before. Tomorrow at this time, he could be dead. If he were, he wondered what his parents would end up thinking. Probably that he had run away. And even if he did beat Jecker, he still didn't know how to get back home. Zrádce had explained to him that whoever won the duel would get to be king. So he might be king. Big Whoop. He didn't care about having a king's power in a place like this. He just wanted to go back home. But what if as king, he started getting the smartest people in the land together to figure out how you could get back to Earth. Then eventually he could come back, maybe thirty years old and try to explain to his parents where he had been.

"What's the matter, Parker?" He was interrupted out of his thoughts by Zrádce.

"It's just, will I ever get back to Earth?"

"My mother used to say to me that all great heroes are rewarded." Puck said sadly.

"Perhaps," Zrádce said, without much confidence.

Parker thought it could be true that all heroes were rewarded, but he had to admit the idea sounded pretty lame to him.

Puck and Parker lay down on blankets that Zrádce had brought for them. The boys lay down on the side, while Zrádce blocked the entrance to the clearing. Parker was exhausted from all the sword practice and pretty soon he had fallen asleep.

In the middle of the night, Parker was awakened by someone tapping his shoulder. His eyes fluttered open and he saw Puck leaning over him. "What's the matter?" Parker asked.

"Parker, don't trust that man. I don't like him and there is something very suspicious about him. I believe his story, but.... there's something wrong. He's been working for Jecker for over thirty years. He's one of his most loyal followers. Why would he just betray him and start helping us?"

"Puck, trust me. I'm a good judge of people." Parker remembered the sadness in Zrádce's eyes.

"No, Parker, we can't trust him, I'm telling you, I'm afraid he'll kill us, first chance he gets."

"How can you say that? He's helped us so much. He trained me how to sword fight. He gave us our food for the whole day."

Puck looked like he was about to argue, but then just nodded. "Fine. Good night."

The next morning when Parker and Puck got up, there was no sign of Zrádce. They searched around but found no trace of him. The only thing he had left was Farthadonos and their blankets. Finally, they found a note, folded inside one of the blankets, written in loopy, cursive writing. This is what it said:

> Dear Parker,
>   Last night, I got more and more afraid that Jecker's men would find me. Finally, I fled to go to a small house I own in the hills of southern Herrin. I know I am a coward for leaving you but I know you can continue without me. Remember everything I have taught you and tomorrow I expect there to be a much better king.
>
> Yours Truly,
> Zrádce

Puck looked at Parker nervously. "I knew we made a mistake, trusting that man."

"What makes you say that? His story is believable. We must leave now, if we wish to challenge Jecker."

Puck winced. "Fine. You're the boss and the one fighting him. It's just, his story seems a bit odd." Inside Parker agreed with him, but he also wanted to get this over with.

Four hours later, two boys stood outside King Jecker's palace. A guard seized Parker.

"You look exactly like the boy His Majesty is looking for."

"Wait a moment," Parker said. "I want to challenge the king to a duel." The guard looked shocked. "Say it again?"

Parker allowed himself the luxury of a smile. "I want to challenge the king to a duel. Isn't anyone allowed to do that?" The guard didn't answer. "Or are you completely corrupt?" The guard suddenly looked scared.

"F-fine. But only one of you may enter. Which one is the challenger?" The boys looked at each other. They hadn't planned this out with Zrádce. Finally, Parker looked the guard in the eye.

"I'm the challenger. Do you swear no harm will come upon Puck?"

"Don't worry, Parker. If he even thinks about attacking, I'll shoot my arrow right through him." Puck grinned at Parker.

"Wish me luck, Puck. Goodbye, until next time." The boys shook hands and then the guard took him through the door.

The dark hallway seemed to go on forever. The good thing about that was it gave Parker enough time to take out Farthadonos, without anyone knowing. If there was anything waiting for him, he would be ready. After walking for about ten minutes, they came out. They went down steps, then up steps, through a locked door and down into a basement. Guards were at every corner. The way got blurred in Parker's mind. He was sure there was an easier way to get there, but the guard was trying to confuse him.

Finally, they entered a large room. Sunlight streamed in from everywhere. The room had guards all around it. In the back was a very comfortable, very fancy throne. Sitting on it was a medium-sized man with thick, greasy dark hair. His face was twisted and cruel. It was King Jecker. Parker looked him over but found no sign of any severe wound on his left ribs. In fact, he looked very fresh.

Then he saw something in the corner that made his face contort in anger. On the far side of the room was a comfortable, sky blue armchair. Sitting in the armchair was a tall man with a withered bright white beard. His hair was tied in a ponytail and his eyes looked very sad. A pretty girl was massaging Zrádce's feet in a small tub of warm water. In his hands was a mug filled with a creamy brown liquid. He had a content smile on his face.

"Yes?" Jecker asked. Parker looked back at the guard who had brought him in. The guard didn't look scared anymore. He had a wide smile on his face. Puck had been right! Zrádce had been a traitor all along. The guard stood up straight and tall.

"This boy would like to challenge you to a duel, Your Highness." The guard said confidently.

Parker shifted uncomfortably. "I......."

"I see; you would rather give up. Well that is fine with me. You shall be hung-"

"NO! I will not give up!" Parker had a fierce expression on his face. "I will let myself be killed, before I give up." He had never been so angry. He was angry at Zrádce for betraying him. He was angry at Jecker for being so cruel. He was angry at Puck for not making him stay in the woods to train. But most of all, he was angry at himself. Puck had tried to tell him about Zrádce. He had tried to protect him from Zrádce. It was bad enough that he hadn't figured out the truth himself, but when Puck had been trying so hard... he should have listened to him.

Jecker stood up. "Very well then. If we are going to duel, we must do it professionally. Come, we will go to the arena." It was clear that he wasn't worried at all about losing. The king and his two bodyguards entered a very primitive sort of elevator and zoomed off. Parker, on the other hand, was taken through more staircases, trap doors and basements, until they got to the arena.

The arena was a large circular room, sort of like a gazebo. It was outdoors but surrounded by walls. There was a small door through which they entered. Around the arena was a field, but it was cut off by high walls on all sides. There were two small windows. Inside, Jecker was already waiting, leaning against the wall, chatting with two guards. He was talking loudly, and it was clear he wanted Parker to hear what he was saying. "Zrádce had the idea, but I was the one who rounded all the corners of the plan. I knew the boy would be idiotic enough to listen to him.

Zrádce was hesitant but I was right." He turned around and with mock surprise pretended to see Parker for the first time. "Oh, so the little champion is here. In most duels whoever surrenders first loses but since this is to the death, surrendering doesn't matter." He smiled a cold smile. Parker swallowed.

"T-to the death?"

"Well of course. This is for the throne, after all." Parker didn't know Jecker well enough to know his weaknesses as a fighter, but even if he did, Parker wasn't sure he could kill him. But now it was too late. A man in a red uniform was already saying ready, set, go. Parker didn't have any sort of plan, and he was ready to lose.

"GO!!"

Jecker was still leaning on the wall waiting casually. Parker was a bit confused, but he charged toward him. As soon as his sword came within striking distance, Jecker did something fancy with his own sleek gold sword and suddenly Parker's sword was lying on the ground and he had a nasty cut. But Jecker didn't try to stop Parker from picking up his sword. This time Parker tried to control his anger. He had to be smart, otherwise he would surely be killed very quickly. He thought about the fanciest move Zrádce had taught him. He pretended to charge, but at the last second stopped. He hoped that Jecker would swipe his sword through thin air, not processing that Parker had stopped. Then Parker could stab him somewhere else.

Instead, Jecker took a step forward and in fact did parry Parker's blow. Parker struck again, but got parried. This time, though, Jecker was faster. He had enough time to parry Parker's strike and also jab his stomach. Parker doubled over in pain, but he tried to shake it off; he had to keep going.

This kept going on for some time, with Jecker just playing defense and Parker getting more and more hurt. Finally, when Parker was completely bruised and bloody, Jecker decided to switch to offense. He swung hard and mixed brains and strength. Parker tried weakly to parry, but it hardly helped.

Finally, Parker was knocked to the ground, begging for mercy. Jecker raised his sword for the kill and Parker wondered how many times he had done this before. Parker closed his eyes waiting, waiting for death. But it never happened, because at that moment a voice yelled from outside, "Nobody messes with my friends!" Parker opened his eyes and saw, to his amazement, Puck, leaping through the window, holding Zrádce's sword that he had let Puck borrow. Out of the five main guards in the arena, two were maimed, two were killed, and one was knocked unconscious.

"You want to go?" Puck yelled. He and Jecker started fighting, but it was clearly going one way - Jecker's. Parker knew that he should help Puck, since now they had a chance, but he couldn't move. He was in a lot of pain and couldn't believe Puck had come all the way here and risked his life just for him.

Finally, Puck too was lying on the ground and Jecker raised his sword, just as he had done to Parker earlier. Jecker glanced at Parker, as if daring him to try to save his friend. At the last second, Parker found his legs. He ran toward Puck, but the king was too fast. He hit Puck's forehead with his blade, hard. It left him just enough time to parry Parker's strike. Puck lay motionless.

No! What kind of hero was he? He knew he wasn't a hero. He had made a friend whom he could trust and who had risked his life to save Parker and he had let him be killed. He tried to focus on beating Jecker, but he couldn't. He wasn't a hero. He wasn't a hero. He wasn't a hero. He just wanted to go home. He just wanted to go home. He just wanted to go home. He felt his consciousness fading, little by little and soon he was in the middle of a dream. Or rather a flashback. It was a time when he was at the park with his Mom. He was on the swing when a big beefy boy came over. It was big Lester, the school bully. Get off! Lester had yelled. Parker looked around for his Mom, but she wasn't anywhere close. Then he expected Lester to beat him up and leave him on the ground till his Mom came. But instead, an arrow came whizzing out of the bushes and Puck came running out. Together the boys ran out of the park together. Then his dream shifted.

He was on a camping trip with his Dad. They had set up camp and his Dad had gone to get some firewood and had left Parker alone in the tent. Suddenly he heard a roar. He had peeked outside the tent and had seen a bear roaring. He remembered being so scared, but again an arrow came flying out of the woods and killed the bear. Then Puck ran out and the boys escaped together. His dream shifted.

He was on a sleepover. When it had really happened, it was with Will, but this time he was with Puck instead. They chatted and laughed as if they were old friends. Then he felt something hard on his head, hitting him over and over again. As he started to wake up, he heard Puck's voice saying, "All great heroes are rewarded."

As his eyes opened slowly, they quickly closed again as Jecker hurled his sword on him again.

"You have good senses, boy," Jecker said. Jecker tried to swing at him again, but Parker managed to weakly deflect it. Anger flowed through him with an intensity he had never felt before. He got up. There was burning pain in his ribs, but that was just a minor obstacle. He jumped up and with surprising strength, parried Jecker's hit and knocked him on the chest. Jecker was still recovering from his shock, when Parker knocked his sword onto the floor and it skittered across the arena.

"Guards," Jecker called weakly. But Puck had killed all his loyal guards, and the others waited and watched.

"There's no one left for you. You have no more tricks. You have no more cheats. I will kill you now." But Parker was a lot less confident than he sounded. He knew he couldn't kill Jecker. No matter how bad Jecker was, Parker couldn't kill another person. He would think about it forever, killing someone, it would drive him mad. Surprisingly, Jecker was smiling.

"Promise me you will leave and never return to Herrin and I'll let you live," Parker said.

But Jecker seemed to sense Parker's reluctance. "Oh no," he said quietly. "I know you can't kill me. You don't have it in you. You are in quite a deadly quandary. You can't kill me and if you let me go, then I'll kill you."

As Parker pondered, a drop of blood fell from his head, and landed on Jecker's mouth. Then another. And another. Parker started to itch where the blood was coming from, and what felt like a huge quantity of blood fell down. Everything seemed blurry, and Parker suddenly felt dizzy.

As soon as Jecker saw what was happening, he tried to jerk the sword away. But as soon as he touched it, Farthadonos slid deep into Jecker's chest.

Parker started losing consciousness, but not before he saw what had happened. The king was dead.

Three months later King Worth could walk on his own. It had taken much time for him to recover from all the many injuries he received while defeating ex-king Jecker. But gradually he recovered his strength and got used to being king. He got used to having servants dress him, to having enormous feasts every night, to having everyone bow down to him. Despite all this, the king was still sad. He wanted more than anything to go back home. Every night he missed his family and friends more. He had changed many laws and the people adored him. He had had Zrádce and everyone else loyal to Jecker put into prison. He had made sure that all mistreated people had a house to stay in. He was even thinking about someday getting married to Raina, the servant girl who had been massaging Zrádce. But at the same time, he yearned to go back. He had the smartest men in Herrin trying to find a way to send cestovatels back to Earth. He had promised anyone who could figure out a way back a free round trip to Earth.

But after three months of getting better from his wounds, and no one coming close to finding a way back, he went for a walk by himself. It was hard to convince his bodyguards to let him go, but after reminding them that he was the king, they let him go.

Soon he found himself in the same spot where he had first arrived in Herrin. The corn fields stretched out all around him. In the distance he saw a small black dot. Parker gasped. Could it be? He started running at full speed toward the dot. As he got closer, the 'dot' seemed to be some sort of tube going into the ground. Excited now, he started running faster, shaking off his heavy gold crown and bracelet of pearls. The tube started flickering as if it were going to close, but Parker had arrived. He knew it! It was the water slide!

He jumped in and it started carrying him down into the ground faster and faster. Soon water appeared, and his heavy clothes started disintegrating and he was left in his bathing suit.

But he was still going faster. As he went, he thought about his adventure in Herrin. Before he had entered the water slide, he had taken so much for granted. His parents, his toys, even the good president of his country. Now he had learned that some places don't have so much comfort. He knew he would never forget what he had learned here. He hoped that after Jecker's death, he had shown the people of Herrin that even the most powerful rulers could fall. Now that he wasn't king, he hoped they would choose a good, just ruler, someone even better than him.

Splash!

He fell out and into a large pool of water. He looked up and saw Dad standing nearby.

"Whoa! That was a long water slide!" his Dad said. "I thought you were never coming out, Parker! You were in there for what, five minutes?"

My Favorite Star

THE DEVIL WALKS INTO A bar and says to a lawyer, "I'll make you rich if you give me the souls of you and your family." The lawyer says, "What's the catch?"

Ha, ha, ha! Hilarious! That joke is so funny I forgot to laugh.

I'm really not into lawyer jokes. After all, I intend to be a lawyer in a few years myself. And it's all up to this debate that I'm going to.

My name is Mark Culverson. I'm in my senior year of college. I've been to twenty-three debates outside of school and won them all. I don't know how many debates I've been to in college. Too many to count.

I step into the auditorium and walk to my seat. I casually glance at the clock as I walk in. 5:15. Perfect, exactly fifteen minutes before the debate starts. My opponent's seat is empty. Good. It always gives the audience a better image of me if I come early.

I'm dressed in a suit and tie, and from now on it's all show. I've often thought to myself how much debates are like acting. Although you're trying to prove your point of view, you want to portray yourself in a way that the audience, and moreover, the judge, agrees with you and wants to help you. I don't mean to brag, but the acting part of debates is something I have mastered.

I weave words together masterfully, and I always try to make others feel for me. And my number one rule, the one thing that I never allow myself to do, is feel for my opponent.

I mean, I think about their point of view in order to think of a counterargument, but solely for that. Because, if ever, if I ever *actually* sympathize with what my opponent says, then my whole show is ruined. Slowly my view will waver, and as a lawyer, that will not do, especially since I won't always be fighting for something I agree with.

If I ever start to think that I might be agreeing with my opponent, I always focus back on something that I know for sure I support. Again, not to brag, but not feeling for my opponent is something I've mastered.

I think about what Professor Connahan told me. Professor Connahan is my professor who is helping me get into law school. He coaches four students on the debate team including me, and he always refers to us as his stars. Even though he knows he shouldn't have favorites, after I won my last debate he said to me, "Mark, don't tell anyone I said this, but you are my favorite star."

He also told me that if I win this debate then my perfect score as a debater would almost definitely ensure that I get into law school. Plus, Professor Connahan told me that an admissions officer from Yale law school is coming to watch the debate today, and impressing her won't hurt my chance for admission.

Professor Connahan is a good teacher. I've learned a lot about law with him. And I'm confident I can win this debate and get into law school and become a professional lawyer.

Especially if my opponent doesn't show up. His or her seat is still empty. The clock says 5:20. Ten minutes left. I murmur something inaudible as I realize that I forgot to check to see who my opponent is. Sometimes it helps me beat them if I know a little bit about them. Actually, I take that back. It always helps me beat them. How could I forget to find out about my opponent on my last debate? But no worries, for I have thoroughly researched the topic. We're debating whether to keep a forty-year-old park or to build apartments. I have prepared for every argument my opponent could make.

Finally, my opponent walks in. There seems to be something familiar about her. She has long black hair falling down to her back and dark brown eyes. She looks almost Indian, but when she says something to a woman in the audience she has no trace of an Indian accent. I slump down into my chair as I realize who this is. Tara. My old best friend.

Suddenly I'm swept back by memories. So many memories, all circulating around this girl. All circulating around Tara.

When I was four years old, she had been my best friend. No, no, more than that. Much more then that.

My only friend.

I saw her every day and we would play together, sometimes at her house, sometimes at mine. We got along well. We signed up for activities together, we did everything together.

Whenever she would come over, she and I would always ask if we could have ice cream. We both loved ice cream, and during the summer afternoons we would sit on my porch steps and lick our ice creams together. In cones, double scooped. One strawberry, one mint chocolate chip. Strawberry was her favorite flavor and mint chocolate chip was mine. We were only four, but we understood each other almost perfectly. If nothing else, we could always talk about our ice cream.

Having it with her somehow made it taste sweeter.

When I went to preschool, I started having more friends. But still I had a best friend - Tara.

I had playdates with her almost every day, even when I turned five. I remember when we joined dance class together and how sad Tara had been when I quit because I was the only boy.

But one day, when Tara was at my house I heard her mom and my mom talking in louder voices than usual. Then suddenly, Tara's mom got up, picked up Tara and walked right out of our house, without even staying for ice cream, even though we were going to have strawberry.

I never had another play date with her again. My mother tried countless times to call her mother, but she never answered. She sent her letters, saying things like, "We are friends, we cannot let something small like this get in the way of our friendship." But she never got a reply.

And me? Well, I didn't just forget about Tara and become best friends with Max instead. I threw my toys that Tara and I had once played with around the house and thought of horrible ways to describe her mother: evil, nasty, bad, mean, and much worse. I learned somewhere that Tara means star in Hindi, so I drew stars and whenever I messed up drawing them I would start crying and shout her name. Because I hadn't learned how to pronounce the "r" sound yet, I would yell, "Tawa, Tawa."

I jerk myself in my seat awkwardly. What am I doing? This girl is my enemy. I must beat her; I must show the judge that we should keep our forty-year-old park. I must be strong; I cannot think about any personal relationship with this girl. It occurs to me that I'm not thinking about what I will say, or rehearsing my argument, which I always do before my debate. I'm loose and distracted, and I realize why. That wasn't the end of Tara.

Before I can stop myself, I'm thinking about that day in the library.

When I was seven, my mother and I were in the town library. As we were looking at the different books, I rounded the corner and saw a small familiar looking girl. Her brown hair was longer than last time, but it was easy to recognize her.

"Hi," I said shyly. I could see the recognition spark in her eyes, only a moment after she looked at me.

I felt like I had gone back in time three years. I felt so comfortable with her, as though it hadn't been three years since we had seen each other. I started talking to her, first nervously, then as I got more comfortable, faster.

Finally, she said, "Do you want to read a book about ice cream?" I got down a book to read with her. It was called *Super Scooper*, with a picture on the cover of a boy scooping ice cream onto a cone with a huge ice cream scoop.

The library had comfortable beanbags everywhere, and we sat down. We started to read the book when suddenly all of our conversation was drowned out as in swept the woman who I hated. It was Tara's mother.

She wore a black coat with a neat row of black buttons, and when she saw what was going on, she took Tara by the hand and led her right out of the library. After that, I thought often about Tara but I never saw her again.

When I was eleven I was told the story of what happened that day at our house. Tara's mother had told my mother, "I really don't want my Tara playing with that boy Will across the street. He has special needs, and I want my Tara to only have clean friends. Your son seems alright, though."

My mother had said, "Now, that's no way to talk about Will. I know he can get a bit wild at times, but it's not his fault he was born like that. We shouldn't stop our kids from playing with our neighbors just because they have special needs."

Tara's mother had gotten up in a rush, very much offended at my mother's words. And that had been the last time I played with Tara.

Now, for the first time in a debate, I'm not sure what I should do. A part of me wants to forget about this whole stupid debate. I want to be with Tara and sit down and eat ice cream with her. I want to forget about these seventeen years when I haven't been with her. I want her to be my best friend again.

And part of me wants to beat her and win the debate.

When I was fourteen, I liked played ping-pong. I would always play my hardest, whether I was playing a friend, a bully, or a beginner. I would always say, when asked, that it was so I wouldn't get out of practice.

I think I have the same attitude now with debate.

In my fourth college debate, I had debated someone named John Baumbach and absolutely crushed him. I had researched well, and every argument he had I would counter with a savage counterargument. I played without debate sportsmanship. Even though I had been given the easier side to defend, I never hesitated. When he would pause to think, I would pile on more reasons. When he would begin to speak, I would interrupt him with a counter to whatever he was saying. When he left, he almost had tears in his eyes. Still, when he saw me, he said, "Good job, Mark." I didn't reply.

I can beat Tara, and I will beat Tara. The fact that we were childhood acquaintances means nothing.

But am I really that cruel? I've often wondered if I should have been nicer to John.

As I ponder this, I look out into the audience and I see Professor Connahan in the front row. Seated next to him is a silver haired woman with a Yale university logo imprinted on her shirt. She must be the admissions officer. I know Professor Connahan doesn't have very much money, yet he spent quite a bit on front row seats. Usually they don't sell tickets for college debates, but for this one, all the money earned goes to charity, so the tickets are expensive. I remember what he had said to me earlier, "You are my favorite star."

At that moment, I decide that no matter what any professor says to me, I will not crush Tara. I will not try my hardest against her; my purpose will not be to extinguish the light in her. Perhaps I will be the winner; no, I will try to be the winner, just to be it in a way so that I do not hurt her.

I can see that boy, John Baumbach, I feel his shame, his embarrassment at being ridiculed in front of his own parents, and I decide that I am not only changing myself for the sake of Tara, I'm changing myself as a person. I will try to win, but not in a way that demoralizes my opponent.

And who knows? Maybe by meeting Tara, my life will change in more ways than just becoming kinder. I see myself sitting at a table for two with Tara, taking a spoonful of mint chocolate chip ice cream from the bowl that we share.

It's almost too much to hope for, but who knows?

Finally, Tara and I rise from our seats, and the white haired judge steps up, gestures at the two of us, and speaks. "Today's debate over the town park will have Mark Culverson defending the forty-year-old grounds and its many historic statues, and Catherine Limegate defending the new apartments."

Fuzz

M ATT AND REENA HAVE ALWAYS been interesting friends. Matt is smart in a different kind of way. He's really into science and is always making rockets or motors or something like that. Reena seems pretty nice, but she's odder than Matt. She always seems calm and contained. I've never seen her get even a little annoyed, but it doesn't seem natural. They're both really into science fiction. They're always talking about how different the world will be in a few hundred years. Also they're twins. I probably wouldn't be friends with them if my mom wasn't friends with their mom. Anyway, I don't resent being their friend. They're the same age as me. They've always been nice to me. At least until now.

We were friends when we lived in Wisconsin, but then we moved all the way to New York because of Dad's work. So when we went back to Wisconsin for the summer, we went to spend the day at their house. At the time, I was going into seventh grade. After dinner, while we were waiting for dessert, the adults talked about golf and philosophy and politics and whatever else they talk about. Matt came over to me and asked if I wanted to go to the park with him. We told our parents where we were going and then started to leave when Reena came running down the stairs. "Where you going?" she asked.

"None of your business," Matt said. Oh yeah, one thing I forgot to mention is that Matt always acts rudely to Reena. But since we were still inside the house, the adults could hear us.

"They're going to the park, Reena," their dad said. Reena put her sneakers on and started running after us as we walked out the door. As we walked, Matt told me about the air bomb Frisbee he was bringing.

"This is the Frisbee of the future, Max," he told me. "I don't know what the record for the farthest Frisbee throw is, but whatever it is, I bet the air bomb record is twice as far."

"That's pretty cool," I said. "I can't wait to try it out in the field."

"Yes it is 'pretty cool'," Reena said coldly. I looked at her for a moment. Her features seemed slightly different to me. Her nose was a little too perfect. Her icy blue eyes seemed to cut into me like daggers. Her thin smile made it seem like she was mocking me. I looked at Matt; he looked the same as always. Same shaggy brown hair, dark eyes and crooked grin. He didn't seem to have heard his sister's sarcastic remark.

When we got to the park I got to try the air bomb Frisbee first. I threw it as hard as I could straight out into the field. It made a sharp turn and immediately landed high in a tree. Although Reena was always nice about things like this, for some reason I expected her to make a harsh remark. So as soon as I saw it disappear into the tree, I looked at her. "That's okay," she said. "We'll try to get it back." I saw the hungriness in her expression; it made her smile seem fake.

For what seemed like hours and probably was, we all took turns climbing the tree. Neither Matt nor I had any luck finding the right branch. Only Reena had been able to actually shake the right branch, so we let her take over most of the time. Matt and I sat on the ground giving directions to Reena. I felt horrible. What could have been a fun evening for all of us had now been ruined. And I wasn't even trying to get it back. But at the same time I knew that if I had been here with my family, we would have given in to the fact that we weren't going to get that particular Frisbee. I got up and stretched my back and started walking around the field, thinking. Finally, I decided that I should suggest to them that we should go home. If they wanted, I could buy them a new Frisbee. Besides it was getting dark.

As I started walking back, I noticed two things that seemed odd. Matt was gone. I couldn't see him anywhere. The other thing was I saw a pink butterfly fluttering and weaving towards the woods.

In a flash, I remembered something that Matt had told me one day, just a few weeks before we moved to New York. He and his family had just come back from a vacation in the Caribbean. We were playing Ping-Pong. It was one of the few times I can remember that Reena wasn't playing with us. I ended the game with a backhand smash and asked Matt if we should invite Reena to play with us. "Listen," Matt said. "Max, I need to tell you something." I crossed the room to listen to him. "When we were in the Caribbean, Reena was acting strange," Matt began.

"So what else is new?" I interrupted, laughing.

"No, she was even weirder than usual, Max. One evening she insisted that I follow her and she showed me a cave. She seemed very interested in it. It was full of butterflies that seemed to be covered with some kind of pink fungus. I thought it was pretty cool, but for some reason it also weirded me out a bit, especially because Reena was so enthralled by them. Anyway, I never saw the cave again.

"Every day we were on that island, Reena would spend all her time with the butterflies. When it was time for us to go to a different island, Reena got very upset. She said she wasn't ready to leave the island. She whined so much that Mom and Dad agreed we would spend one more night there. At the end of the day, Reena begged our parents to stay for just one more day, but they said that she was getting too fussy and that the other island would be great, and we were leaving and that was that.

"The night before we left the island, I got up in the middle of the night. Reena and I were sharing one room and my parents were in the other. I was about to get some water when I noticed no one was in the other bed. Thinking that she was in the bathroom, I knocked on the door, but got no response. I was about to go to my parents' room, when the door opened and in came Reena, dressed in black jeans and a black T-shirt. She obviously had gone out. I was about to ask her something when she murmured that everything was okay and rubbed my forehead. I was still sleepy and I just saw a blur, and then I fell onto the bed, instantly asleep. The next morning, I didn't remember any of it. I spent the rest of our vacation and came back without remembering anything about this. It was three days ago when I started to remember it all, like it was being traced back into my mind. Now I remember everything and I'm worried that something must've happened to Reena, and I'm afraid that maybe she'll start acting strange again."

At the time I had laughed. I told him he should become a storyteller, and he was a liar. But when he had been telling me about the butterflies, I had pictured them in my mind. And now, this butterfly matched my picture. I somehow sensed that the butterfly led to Matt and was about to follow it when I heard Matt's voice from up in the tree, close to where Reena had been climbing.

"I'm fine, Max," he said. But his voice sounded odd, it was tighter and higher pitched than usual.

Already I didn't really believe him, but what happened next made my mind switch from suspicion to just plain scared. Matt's real voice came from a little ways into the woods, where the butterfly was going. "Help, Max!"

"No, I'm fine," came the fake voice from up in the tree.

"Reena," I yelled up.

"Yes, I'm fine, Max," came Reena's voice. "Matt is up here with me. Come up too."

"But Reena, there isn't space," I shouted, slowly backing away toward where I had heard Matt's real voice.

"Help," he yelled again.

The butterfly was hovering over where Matt's real voice seemed to be coming from.

"Get up here Max," Reena said, but this time her voice was much more of a command then a request. By this time, I was running toward where the butterfly was going.

"Yes come on up, Max," came Matt's fake voice. Suddenly I stopped short. Lying at the edge of the woods was Matt's body. He looked normal, except for one thing. His ears. Growing around them was a pink sort of fuzz. There was one part in the lobes where it looked like it had started growing, and then expanded to the rest of the ears, and now was gradually growing across his face.

This was too much for me. I've always trusted my parents a lot, and I was not going to try and manage this on my own. I turned around and started running as fast as I could through the field. I could see the road on the other side of the long grass. From there I could just run down the street and get to the house, where I would tell my parents that Reena had gone crazy and thrown some horrible chemical-infested *something* that had either severely injured or killed Matt. Then I would never go anywhere without my parents again.

I was thinking so hard about this, I didn't notice the butterfly flying toward me from the tree. It hit me on the forehead, but it didn't hurt. Everything felt so comfortable, I lay down on the grass and started relaxing. I could already feel fuzz growing over my face and eyes. I tried to open my eyes and found that it hurt, but that was okay. I closed my eyes gently and let the fuzziness sink over me. Soon even my brain felt fuzzy. I vaguely thought that this fuzz was like the thing that was on Matt, but then I slowly stopped thinking anything at all.

Acknowledgements

I WOULD LIKE TO THANK TWO excellent English teachers for motivating me to write: Ms. Liv Gregor and Mr. Kevin Kuehn. Their enthusiasm and valuable feedback have instilled a joy of writing in me.

Thanks to Dharmendra Kumar, our neighborhood fruit seller, for inspiring the title story and for letting me take his photo to be painted for the cover.

Thanks to Ajit Kumar for painting the excellent cover picture from the photo.

Thanks to my aunt, Lois Weinberg, for her efficient editing and for always encouraging me.

Thanks to my grandmother, Sally Castleman, for her proofreading and for helping me to keep writing when the going got tough.

Finally, thanks to my parents for their ideas, their editing, and, most of all, their encouragement. They have always supported my writing, from telling me stories from the age of four, to helping me make and staple together my first book when I was seven, to letting me have a laptop at age eleven to write these stories.

I cannot thank these eight people enough.

Printed in the United States
By Bookmasters